My Noble Knight

A Medieval Romance Novel

Laurel O'Donnell

CHAPTER ONE
1363 England

Griffin Wolfe summed up his next opponent with a simple indifferent glance. He had seen enough of Rou's practice to know the knight posed no threat to his victory in the joust. The midday sun was hot and a layer of sweat glistened on Griffin's skin as he paused at the fence that surrounded the tiltyard to watch Rou ride by on his brown charger. The war horse kicked up a cloud of dust in its wake which stuck to Griffin's slick skin. He hardly noticed. His thoughts had already moved past Rou.

After Rou's defeat, only one knight stood between him and the winner's purse. Some knight who went by the surname Fletcher. Griffin couldn't even remember his first name. He was the only other competitor who had not yet lost in the tournament. But he would. After Griffin unhorsed Rou, this Fletcher would be next.

He turned and headed back to his pavilion where his squire was preparing his armor. Around him, spectators continued to arrive, the wealthier guests heading for the wooden stands, others staking out their spots in the fields for the best view of the joust. He turned the corner of a pavilion that bore the flapping flag crest of lord Crandall and a small whirlwind slammed into his chest. Griffin grunted and scowled, caught by surprise.

He lowered his gaze to see a pile of wild dark hair at his feet. Two hands emerged into his view and separated the hair to reveal two beaming blue eyes staring up at him. "Pardons, sir." The hands pushed the hair further back to reveal a face and Griffin was shocked to see a woman! If it weren't for her delicate face and full lips, he wasn't sure he would have realized she was a female. She wore brown breeches on her slender legs and a dusty green tunic.

Instinctively, he reached out a hand to her. "Are you hurt?"

Her blue eyes twinkled, and a smile spread across her lips as she reached for his hand. "You're strong, but not a rock. I am unhurt."

When her fingers closed over his palm, a searing jolt raced through Griffin. He almost pulled his hand free of hers, but his upbringing overrode his surprise and he easily lifted her to her feet. There was something instantly intriguing about the woman, even though she was dressed in men's clothing. He withdrew his hand. "Where are you off to in such a hurry?"

"The joust," she answered. "It's already crowded, and I have to get a good spot to watch."

Griffin frowned slightly. Women did not dash around running into men looking for the closest spot to watch a joust. He stepped aside. "Far be it from me to stand in your way."

She nodded and walked past him; her steps more measured.

He watched her walk away. At least she had slowed her pace. His gaze took in her body. Her bottom was hidden beneath the tunic that fell to her mid-thigh. Her legs were covered with knee high black boots. Very inappropriate for a woman, but so very intriguing. Suddenly, she turned and locked gazes with him. A slow smile turned up the corners of her lips into a lovely, knowing smile. It was like the sunrise on a glorious morning. His spirit lifted at the mere sight of her grin. He couldn't help but smile back at her; her grin was infectious.

"Forgive me for crashing into you."

Griffin nodded slightly and then she was gone, swallowed up by the sea of villagers and merchants arriving for the joust. With a strange lightheartedness, Griffin headed for his pavilion to prepare.

Layne Fletcher had found a spectacular place to view the joust. In the center of the field, right against the fence. A tree even offered her shade against the hot sun.

She leaned into the fence, looking from one end of the field to the other for the knights. The victor of this joust would face her brother. She hoped it was Rou. He was a buffoon and she knew Frances could easily unhorse him.

A balding man stepped onto the field of honor, drawing scattered applause from the crowd. Tingles of excitement shot up Layne's spine. It was starting. Her fingers curved over the top plank of wood.

The man held up his arms and the crowd

quieted. He turned around to address the mass of onlookers and announced in his booming voice, "On this final day of the joust, all competitors have been eliminated but three skilled knights. By sunset today, we shall have a victor!"

The crowd erupted in applauses and cheering.

Layne lifted her hands and shouted approval along with them. It would be Frances. It had to be Frances.

"I give you Lord Rou!" the man called and swept his hand out to the side of the field.

Rou rode onto the field, waving and blowing kisses to the crowd. His visor was raised to receive their adoration and muted praise. He rode to his side of the field where his squire was already waiting.

"I give you Sir Wolfe!"

The crowd stood to their feet, applauding, cheering and calling his name. He was the favored knight.

Layne winced. He was favored because he was better, and she knew it.

His visor was down, and he did not acknowledge the audience. He rode directly to his side of the field.

The bald man turned and jogged from the field leaving the two competitors.

They each moved to their squires who handed them their lances. A long moment passed, and Rou lowered his visor. Wolfe spurred his horse. Rou matched his movement. The two knights charged down the field of honor, their lances poised in their arms, the long-blunted tips pointed at each other.

The horses kicked up dust in the field as they rushed forward. The riders sat low in their saddles.

4

Rou's garish red feather flattened in the rush of wind.

Layne studied Rou's form. She groaned inwardly, wondering how he had ever managed to make it this far in the tournament. His form was atrocious. He couched the lance with his hand resting on his leg which bounced at every step his horse took. How could he possibly make a solid strike with such terrible technique?

Layne's gaze shifted to his opponent. Sir Griffin Wolfe. She had crashed into him in her hurry to get to the open spot in the shade. He had been nothing like she expected. After hearing all the grand tales of his glorious victories, she thought he would be snobbish and arrogant. After all, he had never been beaten in tournament. But he wasn't. He had smiled at her. Which was more than most of the other knights had ever done to her.

She watched Griffin ride his steed down the field of honor. His form was impeccable. His armor was spotless and immaculate. He wore no flamboyant colors or feathers. He needed none of those to announce his presence. Everyone knew him. Everyone.

The horses thundered towards each other. Remarkably, at the last moment, Rou lifted his lance and aimed it correctly. The lances struck. Each delivered a solid blow to their opponent. Rou's lance splintered, the shards flying out over the field.

Griffin's lance held, lifting Rou up and out of the saddle. He was suspended over the earth for a long moment at the end of Griffin's lance before he fell heavily to the ground, an explosion of dust erupting all around him.

Layne grimaced. That was going to hurt.

A hush fell over the spectators.

Someone tugged on her arm, but she couldn't bring herself to look away from the fallen knight. Moments ticked by and Rou didn't stand. Layne craned her neck to watch as the dust settled around him. She hoped he wasn't too hurt. She would not wish that on any knight. Defeat, yes. Crippling pain, no.

The tugging persisted at her arm. She finally looked down to see her younger brother, Michael. She swept him with a cursory glance. His moppy brown hair fell into his eyes and over his dirt smudged cheeks. "Better go wash your face or Colin will twist your ears."

She looked back at the field. Rou still had not stirred. His squire raced onto the field of honor.

"Layne," Michael called, yanking at her arm.

Layne scowled and looked at him. For the first time, she saw the intent look on Michael's face and realized something was wrong. She stepped away from the fence, scanning the surrounding crowd behind Michael for her older brother. "Where's Frances?"

With a wave of his hand, Michael signaled for her to come with him.

Layne glanced about and saw a woman holding a baby watching them. A man leaning over the fence swiveled his head to look at them. Layne followed Michael away from the crowd.

Michael stopped when they were out of earshot. "Laynie," he whispered. "Frances is unconscious."

"What?" Layne exclaimed.

Michael shook his head. "He was practicing with the quintain and it spun and hit him in the head. He fell from the horse."

Layne looked toward their pavilion. She couldn't see their tent through the trees, but she knew it was there. She took off running. There were many pathways through the trees, but she took the straightest route, cutting through foliage. Branches snagged her tunic, but her boots protected her feet from the rocks. Finally, she broke through the forest and raced to their pavilion.

She threw the flap aside and entered.

Colin, her oldest brother, sat beside Frances who was prone on his mat. He was not moving. Colin didn't even look up as she entered. He shook his brother's shoulders, calling, "Frances. Frances, wake up."

Michael entered the tent behind her.

Colin looked at Layne. There was helplessness in his gaze, and he shook his head. "We're going to have to forfeit."

"We can't," Layne whispered. "We need the winning pouch."

Colin spread out his hands. "Look at him! He's out. He's not jousting anytime soon."

Layne stood for a long moment, staring at Frances with concern and with anger. How could this happen? How could he be so careless? They needed the winnings! Father needed the winnings. They only needed to win a little more coin. Just a little more and they could go home and buy the land so father could finally rest. But with Frances out cold they had no chance.

Or did they? A tingle of excitement shot up her spine. She grabbed Michael's arm and backed out of the tent, pulling the young boy with her. "Help me."

"Help you do what?"

"Help me get into the armor."

Michael stopped dead in his tracks. "Oh no!" He shook his head and held out his hands in front of him to ward her off. "Colin would quarter me!"

Layne spun on him. "I can't do it alone. It's our only chance!"

Michael shook his head and crossed his arms, glaring at her.

She grabbed his tunic front and shoved her face close to his. "If you don't do it, I'll tell Colin who broke his bow."

Michael's mouth fell open. "You wouldn't."

"Yes, I would. Help me, Michael. We don't have a lot of time."

By the time they had gotten her into Frances's armor, appropriately padding it so it fit, the call was going out the second time for Sir Frances Fletcher. She would have been quicker, but she had to bind her breasts. It was lucky Frances was the same height she was. She had tried his armor on before, secretly many times, so she knew all the places where it was loose. Michael helped her stuff padding into those areas so she should move efficiently in the metal shell that now encased her.

She didn't know if it was just desperation fueling her strength or forbidden excitement over what she was about to do raising her energy, but the armor felt lighter than she remembered. She raised her arm up and down, re-acquainting herself with the feel of the steel.

She chose to use her own horse rather than his. She had never been able to fully control Frances's destrier. The beast was just too big. Her own stallion, Angel, was used to her movements and her direction. She thought it was a better choice. She and Michael had quickly pulled the caparison off of Frances's horse and laid the cloth over Angel's back. The thick fabric would offer good protection to Angel's body during the joust. It was a bit too large for her horse, but it would have to do.

She entered the field to sporadic applause and a few jeering shouts. Michael jogged behind her, acting as her squire. The crowd of people gathered around the field clearly didn't like that she was late. And she could tell by the way Griffin's horse paced impatiently at the other end of the field he was not pleased either.

That's all right. She'd give them a show they wouldn't forget. True, she had never been a participant in a real joust before, anyone who was not a knight was not allowed to participate, but she was confident enough in her abilities. She had practiced dozens of times on her own against quintains and straw dummies when no one else was around. She lifted her chin in defiance, even though she knew no one could see the movement behind the closed visor that covered her face.

As she maneuvered Angel to her side of the field, she passed Griffin. Griffin Wolfe. He had unhorsed all he stood against. This was no man of straw. Far from it. He looked like a massive mountain of glistening metal as he sat tall in his saddle. Her brothers had always told her jousting was dangerous. They would only practice their swordplay with her. And now, as she sat on her horse in the field of honor, her heart beating madly in her chest, sweat running from her brow, she had to concur with them. This could turn out to be dangerous indeed.

Griffin's horse pranced up to his squire at the other end of the yard.

All she needed to do was find his weak spot. Just one flaw. She knew she couldn't beat him with strength.

She would have to beat him with speed and angles. Layne licked her lips beneath the helmet. The helmet was slightly too big for her, but she had stuck cloth into the top so it fit better. It barely jostled at all when she moved her head.

There was no going back now. She urged Angel forward with a slight kick. Luckily, Frances had used Angel before to joust in other tournaments when his horse had taken ill so the noise and ruckus from the spectators didn't spook Angel.

Michael handed her the lance with a slight shake of his head. She narrowed her eyes at him, repeating the silent threat that she would tell Colin about the bow, if it came to that. But she knew Michael would do his part. It was too late for him to turn back.

She whirled Angel about and spurred him hard. The sound of the crowd died about her, muffled by the helmet and the thunder of Angel's hooves. Her breathing was loud in her ears. She concentrated on Wolfe. Through the thin slit in her visor, she saw him closing on her, the lance held firm in his arm, the tip pointed directly at her. She lowered her own lance.

At the last moment, Angel balked, and the lances missed completely.

They rounded the ends of the field and cantered back to their sides. Wolfe passed within two feet of her. He really was an excellent rider. His control of his steed was excellent. But she was better.

What was wrong with Angel? Layne patted his neck reassuringly. Angel snorted and tossed his head. "Don't you start," Layne whispered to him. "I can do this. No one need know."

Michael handed her the lance, still shaking his head.

Layne grimaced. It wasn't enough she was facing the best knight she had ever seen in her very first joust, but no one had faith in her. Not Michael. Not even her horse. Well, she would show them. She would show them all!

She rounded Angel, the lance held up. It was easier to control Angel with the lance out of the way. Once Angel fell into rhythm, Layne lowered the lance, tucking it beneath her arm. She leaned forward, racing down the list.

Wolfe rounded the tilt barrier and charged forward.

At the last moment, Layne leaned away from his lance, making him miss completely. She held her lance firm, aimed directly at him. It struck his shoulder. The impact jarred her arm, sending sharp tingles through her limb, and she dropped the lance.

The two horses sped past each other.

She opened and closed her hand again and again to get the blood flowing into her limb and force the numb feeling to fade. She had struck him! Jubilant, she turned to look at him down the field. He had thrown up his faceplate to stare at her.

The crowd around them was silent in shock.

She cantered Angel down the field, passing Wolfe. His startling blue eyes were locked on her, his jaw tight. Maybe hitting him wasn't such a good idea.

As she reached the end of the field where Michael stood, she glanced into the audience and almost fell off Angel. Standing at the fence with his arms crossed was Colin. His gaze bore into her with the promise of punishment. Severe punishment.

Even with trepidation snaking its way up her spine, Layne couldn't stop. She wanted this opportunity. She had always wanted to joust, but it had been forbidden to her. This was her only time to try it. The opportunity had presented itself to her and she had seized it. And her family needed her to win! She couldn't back out now.

She turned to look at Wolfe. He had reached the other side and stretched out his hand for his lance.

Layne held out her hand and Michael handed her the lance, whispering, "You are in so much trouble."

Layne glared at him but said nothing as she cradled the lance. She turned away from her younger brother and yanked the reins. Angel reared slightly before starting off down the field. Layne lowered her lance, focusing on Wolfe. He was angry now. She had seen it in his face. He would make a mistake. Or he would knock her silly. Either way, she had to be alert. As they closed, she saw an opening. He had taken off his gloves. She could hit him in the hand! She aimed the lance at his unprotected hand.

But then she hesitated. She could seriously hurt him, perhaps injure him so severely he would never joust again. She could never do that to a knight. She turned the lance away at the last moment. It was unchivalrous to do something like that.

His lance struck her a light blow. She saw his plan. She was so intent on his hand that she didn't see him turn the lance in at the last moment. Only by moving her lance did she bump his and cause the glancing blow instead a full unhorsing.

She tossed the lance down. He was clever, she would give him that. She had noticed something else, too. Something she bet the others never saw. It was just a minor mistake. He held the lance slightly tilted to the inside until he was very close. Then he adjusted his aim.

It was not necessarily a flaw in his technique, but it was something she might be able to take advantage of.

As they moved past each other, crossing to the other side of the field, she could see his blue eyes through the visor of his helmet. She couldn't read the emotion and they passed before she could figure out what it was.

She rounded the field, her gaze on Wolfe. She did her best to ignore Colin's glare of fury, forcing herself to concentrate on the immediate task at hand. She had an idea that would play on the subtle weakness she saw in Wolfe's technique. It was a dangerous move, but if she was right, she would unhorse him. And win. It was a chance she had to take.

She took the lance from Michael and spurred Angel. Through the small slit in her visor she watched Wolfe charge toward her. He sat low in the saddle, leaning over his horse's head. Like she had seen him do before, he held his lance aimed toward the inside.

She matched his movement. Let him think she thought he was aiming for her stomach.

They raced toward each other, Layne's breath coming in small huffs matching the thundering pace in her horse's steps. Wait, she told herself. Don't move the lance. Wait until he does. Then move and aim for his stomach.

He drew closer and still Wolfe did not move the lance.

Layne forced herself to wait when every instinct was telling her to protect herself, not to leave herself so wide open.

The horses thundered closer. The distant roar of the crowd sounded like the wind in her ears. Her heart hammered hard in her chest.

At the last moment, she saw Wolfe shift his lance. Immediately, she followed suit and then closed her eyes, preparing for the impact. The force of the collision was brutal, slamming into her shoulder with enough force to spin her around in a complete circle, flinging her from the saddle. She landed hard on her back on the dirt ground.

She didn't know how long she lay there staring at the sky. It was blue with no clouds. Just simply blue. Slowly and groggily, noise filtered into her senses. A horse whinnied somewhere. Birds chirped. The realization she wasn't on Angel seeped into her mind.

Unhorsed. She had been unhorsed.

With a groan, she boosted herself onto her elbow. Aches exploded to life all over her body. Her left shoulder was numb and throbbed with explosive pain. She mentally took stock of her body. Her shoulder and her pride hurt the worst. Her back was sore, from the fall she guessed, but the pain was tolerable.

She slowly sat up.

Unhorsed. She shook her head, trying to clear it. She would never hear the end of this from her brothers. They would tell her that was why women did not joust. Now, her head hurt, too. She looked around.

For the first time she noticed the strange silence that had settled over the field. Everyone just stared. All the villagers leaning over the fence, all the nobles in the grandstands, all the knights, all the squires, they all just stared.

Layne climbed to her feet. A gasp came from the crowd. But it wasn't accompanied by applause. Something wasn't right. Her shoulder ached. She couldn't move her left arm; it was completely numb. A wave of light-headedness fell over her and she hesitated a moment, wanting to sit back down. She blinked, forcing the sensation away. She spotted Angel a few yards away, the horse standing still, watching her. She turned. Michael stood near Colin, both staring at her with an open-mouthed expression. They probably thought she was hurt. She should wave or something...

That's when she spotted the other horse, Wolfe's horse at the end of the field where Michael was.

The horse was riderless!

Shocked, Layne spun, searching the dusty field for Wolfe. Sunlight reflected off of armor in the dirt of the field of honor. Wolfe lay on the ground.

For a moment, she couldn't move. For a moment, she stared like everyone else. He was unhorsed! He was lying on the ground. Unhorsed. By her!

She started toward him in disbelief. Was he hurt? Had she harmed him?

Michael raced up beside her, whispering, "Colin said let him be. He said to get out of the field of honor."

Layne still couldn't believe she had unhorsed Griffin Wolfe! No one else had done it! "Get me a sword."

"Layne," Michael begged.

She glared at him. "Sword!" She could beat him! Didn't they understand? She could win!

Michael's lips thinned and he reluctantly handed her a sword.

Frances's sword was heavy, and her arms ached with the effort to hold it. She had to use both of her hands. The tip of the sword dragged in the dirt for a moment before she was able to bring it up. Her left shoulder shrieked in agony, but she fought back the pain as she approached Wolfe. The nearness of victory deadened any agony. He still did not rise to defend himself.

She stood over him for a moment, the sword held out. Her left shoulder throbbed.

Nothing. No movement. She reached out with the sword and flicked up his visor.

His eyes were closed as if he were sleeping.

Layne scanned his body, unsure of what to do. She was about to look over her shoulder at Michael and Colin when she spotted blood dripping from the gap above his breastplate onto the dirt below. She dropped the sword and fell to his side. She tried to unbuckle his breastplate, but with the gauntlets on, she couldn't. She ripped them off and cast them aside. She unbuckled his breastplate, first from one shoulder and then the next, wincing at the pain in her own shoulder. She lifted it and peered beneath it. Red soaked the doublet below his shoulder.

She couldn't see! Sweat trickled down her forehead into her eyes. She tried to wipe it away with the back of her hand, but her fingers brushed the cold metal helmet. She ripped the helmet from her head and cast it aside.

Cool air kissed her sweat-drenched brow. She leaned over him to unlace the other side of the breastplate. No, no, no. This couldn't be happening. He had to be all right.

Michael raced to her side, joined by Wolfe's squire.

"He's hurt," she stated, unbuckling the side. She pulled the breastplate from his torso. Blood seeped through his doublet, soaking it. She pushed the padded material up over the flat planes of his stomach, up over the ridged muscles of his pectorals. "Help me," she commanded the boys. Fingers worked together to lift the doublet higher. A gash about a hand's width seeped blood near his shoulder. She pressed her hands against it, commanding Michael. "Get me clean towels. He needs –"

Wolfe suddenly gasped a sharp breath, his eyes flashing open. His hands grasped at his wound, touching Layne's fingers. Her eyes locked with his.

Then, hands pushed her back, away from him. People crowded around, shoving her out of the way.

Slowly, she climbed to her feet.

Someone roughly grabbed her arm, pulling her back. "Let's go."

Her shoulder screamed in pain at the rough movement and she looked up to see Colin's angry brown eyes glaring at her. She didn't fight as he led her quickly from the field. Disoriented and frightened, it took until they reached the outskirts of the forest for Layne to recover. She glanced back over her shoulder. "He'll be all right."

"Which is more than I can say for you," Colin growled.

Michael rode Angel up to their side. "He's on his feet. Physicians are helping him."

Layne felt a wave of relief wash over her. She stopped trying to look backward and walked with Colin.

"Pack up," Colin ordered Michael. "We leave immediately."

His words stopped Layne in her tracks. "But I won!"

Colin whirled on her. "Do you realize what you've done?" he demanded in a harsh growl.

"Yes!" Layne exclaimed. "I won the purse for us!

I beat the knight who couldn't be beaten! We can go home!"

Colin grabbed her breastplate and pulled her toward him, shoving his face close to hers.

"My shoulder," she gasped. "You're hurting me."

Colin released his grip, but his face remained full of rage. "You removed your helmet! Everyone knows you're a girl!"

His words slowly soaked in. Not only was she not a knight and forbidden from entering tournaments, but she had beaten their best knight. A woman had beaten a man. They would never get the purse. They would be lucky to leave with their heads intact. Oh, this was bad. "I couldn't see... He would have died if I didn't..."

Colin turned to Michael. "Michael, run ahead and get Frances to help you start packing."

Michael nodded and rode off through the forest.

Colin whirled on her. "Of all the stupid ideas! What were you thinking?"

Layne gaped at him. She had never seen him so angry. "I... wanted to win..."

"You wanted to joust! That's all you've been asking me for lately."

Layne scowled. "And why shouldn't I be able to? I won!"

"Because you're not a knight!" he exploded, stepping toward her.

"Well... I could be."

"But you're not!"

Her brows came together. "I was better than all of them! Better than Frances! Better than Wolfe! Better than you!"

Colin's jaw clenched tightly, and Layne knew she had gone too far. "You got lucky, that's all." Colin turned and stormed toward their tent. "I'm sending you home where you belong."

It was like a crossbow bolt to her heart. "No," she gasped. "Colin!" She raced after him. Not home! To live with her cousins. With her father. To tend him like some servant woman. He would never let her touch a sword. Never... She grabbed Colin's arm.

Colin spun on her. "You don't listen anymore. You've endangered all of us! You shouldn't be here." He stalked back to the tent.

Layne watched him go, tears rising in her eyes. He's right. It was foolish what she had done. Foolish and reckless and... Stupid! She glanced back toward the forest. The large trees blocked the field from her view.

Women didn't belong in the field. Not jousting. Not sword fighting. It didn't matter how good they were. Angry and hurt, she pulled at the buckles on the breastplate. They didn't belong in armor or on a horse. She tugged the buckles open and when the last one caught and wouldn't open, she lifted the armor over her head, tugging and yanking it. A lock of her hair snagged, but she didn't stop, she continued panting and pushing and pulling at the armor until it ripped the strand from her head. She tossed the armor aside with a shout of agony and landed on her bottom.

Huffing, she stared at the armor. It glistened dully in the early morning sun. She would never joust again. She would never touch a sword and lift it in challenge. The only problem was she enjoyed it. She enjoyed riding Angel; she enjoyed wielding a lance and she had relished jousting. She looked down at her hands to find them still covered in Wolfe's blood. It could just as well have been her own.

Michael emerged from the tent. He saw her sitting in the dirt and signaled for her to come over. When she didn't move, he cast a glance at the tent and then hurried to her side. "They're as hot as a boiling pot of stew. You'd better start helping."

Layne stared down at the blood on her hands. She had hurt Wolfe, but she had won. A woman had won the joust. They would never let her get away with it. Not Colin. Not Wolfe. Not Lord Dinkleshire who had sponsored the tournament. They would make up some excuse to deny her victory and then they would punish her and her family. "What have I done?"

CHAPTER TWO

𝕮arlton leaned over Griffin, pressing the cloth against his wounded shoulder. Physicians fussed over him as if he were an old lady. Griffin sat up and shoved his squire away, motioning for everyone to leave with a wide sweep of his arm, ordering them out of his pavilion with a growl.

When they had fled, his mind was finally able to focus on what had happened. He remembered opening his eyes and seeing twin beacons of blue gazing down at him. For a moment, he thought he had died, and she was an angel. Then, he recognized her slim face and full lips. The girl he had knocked over before the start of the joust. It took a moment longer for him to realize that she wore armor. And now, now, he realized what had happened and the full extent of her treachery. Dressing as a knight to joust against him! His fingers curled over the edge of his straw mattress. It was impossible! He had been knocked from his horse, senseless. And if that weren't maddening enough, it had been by the hand of a woman!

He swung his legs from the raised mat and pain flared through his shoulder. He looked down, peeling away the cloth his squire Carlton had placed over the wound. He studied the gouge. He must have received it from the lance. A lucky shot, that much was certain. It was bleeding, but it was no death wound. He would survive. He tossed the cloth aside.

A woman! What type of joust was Dinkleshire running? How could he allow this? It wasn't chivalrous to face a woman in a joust! It wasn't chivalrous to raise any weapon against a woman! Griffin rose. He planned to have words with Dinkleshire. He grabbed a tunic and pulled it over his head, marching from his pavilion as he tugged at the cloth.

"M'lord!" Carlton greeted as he exited. He was a young man of seventeen, standing a hands-breadth shorter than he, a valuable aide always eager to learn the ways of a knight. His dark hair was uncombed, looking like brambles of thorns were entangled in it. He brushed strands from his eyes. "Sir, your shoulder –"

"It will be fine," Griffin insisted. He was grateful those pesky physicians had departed.

He looked up to see Lord Dinkleshire hurrying across the grassy plain toward him. Short and stocky, the host of the tournament reminded Griffin of a nervous rat. He wrung his hands as he approached. "Sir Griffin!" he called. Other participants of the joust followed him, with a crowd of onlookers behind them.

Vultures, Griffin thought with distaste. Wanting to see what punishment would be levied.

"I am truly sorry about this. I---"

"As you should be," Griffin interrupted.

Dinkleshire puffed up his chest. "This shall be remedied immediately. I shant stand for such insult in my tournament. You shall be proclaimed winner and the purse shall be yours."

Griffin nodded, but he couldn't get past the fact he had not won.

Dinkleshire urged a small boy on with a quick wave of his hand, and then followed the child as he scampered around the tents. Four armed guards followed the boy.

With a scowl, Griffin joined the crowd, moving up to Dinkleshire's side. Around him, he recognized some of his opponents. Their jaws were tight, their brows furrowed. Some mumbled about hanging.

Prickles raced across Griffin's neck. This could quickly get out of hand. Dinkleshire wasn't strong enough to command this rabble. They were angry and wanted retribution. When Carlton joined him, he whispered, "Bring my sword."

Carlton disappeared immediately, racing back to the tent.

The small boy they were following burst through the edge of the forest. "There!" the boy shouted, pointing his slim arm. It was obvious which tent was theirs. It was the only pavilion being pulled down. Dinkleshire marched up to the tent, his fists clenched at his sides. The crowd followed behind him.

Two men who had been yanking the tent fabric down looked up at the crowd. They stopped their work and the one with dirty blonde hair stepped forward.

"Where is she?" Dinkleshire demanded.

"She?"

"The woman who injured Sir Griffin. You know women aren't allowed to joust."

"Of course I know that," the man replied.

"Then present her this moment."

Griffin was impressed at the manner in which the nervous little Dinkleshire ordered the man. He had seen this knight at other tournaments. He was the elder brother. There were two Fletchers that jousted, he vaguely recalled.

"Lord Dinkleshire, what my sister did is unforgivable. She did it without my knowledge," the Fletcher brother said.

"It is not my concern that you cannot control your family. Where is she?"

A moment of heavy silence spread through the clearing.

Griffin glanced over his shoulder at the crowd. Scowls of disapproval, and even anger, marred more than one man's brow. One knight had his hand on the pommel of his sword. Where was Carlton with his weapon? When he looked back at the dismantled tent, he saw her, the woman he had seen leaning over him in the field of honor. Long brown hair hung in waves down her back. Her nose was pert and delicate. Black leggings fit snugly over the womanly curves of her thighs and lower hips. Her torso was covered by a green tunic. The whirlwind who had slammed into him before the joust. He stared at her face, looking at her large eyes, wanting to see if they were truly so blue as he remembered, but she was gazing at Dinkleshire. Griffin's gaze swept her again. She was so young. But it was her, there was no doubt in his mind. Griffin's surprise and distress only added to his anger and humiliation.

The crowd around him grumbled as one, their voices crashing over him in a sea of displeasure.

A younger boy stepped beside her.

She hung her head and a lock of her hair fell

forward.

"Lord Dinkleshire, I take full responsibility for my sister," the eldest brother stated.

This drew the gazes of the rest of the Fletcher siblings.

"As you should, Sir Colin," Dinkleshire said. "You will be fined. Fifty shillings."

A collective gasp moved through the crowd like a small breeze.

Griffin's eyebrows rose. That was a hefty fine. One could buy a war horse for fifty shillings. But it was a fair price for the crime. He nodded in agreement. The matter was settled. They would pay the fine and hopefully the little chit would be put in her place and never joust again.

Colin exchanged a glance with the other brother. Griffin realized he must be Frances, the one that should have jousted. Colin straightened as he turned back to Dinkleshire. "We do not have that much coin."

Griffin shifted his gaze from Dinkleshire to Colin.

"We cannot pay that fine. We can work it off, but…"

Dinkleshire's face turned red.

Griffin realized Dinkleshire knew they wouldn't be able to pay that much coin. He had hoped to drive them off, send them back to their lands. He had wanted to punish them all and had set the fine incredibly high so they would never be allowed to compete in future jousts. Griffin knew he should be grateful. Ridding the tournament of the likes of the Fletcher girl and her brothers was a boon to all righteous knights. But there was also a nagging feeling of disappointment. He had never shied away from a challenge. If the girl had been so talented in the joust, surely her brothers would be even more so. If this heavy fine drove the Fletchers out of the tournaments entirely, he would never have a chance to face them on the field of honor.

"You know the alternative," Dinkleshire warned.

Colin drew himself up. He lifted his chin, a mirror image of the girl's defiant tilt.

"Colin," the girl hissed, taking a step forward.

"Layne," Frances called. "Haven't you done enough?"

"I do," Colin answered Dinkleshire.

Dinkleshire stared at him for a moment. Then, he signaled his guards with a wave of his hand. "Take him to the dungeon."

Griffin sighed quietly. A severe punishment, but a deserved one. The sanctity of the tournament had to be preserved.

"No." The denial ripped from the woman's very soul. It touched something primal inside of Griffin. She stepped forward as the guards came to surround her brother.

Her youngest brother tugged pleadingly on her arm to keep her back.

As the guards moved aside to usher Colin forward, the woman took another step. "No!" Her cry froze everything.

"Layne," Frances snapped.

"No," she repeated. "You can't take him. This isn't his fault."

"No, it's not," Dinkleshire said. "Maybe you'll remember your place in the future." He turned away.

Griffin saw the anguish in her large blue eyes, the agony in her parted lips, and his heart skipped a beat.

Her shoulders dropped. "It's my fault. I did this." She lifted her chin. "Take me instead."

For a moment, time seemed to stop as everyone looked at the girl. Then, Dinkleshire began laughing. "Surely you jest!"

Griffin saw the spark in her eyes as her teeth clenched. "If you don't, I might joust in a tournament again and all of this will be for naught."

That stopped Dinkleshire's laughter. His lips thinned. He poked a finger at the girl, signaling the guards to take her. As they left Colin's side and moved to the girl, Frances cast a quick glance at his brother.

Colin held up his hands in helplessness and shook his head. "You can't take her!" he called. "She's just a foolish, impulsive child. She doesn't know what she's doing!"

"She knew enough to get past you," Dinkleshire retorted.

Griffin's fists clenched. A woman in the dungeon. It went against his code of chivalry. Women were to be protected, cherished. Saved from harm, not put into harm's way. Even those who were foolish enough to joust against him. He winced at the last thought. She had won. And that pricked his pride. But he could not allow them to throw her in the dungeon. "Wait." The command seemed to come out of his mouth before he had even decided to utter it.

At first, no one heard him.

The two brothers stood together, speaking fervently.

The youngest brother watched from near the horses.

The girl stood in the midst of the guards, just

starting to move off toward the castle and her permanent home in the dungeon. The knights from the joust parted to let them through.

"Stop!" Griffin called in a booming voice, drawing all the attention to him.

The talking ceased.

He walked toward Dinkleshire.

Dinkleshire met him halfway. "Surely this meets with your approval," the stout man said, a half smile on his lips.

"I will pay the fine," Griffin proclaimed.

Dinkleshire paused, his mouth dropping in surprise. "But Sir Griffin... You were the one wronged! It's not right..."

Griffin couldn't believe he had uttered the words. No, it wasn't right. "I will make sure the girl is punished properly," Griffin added. "I will pay the fine and she will work it off."

 CHAPTER THREE

Layne heard Griffin's proclamation and couldn't move. She was numb. First the dungeon, now this!

"No!" Colin exploded and stalked toward Griffin. "Layne will not be a plaything for this man's sexual appetite."

Griffin's face darkened, his lips thinned, and his jaw clenched tight. "I have purely chivalrous motives in mind. Are you saying I am anything but honorable?"

"What could you possibly want with her? She is a woman who thinks she can wield a sword as well as a man!"

"I aim to teach her her place," Griffin rumbled, towering over Colin. "Something you could not do."

Colin's eyes widened in outrage.

Layne had seen that murderous glare only one other time from Colin. When he was standing at the fence in the field of honor, watching her joust Sir Griffin. She pushed her way out from between the guards. She had to stop this before Colin did something foolish like challenge Griffin. She stepped between the two men, placing her arm on Colin's. "It's all right, Colin. I can take care of myself. You've taught me this."

Colin grit his teeth.

Layne leaned in closer to him. "You have to look out for Michael," she whispered. When he continued to glare at Griffin, she called, "Colin."

He snapped his gaze to her.

"Michael. You have to look out for him." She shook his arm. "How many times have you told me jousting and swordplay was a man's world? How many?"

Colin shook his head and then dropped his chin to his chest, muttering a soft curse.

"Michael. Look out for him. He'll be lonely. You have to take care of him. Don't push him away."

Colin shook his head. "I won't let you do this, Layne."

She looked over her shoulder at Griffin. The man stood tall, his blonde hair glinting in the sun. His jaw was hard, his eyes narrowed. "I suppose it's better than the dungeon." She glanced at Colin. "For both of us."

Colin began to shake his head.

Layne ducked her head, catching his eye. "This is my fault. I want to make it right."

Colin grimaced, but stopped shaking his head. His shoulders drooped slightly. "Laynie..." he protested weakly.

She threw her arms around his neck. "I know you would have gone to the dungeon for me. And I would have gone for you."

He squeezed her for a short moment.

"Please don't tell father," Layne whispered.

Colin released her, staring into her eyes for a long moment. Agony, resolve and bitter determination

30

glinted in his orbs. He turned to face Griffin. "When we have the coin, I will pay you back and Layne will return to us."

Griffin nodded once. "Agreed."

Colin stepped forward, jabbing a finger into Griffin's chest. "I swear Wolfe, if you mistreat her in any way..."

"She will not be mistreated," Wolfe promised.

Colin's jaw was firm, his eyes distrustful as he stared at Wolfe. Finally, he sighed softly and locked gazes with Layne. It was as if he wanted to tell her something, as if he wanted to bestow on her some brotherly wisdom. Instead, he simply bowed his head and turned away.

Griffin's squire rushed up, panting. He handed Griffin his sword.

Griffin sheathed the weapon and joined Layne. "Carlton, show the lady to our tent."

Layne stared at Colin's retreating back for a moment, then she heard Griffin's words and snapped herself out of her trepidation. "I have to get my things from my tent."

"You have no further need of your things. Everything you need will be supplied by me."

Layne's brows rose in surprise. "But my dagger. I can't..."

"Ladies have no need for weapons. You will learn that in my care."

Surprise gave way to anger and Layne scowled. She didn't like this presumptuous arrogant cad. He wasn't at all like the man she had crashed into. She stood for a moment, staring Wolfe in the eye. It would not do to defy him here. Not in front of the others. She was already in enough trouble as far as they were concerned.

She turned and followed Griffin's squire into the mass of onlookers. Some men mumbled insults as she passed, but none dared to touch her. She glanced back at Griffin Wolfe to find him speaking with Dinkleshire. He towered over the short lord, his face set in consternation.

Layne continued after Griffin's squire. One of the men before her spit on the ground. Shivers raced through Layne. She had made enemies by jousting. By winning. She carefully brushed past him, hurrying after Carlton. The crowd was like a group of poisoned daggers poised to prick her flesh; the hatred and animosity were almost a physical manifestation. When they broke through the crowd, she breathed a small sigh of relief. The fresh air was cool and refreshing...and safe. She wished she could have taken at least one of her daggers.

"Come on," Carlton called.

Layne glanced up at him. He stood five horse-lengths before her, his hands on his hips. He was about her age, she surmised. She picked up her pace, moving quickly after him as he turned to continue on.

"I'm sure Sir Griffin will tell you your chores, so ya don't have to worry about that."

Chores? That should have been expected. He did say she would have to work the coin off.

"The armor, weapons and horses are my responsibility, so I expect ya to keep yer hands off."

That was insulting, but Layne kept her mouth closed. She was a skilled horsewoman and knew how to handle both animals and weapons. She would have to remember she was here to work. To do as Griffin said. And he was most assuredly angry she had beaten him. She had to assume this would not be a pleasant experience.

Carlton stopped abruptly and turned to her. "And let's get something else straight. You take orders from me, not the other way around. I'm Sir Griffin's squire. Not you."

Layne grit her teeth. "As if I would want to be."

Carlton's eyes narrowed. "Sir Griffin is an honored knight. He has won every tournament he has ever entered."

"Except one," she couldn't help adding. She didn't like the smug superiority of this squire.

Carlton stepped closer to her. "Witchcraft and sorcery aside, he has won every tournament."

"Is that what he told you? That I was a witch?"

"There can be no other explanation."

"Except one." She lifted her chin. "That I am better than him."

"There will be no more talk like that."

Layne whirled at the booming voice. She blushed from head to toe. Wolfe stood behind her.

"You will learn that a woman who is not a knight does not have a place on the field of honor."

Layne lowered her head so she could scowl without him seeing her. She felt horrible at having him hear she thought she was better than him. Truth be told, she thought she got lucky. She should never have been able to defeat him. He was more skilled than she was, more experienced.

Carlton beamed happily and righteously at her.

Griffin walked past her and headed toward a large tent in the center of the others. A white warhorse was tethered beside a dappled horse at the side of the tent. The warhorse was beautiful. Its silky white coat shone in the sunlight. Layne marveled at the animal, and every instinct demanded she rush to the horse to touch with reverence and admiration.

Griffin cast a glance over his shoulder at her. He followed her gaze. "Adonis."

The horse looked up, whinnying.

It took all of Layne's will power to remain where she was.

Griffin must have seen this. "It is Carlton's responsibility to see to the horses." He looked at his squire. "Begin packing. Leave the tent for last."

Carlton nodded and moved off toward the tent.

Griffin looked at her. "I have other responsibilities for you."

Layne nodded and cast a last look at the beautiful steed as she followed Griffin into the tent.

And stopped. Two simple beds made of straw and blankets were against the far wall of the tent. Her eyes moved to the weapons against the wall to her right. A sword, crossbow, bow and arrow, all lay out neatly positioned. She longed to run her hand over them, to lift them and test their balance.

"You shall make our meals," Griffin said. "Mend our clothing. And tend our wounds."

Layne glanced at him. He stood with his hands on his hips, watching her. She could do that in the blink of an eye. "What else?" she demanded.

He cocked his head.

"I can finish those in a matter of hours. I am skilled at cleaning and sharpening weapons. I have --"

"Carlton will do the chores required of a squire."

She lifted her chin. "I am to be a servant?"

Griffin opened his mouth and then closed it. "You will be what I require."

Layne's jaw clenched. He was not going to make this easy on her. And he shouldn't, she reminded herself. Colin would have sent her back to her father. This was not worse than that. Nothing could be worse than being sent back home to face her father's wrath. She nodded.

"You will keep the tent neat. Clean up our meals, wash our clothing."

"Anything else?" she asked.

"If I require more of you, I will tell you. You will start by tending the wound you inflicted on me." He lifted his tunic over his head.

Sculpted firmness met her eyes. Every line, every curve was perfection. His muscles rippled as he lay on one of the mats. It wasn't that she had never seen a man with his shirt off, because she had, many times. Her brothers often took off their tunics to practice or labor. But Griffin was different. He looked stronger and in better shape than her brothers.

He lay on his mat and looked up at her. "Do not be afraid. I will not hurt you."

Layne swallowed. She had tended her brothers many times, cleaned and wrapped their wounds. This was not new to her. But somehow this felt different. Very different.

Griffin pointed to cloth and a water basin near the foot of the mat.

She dragged them over to the side of the bed and dropped to her knees. She shoved a cloth into the water and wrung it out. Her gaze moved over his torso to his shoulder where the wound was. For a moment, she wondered what it would be like to touch him. She mentally shook herself. What was she thinking? She leaned over him and carefully dabbed at the cut. The wound was an ugly gash in his tanned skin. Blood still dripped freshly from the very center of the cut. But it was slowing. It was not fatal, and for this Layne was grateful.

He relaxed back.

Layne rinsed the cloth in the water and carefully cleaned the area. It looked like the lance had gotten under his armor, scraping his skin. Guilt assailed her. She had done this to him. It had not been her intention. "I'm sorry," she whispered.

"For the wound?" he wondered.

She didn't respond, but continued to clean his injury, carefully tending the open cut.

"I've had worse. 'Tis nothing," he insisted.

She ran her fingertips over the skin around the cut to check for warmth. That could be a sign of infection. A soft breath rustled a lock of hair that had fallen forward to brush his shoulder. She glanced up. He was close. So very close. The absolute blue of his eyes seemed to take up her entire vision.

"This could have happened to you," he whispered.

She hadn't thought of that. She had only wanted to face someone on the field of honor, to see what it was like to joust. Her gaze dipped to his lips.

"You could have been hurt just as badly. Or worse."

His lips moved, forming each word. What had he said? She could have been hurt. Yes. For the second time, she had to pull herself from her musings. She sat back, separating herself from him, breaking the spell. She glanced around and found the clean cotton cloth at the foot of the mat. She carefully pressed it to the wound.

"If I had hurt you like this, I would never have been able to forgive myself."

Startled, Layne shifted her gaze to his. Sincerity shone in his blue orbs. Layne's heart fluttered like a baby bird waking up to a ray of sunshine. She didn't like the warm feeling washing over her.

"You must never joust again." His commanding tone returned. "And I will see to it that you do not."

 CHAPTER FOUR

riffin didn't know what to make of the woman. He was shocked that she seemed sincere in her apology. What had she expected of a joust? Men were stronger and able to withstand the injuries that came with a tournament. Women were fragile, delicate even. God's blood! If he had struck her with the lance, she could easily have been killed! His gaze moved over her. She was only a slip of a woman, from what he could see. To don a man's armor and to take up a lance against him was folly.

She ran her tongue over her lips as she picked up the corner of the cloth to check on the wound.

For a moment, he was stunned, captivated by her presence. Perhaps it was the unexpected glistening of her moist lips. Perhaps it was the brush of her hair across his nipple. Whatever it was, he had a sudden and unanticipated picture of her lying beneath him with her lips parted. He shifted his position and turned his gaze to her hand on his wound. Her fingers were so small. Another image flashed into his head. Of those small hands wrapped around...

He cleared his throat, drawing her gaze. "Did your brothers allow you to joust?"

She shook her head, looking back at the wound. "No." A smile slowly curved her lips. Then, she froze and looked at him. Her chin lifted a notch. "Frances hit his head and I took it upon myself to take his place."

"Took it upon yourself?" he echoed in disbelief. He shook his head as she pressed the cloth against his wound again. "Then you must have jousted elsewhere, in other tournaments?"

Again, she shook her head. "I've watched my brothers in practice and on the field." She looked at him and a lock of her dark hair hung over her cheek. "I've tried the quintain..."

He scowled. The quintain? But his concentration was held by that stray lock of her hair out of place against her rounded cheek. He found it difficult to concentrate. He wanted to brush that hair from her face, run his fingers along her skin.

She sat back, brushing the lock from her cheek, and lifted the cloth from his shoulder. "I'm skilled with a horse. I've often trained with my brothers sparring with swords."

"Swords?" The word seemed to come from her effortlessly. It should have been foreign on her lips. He sat up, his brows furrowing. She should have been speaking of French fashion or embroidery. "Your brothers allowed you to use a sword?" he asked in disbelief.

She shrugged. "They needed the practice. Michael is too young, although he is learning quickly. And there were occasions where either Colin or Frances could not practice when the other wished. Frances was more likely to spar with me than Colin."

Griffin looked at her hands. He imagined them...wrapped around the handle of a sword. "Where is your mother?"

"She died when I was young."

He lifted his gaze to her eyes. "And your father?"

"Why do you ask me so many questions?"

Griffin cocked his head. "If you are to be with me, in my care, I must know your character."

She straightened. "I should find that insulting. You mean because I am a woman who likes to joust and sword fight there is a flaw in my character?"

"Hmm." He shook his head. "Because you disobeyed your brothers and jousted anyway, there is a flaw in your character."

She sighed softly and dropped her chin to her chest. "Yes. I suppose that could be true." She looked up at him and there was something in her deep blue eyes that held more mystery. "If you truly think that, why did you stop them from throwing me in the dungeon?"

"Women should be protected and cherished. The dungeon is no place for a woman."

"Even a woman with a flaw in her character?"

His gaze swept her face, from her long lashes to her full lips. "Any woman."

She nodded and began to collect the cloth. "I thought you saved me from the dungeon because you wanted to know how I could have possibly unhorsed you."

He reached out, grabbing her arm and preventing her from moving away from him. "I do want to know how you beat me." No real training, never jousting in a tournament before. It irked his pride beyond all measure.

Her lips curved up in a grin. "With a lance."

He stared at her curved lips. Those insolent, mocking lips. He remembered his father teaching a servant woman her place. He had used his fist. Griffin released her and leaned back. He glanced at his shoulder. "Finish," he commanded.

Her gaze dipped to the juncture of his thighs. Or was that his imagination?

She put down the cloth and picked up a fresh one. She moved closer to him and placed the cloth on his wound. He lifted his arm as she began to wrap a thin strip around the clean cloth to hold it in place.

Griffin's gaze slid from her hands to her lips. She was very close. He could just lean in and sample her lips. He gritted his teeth. What was he thinking? That would dishonor her and her brothers. He was trying to teach her a woman's place and all he could think about was her naked body and her lips. God's blood!

Finally, she sat back with a nod.

He inspected her work and found it satisfactory. He rose, towering above her. She knelt before him; her hands folded in her lap. His gaze moved over her. This was going to take a lot more will power than he had thought. He brushed past her, toward the exit.

"I found a flaw in your style."

He froze. Impossible. There was no fault with his style. It was perfect. It was… He turned to her. She was just a woman. What did she know about jousting style? She was only trying to punish him for insulting her. Still… she had unhorsed him. He clenched his teeth, leaving his biting retort unspoken. He spun and strode from the tent.

Layne sat in the middle of Griffin's tent. How many times had Colin told her she was not to joust? How many times had her father chastised her for picking up a sword? Again and again she had been warned. But none of them had told her that her disobedience was a flaw in her character. A flaw in her character. A flaw. She had accepted long ago that she would never be the perfect woman like her aunt. She didn't like embroidery or playing an instrument. She didn't care at all about fashion.

Her father would often punish her by banning her from the fields or from the stables. It had never worked. She had simply waited out the punishment, endured it without bemoaning the injustice of it all. As she did now. Be a good little girl. Follow the rules until all is forgotten and forgiven. Or until Colin saved enough coin to pay Griffin back.

She looked around the tent. The weapons gleamed invitingly on the floor, the reflection of the setting sun flashing off the polished metal. Every instinct demanded she touch them in reverence, pick them up, swing one of them. But Griffin had forbidden it. She clasped her hands in her lap tightly. Not one touch.

But she could look. She forced herself to stay where she was and just look at the weapons. These were either winnings from recent melees, or Griffin was wealthy, and these were his personal collection. They were not like the swords her brothers had. These were beautiful with finely etched details in the hilt. They were works of art. Perfect. Much like their owner. She brushed that last thought away lest it start to really take hold of her senses. The man was far from perfect. His body, though, was truly a work of art. Stop it, Laynie.

She glanced around the tent, forcing her thoughts elsewhere. It was so different from the Fletcher tent. Here, everything had a place. There was no clutter. In her family's tent, her brothers were not so...meticulous. They threw blankets and bags everywhere. Clothing was scattered over the inside of the tent. Here, the blankets were folded neatly on the bed. Granted, the tent was larger than hers, but that made it seem all the more organized.

She stood and slowly moved about the tent, familiarizing herself with the layout. The area closest to the door was where Griffin's armor was laid out. Layne bent down and inspected the small dent in Griffin's breast plate. This was where her lance struck him, giving him the wound she had just tended. She reached out and ran her fingers over the indent. She had not meant to hurt him. She had never really thought she would unhorse him.

She continued on. Next was a pile of clothing that Layne was sure was the clothing Griffin wore beneath his armor. It would have to be cleaned. That was her duty. She would get back to it. She continued to survey the tent.

Next came cleaning supplies, candles, kindling for a fire, as well as Adonis's comb. Then Carlton's bed, then Griffin's. She wondered briefly where she would sleep, but that didn't concern her as much as starting her duties. At least it would give her something to do!

Layne picked up the pile of clothing and the soap she found near the supplies and left the tent.

"Where do you think you're going?"

Layne whirled to find Carlton sitting on the ground, running a stone against the edge of a sword.

"To the stream. To wash clothes. My chores." She turned to head toward the stream. Carlton stood and followed her. She stopped and turned to him. "I am more than capable of washing clothes."

"I'm sure you are. My orders are to make sure you are safe."

Layne looked back at the tent. "Where is Sir Griffin?"

"Practicing."

Layne turned and walked toward the stream. "Does he always practice this late?"

"No. But he's never been unhorsed before."

The last rays of the sun were fading from the sky when Layne finished washing the clothing and began to carry them back to the tent. Carlton advised her to go around the tents of the other knights to avoid any unwanted confrontation. She silently agreed. She knew the other knights were not pleased with what she had done.

The path around the tents led her close to the field of honor. She heard a smash of wood against wood and wondered if Griffin was still practicing. Layne glanced at the field and saw one rider. As night took over the sky, she saw he wore no armor. His horse thundered toward the quintain; the long lance pointed straight toward the wooden structure. His form was perfect, his concentration fierce. Tingles danced across the nape of her neck and she took a step closer, hugging the wet clothing to her chest.

The lance struck the quintain and it spun. For a moment, she thought it was going to strike Griffin, but he ducked and rode past. She found herself grinning. He was spectacular. The ease at which he moved made it look easy. He lifted the lance and reined his white stallion into a canter.

He threw the lance down as he maneuvered his horse around the field. Griffin and Adonis moved together as one. They were elegant and wonderful to watch. But then Griffin did something she had never seen anyone do before on such a big horse. He dropped the reins and sat up straight, crossing his arms over his chest. What was he doing? Surely without control of the horse, Adonis would balk or refuse his commands or simply stop. But to her amazement Adonis continued his canter around the field, taking the turns as if Griffin still held the reins in his hands. It took Layne a moment to realize Griffin was controlling Adonis with subtle movements of his legs and knees.

Astonished, Layne could only stare. He truly was amazing and very skilled. Much more so than she was. And yet, she had beaten him. How had that happened? She wasn't that good. It had been her first time jousting! It shouldn't have happened. She thought back to the joust and his 'flaw'. She had seen him list to the side. What could have caused that? He wasn't doing it now. Had Adonis stumbled?

"He's a great knight," Carlton said from beside her.

Layne could only nod. He was marvelous. It was like watching living art. His blonde hair waved behind him like a small flag. He moved in smooth cadence with Adonis, each gentle movement a rhythm of elegance and power. He was magnificent.

Griffin stopped and dismounted, throwing a leg over the side and sliding to the ground. He picked up the lance and shoved it into the ground so it stood upright. Then, he swung himself up into the saddle easily. He grabbed the lance. Neither horse nor rider seemed to have any flaws now. Was it only something you could see when you faced him? Something no one else had seen except her?

The hairs on the back of her neck prickled and chills raced down her arms. She had observed many jousts, but there was something about this… Something that didn't seem right.

"Let's go. We still need to set up your sleeping mat." Carlton walked up the slight rise toward the tent.

Layne glanced at Griffin again. Warmth flooded through her. He was such a valiant sight. She reluctantly turned away from him and followed Carlton, holding the clothing to her chest. "His form is…very good," Layne said hesitantly.

"His form is faultless," Carlton countered. "Sir Griffin perfected it a long time ago and he practices it for hours a day."

"His control over Adonis is amazing."

Carlton nodded. "He raised him from a foal. He trained him alone. No one else cared for him. It was all Sir Griffin. Even now, he is the one to comb Adonis and see to his needs."

Layne glanced back at the field. Griffin obviously knew Adonis well. The chances of Adonis balking or sidestepping would be slim. But it could happen. "During our joust, Sir Griffin and mine, did you see Adonis step into a hole or twist his ankle?"

"No," Carlton said firmly. "Adonis did nothing wrong."

"But Griffin is such a talented rider, something must have happened. I shouldn't have been able to unhorse him."

Carlton stopped and looked at her with harshness in his eyes. "No. You shouldn't have."

"Have you checked everything? Maybe Adonis has a stone in his shoe. Maybe –"

"That is not your concern!"

Layne was startled by the agitation in his voice.

Carlton began forward but stopped suddenly and whirled. "And don't get any ideas about inspecting Sir Griffin's armor or weapons. You are to stay away from them."

Layne drew herself up. "I know!"

Carlton narrowed his eyes in disbelief and shook his head. He stalked toward the tent.

Layne glanced one more time in Griffin's direction. He was too good to be unhorsed by her. There was something else going on. Something else must have happened on the field of honor to cause him to falter and take a misstep. She turned to follow Carlton.

As they approached the tent, Layne saw a group of about five men standing near their pavilion; some she recognized as competing knights in the joust, some she didn't.

Carlton slowed before they reached the tent. He grabbed her arm, halting her. "Go and get Sir Griffin," he said in a quiet voice. He gently eased the wet clothing from her arms.

Layne looked back at the men. At first glance, she didn't see anything to be apprehensive of, but she quickly realized they all wore their swords strapped to their waists. One stumbled as though he were drunk, and the others laughed. She nodded and backed away, turning to dash toward the field. She ran as fast as she could, hating to leave Carlton alone with the men.

She didn't slow as she emerged from the forest, running toward the field. Her heart pounded.

Griffin was still the only knight in the field. He thundered down the field, holding his lance.

Layne called his name. She stood at the fence, waving to get his attention. When he didn't pause or turn in her direction, she ducked through the planks of wood and ran onto the field.

Griffin hit the quintain and rode by. The sandbag whirled around but didn't come close to hitting him. When he reached the other end of the field, he turned Adonis. He saw her and cantered the steed toward her, his brow furrowed in unhappiness.

They met in the center of the field.

Layne's heart thundered in her chest as Griffin neared and she wasn't certain whether it was because of the knights at the tent or Griffin's disapproving scowl.

"I told you it was forbidden to come to the field," Griffin warned quietly.

"There are five knights at the tent looking for trouble."

Griffin's lips thinned. He reached a hand down to her. Layne stretched her hand up to him, grasping it. Griffin swept her up before him, his arms around her to hold the reins. As soon as she was seated, he spurred Adonis out of the field.

When they came within sight of the tent, Layne saw Carlton surrounded by the men. He shook his head and said something indiscernible to them. One of them answered, pointing to the ground as if making a point.

Griffin urged Adonis between Carlton and the knight, pushing the knight away from Carlton with the animal's mass.

Layne recognized the knight from the scar

running along his cheek to his jaw. Sir Osmont. He sneered when he locked gazes with her.

"Is there something you would say to me, Sir Osmont?" Griffin demanded.

When the other knights turned from Carlton to Griffin, Carlton backed away to the tent, his anxious eyes searching out Griffin.

"You can't let her get away with it!" Osmont hollered, pointing a finger at Layne. "A fine is not enough punishment."

Griffin dismounted easily and walked to Osmont until he stood directly before him. Osmont was half a head shorter than Griffin. "And what would you do?"

"Flog the wench! She will understand that a woman does not dress in armor and pretend to be a knight."

Layne's fingers curled anxiously around Adonis's reins.

"I could show her the proper place for a woman," one of the men behind Osmont said and grabbed his crotch. The movement put him off balance and he stumbled into another knight.

Griffin's gaze never left Osmont. "Is this the type of treatment you condone for a woman? Hardly befitting of a knight."

Osmont's cheeks colored and his jaw tightened.

"A woman is to be treated with reverence, not scorn."

"She broke the rules!" Osmont sneered.

"And Dinkleshire proclaimed the punishment of a fine."

"Which you paid. She knocked you on your arse." Osmont spit out the words. "Where is your pride, man? At the very least you should have let her rot in the dungeon."

Griffin's eyes narrowed. "And now you tell me how to behave? Careful, Osmont. You overstep your bounds."

Osmont met Griffin's glare, puffing out his chest. "You can't let her get away with this."

"The offense was against me, not anyone else."

"It was against all knights! All men! You were humiliated! Unhorsed by a woman!"

The four knights behind him grumbled in agreement. "And you even paid the bloody fine!" one of them grumbled.

"I did," Griffin agreed. "I will not have a woman locked away in a dungeon because of me."

"This is not over, Wolfe. She will be punished," Osmont growled.

"This woman is mine until her brothers repay me."

An odd thrill rushed through her at his words. *This woman is mine.* She knew he had said other words after that, but she didn't hear them. The thrill evaporated just as quickly as it had formed, replaced by a gnawing fear of what her future held under his command.

"She is under my protection," Griffin continued.

Shocked exclamations met his proclamation.

"If you chose to do her harm, then you do me harm." Griffin's eyes narrowed. "And there will be no mercy from me."

Osmont spit on the ground, but he took a step backward. "You're growing soft, Wolfe."

"Your words mean nothing to me. Prove it on the jousting field," Griffin said, turning his back on

Osmont to lock gazes with Layne.

"Oh, I intend to. If a woman can unhorse you, then I should have no problem." He whirled and stormed off. The other knights followed Osmont toward the castle.

Adonis snorted and tossed his head.

Concern washed over Layne. She had humiliated Griffin. And now, every knight would think he was easy to unhorse. He would be a target for the other knights, both physically and for their scorn and ridicule.

Griffin let out a soft sigh and stepped toward her, lifting his hands to help her dismount.

"Sir Griffin, I apologize. I could have –" Carlton said, his head bowed.

"There is nothing to apologize for."

Layne leaned down into Griffin's hold. For just a moment, his hands spanned her waist and her hand lay against his shoulders. She could feel the muscles beneath his tunic, the rippling power.

"You are wet," he said. His gaze shifted from her eyes to her chest.

Layne recalled the wet clothing she had been holding in her arms. "Oh. Yes. I was doing my chores. Cleaning your clothes."

Griffin's smooth brow slowly furrowed. "You went to the stream alone?"

"Carlton accompanied me."

Griffin nodded in approval. "It is not wise for you to leave the tent unaccompanied." He looked at the path the knights had taken. "There are some who would do you harm."

Layne nodded and chanced a glance in the direction the knights had taken. These were men that followed the circuit of tournaments. She knew them by sight, at least. She knew she would come into contact with them again and again.

"It's not only here. We are participating in the Norfolk Tourney. By then news will have reached them about you."

Layne hadn't thought there would be this much controversy surrounding her jousting. She hadn't thought it through. And now she deeply regretted her actions. It brought embarrassment to her brothers, and if her father heard about what happened he would send for her. That thought sent shivers of apprehension through her.

"It will be dangerous for you," Griffin said softly.

Layne looked up to see him staring at her. She blushed slightly and nodded.

"You will sleep in the tent with Carlton and me."

Layne's mouth dropped. Sleep in the tent with them? But they were not kin. "That isn't appropriate."

"Dressing in armor and jousting like a knight isn't appropriate. This, I do for your safety."

# CHAPTER FIVE

Layne had done everything Griffin asked her without protest. He was having trouble reconciling this Layne with the one that had defied her brothers and jousted.

They sat in the main room of the Boar's Head Inn, eating. Carlton sat next to him; Layne sat opposite on the other side of the wooden table. As they ate, Griffin watched Layne. Layne sipped at the soup in the trencher. A lock of dark hair brushed her hand as she lifted a piece of bread to her mouth. She was unlike any woman he had ever met. Intelligent, opinionated. Nothing like his sister, Gwen. Long ago, Gwen had learned the art of fake tears, pouting and manipulation to get her way. Layne seemed to be more of a fighter, a woman who didn't need to resort to manipulation to get what she wanted.

She lifted her eyes and locked gazes with him. Her eyes were wide and blue…

"What?" she demanded. She quickly moved her arms from the table. "Are my elbows on the table? My brothers always chastised me for that. I'm sorry, if they were."

Griffin was pleased that her brothers attempted to guide her in manners. "No," Griffin said. "You look tired."

She smiled slightly. "Perhaps I am, a little."

Griffin lifted a piece of bread to his lips and took a bite. "Women are naturally more delicate than men. If you are tired, you should –"

She leaned forward. "I find it insulting that you continually try to remind me how weak I am. Perhaps men are physically stronger. They were built for heavy lifting and wielding mighty weapons. But it is not always the better weapon that wins the fight. It is the intelligence of the person wielding it."

Griffin stared. Carlton stared.

She gave a puff of exasperation and shook her head. She pushed herself from the table to stand. "I will retire since I am so weak and frail."

Griffin watched her walk up the stairs. He had meant no disrespect. And yet, she had taken offense at his comment. He watched her shapely bottom as she moved up the stairs, unable to take his gaze from her.

"Sir Griffin," Carlton said carefully, "if any other man spoke to ya as she does, ya would have them at the end of your sword."

Griffin lifted a cup of ale to his lips. He took a long drink. When he lowered the mug, he looked at Carlton. "Layne is a willful young woman, that is certain. But she is still a woman. I would no more draw my sword against her than I would a child."

Carlton scowled.

"You don't agree with this?"

Carlton considered his question, quietly staring at his trencher.

He was a young man who could be rash at times. Griffin had seen him get angry when sword fighting. And then make mistakes that in a real battle could cost him his life. Griffin knew when fighting, whether it was in a joust or with sword, one must always maintain a clear head.

"I do," Carlton said slowly. "The Code of Chivalry says to respect the honor of women, I know this." He looked up at him. "I must wonder if this woman has honor."

Griffin scowled. He had been asking himself this exact question over and over, trying to decide what type of woman Layne was. "Has she said something that makes you question her honor?"

"It is what she did that makes me question it. Any woman who disguises herself as a knight and sneaks onto the field of honor to joust with a renowned knight..." Carlton shook his head in disapproval. "That is not a woman with honor."

Griffin nodded. "And yet, she was willing to give herself up, to go to the dungeon in her brother's place. That is honorable."

Carlton dropped his gaze to the piece of bread he held, a thoughtful scowl on his brow.

"We must give her time to reveal the true woman she is."

"Did someone say woman?"

Griffin glanced up at the dark-haired man standing beside the table, a lock of dark hair falling into his eyes. He recognized the man immediately and a grin spread across his lips. He stood, extending his hand. "Ethan Farindale!"

"Griffin Wolfe." Ethan grasped his arm in the typical warrior fashion, clasping it just below his elbow.

His blue eyes sparkled; his dark hair and complexion gave him that typical rogue appeal all the women seemed to love. "Tell me it's not true! Tell me mine ears hath deceived me. Tell me you were not unhorsed!"

Griffin groaned inwardly. His friend would never let him live that down. He hoped Ethan didn't know the entire truth. "Aye. It was a lucky blow."

Ethan closed his eyes and clutched his chest. "I thought I saw a lightning bolt strike the earth."

Griffin grinned. Lord, it was good to see his friend! It had been years since he had last seen him. How had they drifted apart?

"I heard it 'ad nothing ta do with a lightnin' bolt!" another voice said.

Griffin cringed, suddenly remembering why he and Ethan had drifted apart. He turned to a second man who approached the table. Gill Daunger. The man swaggered; his chest puffed out. The top of his shiny bald head came up to Griffin's chin. Ethan had taken another path, going off with Daunger to compete in a different sort of tournament. The melees, where dozens of men fought each other in bedlam and pandemonium. Total chaos, as far as Griffin was concerned. He enjoyed a much more civilized show of arms in the jousts.

"More like a couple of tits," Gill said with a lecherous grin. "Did she flash ya as ya rode by?"

Ethan chuckled. "A woman? A woman unhorsed you? You must be getting soft in your old age." He circled, looking him over thoughtfully. "I see no sign of laziness around your girth." He peered at his head, scrutinizing his skull with blatant skepticism. "Perhaps the softness is in there."

Griffin ignored him. "What are you doing here? I thought the last melee was in Derby."

Ethan nodded condescendingly; his lips quirked into a grimace of a half chuckle, half displeasure. "We're heading up to Norfolk for the Pas d'armes."

A tremor of unease snaked its way through Griffin. "I thought you enjoyed the melees."

"Didn't do so well in the last one. So Daunger and I thought we'd check out our competition in Norfolk and then head over to Woodstock Palace to join that one."

Dread slithered across Griffin's shoulders and he retook his seat, trying to appear casual even though chills of foreboding shot up his spine. It was exactly what he was doing. While Ethan had once been his friend, Daunger was nothing of the sort. Griffin didn't like the man. He was crude, lecherous and untrustworthy.

"Huge purse in Woodstock," Daunger marveled, taking a seat beside Carlton. He reached over and dipped his fingers into Carlton's stew to pull out a large piece of meat. He shoved it into his mouth.

Griffin ripped a piece of bread from his trencher.

Ethan placed a hand on his shoulder. "You know, don't you?"

Griffin paused. "Know what?"

"Your brother is hosting the Tourney at Woodstock Palace."

Griffin stiffened. "With Prince Edward?"

Daunger chuckled softly, his keen eyes locked on Griffin.

A bottomless pit opened up beneath Griffin. His brother hosting. Griffin shoved the piece of bread into his mouth, forcing himself to chew. He hadn't heard. How had his brother weaseled his way into hosting the tournament with the prince? That could only mean one thing. His father would be there. It suddenly sounded more like a trap than a glorious event.

Griffin couldn't shake the feeling of impending doom. What was his brother up to? He waited until Ethan and Daunger retired for the night before heading upstairs with Carlton. He didn't trust Daunger. Things went missing when Daunger was around. Coin and items, both. He had heard things, but there was never any proof. The man also had a gruff, overbearing demeanor that often put him at odds with others. More than once, Daunger had been the center of brawls.

When Griffin came to his room and opened the door, he scanned the small room for Layne and found her curled up in a blanket on the floor. He crossed the room and scooped her up, ready to reprimand her when she woke. She stirred, nestling against his chest, but did not awaken. Griffin stared down at her. It gave him a moment to truly look at her. Her dark hair was riotous about her face in gentle waves. Her nose was pert. Her lips full and slightly parted revealing a glimpse of white teeth. She was very pleasing to the eye. He was shocked at the sudden tender feelings that arose inside of him. She should be terrified, alone with two men she knew nothing about. But she had not complained. Not about the long, hard ride. Not about the chores. Perhaps she was used to such with her brothers. Either way, he felt a warmth of pride bloom in his chest. Yes, he was proud of her, of the way she carried herself.

He strode over to the bed and eased her into it. He stood looking down at her for a long moment before turning to Carlton. He pointed to the opposite side of the room. Carlton would sleep there.

As he walked to the opposite wall from Carlton, the spot he had chosen to sleep, he couldn't help wondering what his brother was up to. And what he had gotten himself into saving a woman who didn't want to be saved.

CHAPTER SIX

Sir Talvace charged down the field, his body leaning forward over the horse's neck. He struck the quintain hard enough to make it spin and ducked beneath the counterweight bag of sand that swung around.

Cheers went up around the yard as other knights encouraged him. They had reached the Norfolk Tournament grounds without further incident and now stood at the field where the Tournament was to be held.

Layne looked across the field to see three women leaning over the fence, waving to Sir Talvace. He rode past them in a show of bravado. Layne grimaced. It was all a game to him. He didn't care how good he was. Only that he won the attention of the noble women.

She looked at Griffin and Carlton beside her. Griffin had allowed her to come to the field, grudgingly admitting she was safer with him than being left alone in the tent.

Sir Talvace took up another lance.

"Watch," Griffin told Carlton.

Layne looked at Talvace. He wore only his

breastplate armor and Layne guessed it was to impress the ladies more than he needed it for protection. Most of the other knights practiced in a tunic.

Talvace lifted his lance to an upright position in preparation. His horse reared slightly, and he spurred it, lowering the lance and beginning his charge down the field. His lance bobbled for a moment before he regained control of it and leaned over the horse. He hit the quintain and it spun. This time he hadn't been quick enough, and the bag of sand twirled and knocked him in the arm.

Groans came from the audience.

"What did he do wrong?" Griffin asked.

Carlton leaned forward as if studying Talvace. "He couched the lance too far up. Too much lance was sticking out behind him."

Griffin nodded.

Layne stared at Talvace as he galloped past the ladies.

"He didn't punch forward with the lance," Carlton added.

"Punch forward?" Layne asked.

Carlton leaned forward so he could see her past Griffin. "Ya know..." He jerked his body forward. "Punch forward."

Layne nodded and looked again at Talvace.

"Very good," Griffin said. "What else?"

The silence stretched as Carlton watched Talvace.

"His grip on the lance was lazy allowing the lance to fall so it was not perpendicular to the quintain when he struck it," Layne said, watching Talvace as he greeted some of the knights at the other end of the field. She and her brothers had often made a game of finding the reason for the loss in jousting or the mistake in practice. As the silence stretched, she glanced at Carlton and Griffin. The two men stared at her, Griffin with a thin-looked steely gaze and Carlton with his mouth open slightly in shock. She realized her mistake and looked back at Talvace. She closed her mouth and bit her lower lip. She shouldn't have said anything. Griffin would tell her it wasn't her place.

"His horse was also going too slow," Griffin added.

Layne swung her head around to meet his gaze in surprise. Yes, it had been. If Talvace had spurred it on, regardless of everything else, he would not have gotten hit with the sandbag.

Griffin stared at her with a calm, cold gaze. She wished he could see how much she enjoyed the joust, how much she enjoyed watching and figuring out what went wrong for the loser, and what was done well by the victor. And nothing was a bigger challenge to her right now than finding out how she had knocked Griffin from the horse.

Griffin sent Carlton to the castle to enter him in the lists. He then accompanied Layne to the tent. "You were correct in what you noticed with Talvace."

Layne nodded. She knew she was.

"You are very skilled when it comes to seeing the flaws in other's jousting."

Layne shrugged, but kicked a rock as she walked. None of her brothers would admit that. "Colin would often make it a game. Who could find the most faults?" She shrugged. "I was the reigning champion."

"Not everyone would notice that Talvace lowered his lance a few finger-widths too much."

"Maybe."

He stopped, forcing Layne to look at him. The wind swept through his blond hair.

"Tell me," he ordered. "When you jousted against me, what flaw allowed you to unhorse me?"

Layne cocked her head to the side, her eyes narrowing in disbelief. "You're asking my opinion?"

Griffin pursed his lips and looked at the ground. "After what you noticed with Talvace, I am curious."

"Are you sure that's it? And not that I am the only one to unhorse you?"

He remained silent.

She quickly reviewed their joust in her mind and admitted, "Maybe it was just luck."

"Perchance. Except you told me there was a flaw in my style."

She shook her head. "It wasn't really a flaw. More like something you did that I took advantage of."

"I would know what that was."

A suspicion rose inside of her. What if Griffin had paid her fine to find out how she had beaten him? What if once he discovered it, he had every intention of allowing Dinkleshire to throw her in the dungeon? She continued walking back to the tent, an uneasy feeling in the pit of her stomach. "Would you believe it coming from a woman who was not a knight?"

He followed her. Silence settled around them like a cloud of distrust. "No. But I would take it into consideration."

"Are you sure Adonis did not stumble? Or a stirrup was broken?"

His gaze snapped to her. "How did you know

that?"

"Know what?"

"That a stirrup was broken."

"I didn't," she admitted. But it made sense. She remembered how angry Carlton had gotten when she questioned him about Adonis. He had probably missed the frayed leather when he was checking the horse before the joust. He was being defensive of his mistake. She knew she couldn't have beaten Griffin without help.

Griffin's eyes narrowed slightly. "Carlton is taking the stirrup to the leather maker in town on the morrow after the first round of jousts."

She nodded, but she couldn't quite stop the disappointment bubbling up into her throat, swallowing her words. A broken stirrup. Not her talent, not her skill. She had known as much, but to hear it aloud was heartbreaking. She turned and continued into the tent.

Griffin entered the pavilion after her, grabbing her arm. "Layne."

She couldn't turn to him. She didn't want him to see the disappointment brimming in her eyes.

"All knights I have come against have fallen. There have been broken stirrups before."

Startled, she turned to him. Was he trying to make her feel better?

"A good knight trains for a broken stirrup. It is not the reason I lost to you."

She stared at him. A tremor moved through her. Her gaze dipped to his lips. "Then...why?" His hand still held her wrist as though he didn't want her to move away. His fingers were warm against her skin. Firm. He was used to getting what he wanted.

Silence again fell about them.

Awareness sprang to life inside Layne. Her nipples tingled; warmth spread through her body, heating her. They were alone. The thought was instantly exciting. He could do something that would not be proper. "Should I be..." Her gaze swept his face as his hand moved up her arm, drawing her closer.

"A young woman should not be alone," Griffin whispered, "with a man."

Layne watched the way his lips formed each word. "Why?" was all she could say in a breathless sigh.

"He might..." Griffin gathered her in, pulling her closer.

Her hands rested against his strong chest. She should push him away. She should resist. But she couldn't take her eyes from his lips. How she wanted to feel them against hers. How she wanted him to kiss her. "What?" she asked softly.

He hesitated a moment, his gaze sweeping her face in a heated stroke.

She was almost desperate. What if he didn't kiss her? Her breasts pressed against his chest. "What might he do?" she demanded in a frantic whisper, almost a dare.

With a growl, he lowered his lips to hers, slanting them across her mouth. His lips slid gently over hers, coaxing. Layne sighed and Griffin plunged his tongue into her mouth, pulling her tight against him, exploring her mouth.

Layne wrapped her fingers up his back to the nape of his neck, curling them in the thick strands of his hair.

Suddenly, Griffin pulled away, taking a step from her.

Layne stumbled, but caught herself.

"He might do that," Griffin said coarsely.

Shocked, she could only stare at him. Cold suddenly seeped in around her, putting a chill on her heated body. Anger quickly replaced her shock as Griffin whirled and stalked from the tent. She wanted to grab something and throw it at him. He had kissed her as an example of what might happen! She wanted to twine a stirrup around his neck. He had kissed her so she could see how dangerous it was to be alone with a man. She wanted to kiss him again. The thought was so appalling and surprising that she could only just stand there and take no action at all.

He was trying to teach her to be a proper lady, she reminded herself. She had to keep that in mind.

Griffin paced before the tent. Where the devil was Carlton? He looked toward the castle, passed the competitor tents that dotted the hillside. But there was no sign of his squire.

God's blood! He had given his word not to mistreat her. And here he was kissing her at the first opportunity! Kissing her. He stopped pacing. Her lips were warm and soft and so very inviting.

She had provoked him! He began pacing again. Yes! By simply asking what would happen if a woman was alone with a man. How could he not show her? How could he not kiss her? He was only human!

Adonis nickered softly, drawing Griffin's gaze. He moved over to the horse's side and patted his white nose. The problem was how could he resist doing it again? Griffin clenched his jaw. He was no youngster. He knew how to behave with women. And he knew well how to kiss them. He shook himself. He knew how to respect them. He knew what was allowed in polite society and what was not.

"I should apologize," he announced to Adonis.

Layne emerged from the tent. They locked eyes and she lifted her chin slightly.

She was not embarrassed, not humiliated. She was confident, radiant, alluring. Griffin could not apologize. Because he knew he would kiss her again. And again. She brushed by him to Adonis's saddlebags.

Griffin bowed his head as if whispering to Adonis. This was going to take more will power than he thought. Much more will power.

CHAPTER SEVEN

𝕴t was almost midday when Layne knelt down, removing bread from a satchel. Something slammed into her from behind, almost tumbling her over. She glanced at the little brown head of the boy clutching her. "Michael!" she cried and threw her arms around him.

Griffin and Carlton rushed out of the tent.

Over Michael's head, Layne saw Colin and Frances leading the horses forward. She released Michael and raced forward, launching herself into Frances's arms. She almost toppled him, but he managed to stay upright, a bright smile on his lips.

Grinning, she turned to her oldest brother.

Colin held out his hands. "Laynie."

Layne marched into his arms and squeezed him tight. She could smell the scent of home, the rich woodsy scent that was Colin's.

Colin glanced at Griffin over Layne's head and his eyes hardened. "Has he mistreated you?"

"No," Layne admitted.

"That is offensive," Griffin warned.

"She's my sister."

"And she is under my protection."

"Glad to hear it." He pointed to the spot right next to Griffin's tent. "We'll set up camp there."

Michael giggled and ran in circles around Layne as Colin stepped past her, leading his horse to the indicated spot.

Layne hugged Michael again. "You should see Griffin's weapons!" she said softly and leaned close to him. "He won't let me touch them."

Michael's eyes narrowed. "You are a girl."

Layne put her hands on her hips. "Don't you start with me, too. I can still beat you in hand to hand."

Michael nodded. "Not for long. Colin is teaching me some moves that will have you flat on your back."

Layne's mouth dropped open and she glanced at Colin as he pulled a saddle bag from the horse. She was happy Colin was including him, but she missed their practices. She wanted to learn the moves, too. How embarrassing if her younger brother beat her in hand-to-hand combat.

"Come on, Michael," Colin ordered.

Michael glanced at Colin and then back at Layne. He leaned in to whisper to Layne, "Frances and Colin are both in the lists. They are hoping for a round against Wolfe."

Layne glanced at her brothers. In her eyes, what Griffin had done had saved both her and Colin from the dungeon.

Michael scowled. "Then they can win the purse and you can come back with us again."

Layne nodded, but she couldn't help wondering... if they won the purse for her, they wouldn't have enough coin to purchase the land for their father. What would happen to him? What would happen to all of them? As Michael walked over to Colin, she caught sight of Griffin. He sat beside Carlton, instructing him on the proper way to hold the stone for the best results at sharpening his sword. She watched the way he turned his hand to demonstrate. Such strong hands, such dark hands. Such skilled hands. What would they feel like on her body?

He suddenly looked up, locking eyes with her.

Heat suffused her cheeks. She turned her attention back to the satchel and continued to remove the bread for their meal.

Griffin came up behind her, catching her hand to still her movements. "Layne. I must practice and I need Carlton's help. As much as I don't think the field is a place for a woman, I hesitate to leave you alone. I wish you to accompany us to the field for practice."

Her face lit up. She would get to see him practice. Maybe he would let her help! Maybe--

"To watch."

Her joy plummeted. She grimaced and nodded, dropping her gaze to the ground to hide her disappointment. At least she would get to see him practice.

He stood over her until she lifted her gaze to him. The sun shone above him, casting a halo of light around his head and shoulders. His shoulder-length blonde locks glowed in sunlight like a halo. And his eyes, they sparkled! Breathlessness caught Layne by surprise. She couldn't help but stare. He looked as though he wanted to say something, but in the next instant he turned away.

Layne watched his retreating form. What was wrong with her? She never felt this way. She never struggled to find words. No one had ever affected her the way Griffin did. When he disappeared into the tent, she stood for a long moment, baffled. Why had she responded to him like that?

She looked around. What had she been doing? She saw the saddlebag at her feet, the satchel open. Yes. Bread. She was getting the meal ready.

She moved to the side of the tent where the other saddlebag lay on the ground. She opened it to retrieve a flask of ale. Instead, her hand wrapped around a leather strip. She pulled it out. It was a piece of stirrup leather. It wasn't the actual stirrup, the place Griffin put his foot, that had broken, but the strap that held it. Sometimes things like that happened. The leather wore out and simply failed. She was about to put the stirrup leather back when something caught her eye.

She studied the spot where the leather had failed, the bottom of the broken piece of leather. She lifted it to inspect it. The spot of the break began with a clean cut. A straight line. It ended with a ragged rip. She expected the worn-out leather to be frayed and worn, like it was at the end of the break. But the beginning was clean. Tingles raced along her neck.

Layne stared at the stirrup. It had not been natural wearing of the leather. It had been cut.

CHAPTER EIGHT

Shivers shot through her body. She heard heavy footfalls and quickly shoved the stirrup leather into her tunic. Then began rummaging through the saddlebags. For a moment, she couldn't remember what she had been looking for.

The footfalls stopped.

She glanced over her shoulder.

Carlton stood in the tent opening, his arms akimbo. "Do you need help?"

"I can't find --" Then her hand closed over the ale flask and she took it out victoriously. "No." She brandished it happily, containing her nervousness behind a smile. "I've got it."

Griffin refused to be distracted by the woman who sat on the top of the fence, her booted feet hanging loosely below her. She clutched the top rail. He had to get a dress for her. It was inappropriate for her to be dressed in breeches and a tunic. A man could see all her curves! *He* could see all of her curves and it was distracting. Very distracting.

Griffin tore his gaze from her and reined Adonis around. He took the lance from Carlton and spurred his stallion, charging down the field toward the quintain. He hated the static quintain. It swung around in a circle and hit less experienced knights in the back hard, but it was useless for a knight of his caliber. When he had been at home, practicing with his brother, they had developed a quintain that rocked. The object of their passes was to hit it hard enough to knock it over. It was a difficult thing to do as the quintain weighed almost as much as a fully armored opponent. But Griffin had mastered it. And challenged himself to hit it just hard enough to teeter it, without knocking it over so that it would return to its original position. That was a challenge! He missed that.

Griffin couched the lance beneath his arm and charged toward the quintain. He held the lance firmly, aiming for the center of the quintain. He leaned in slightly, expecting the moment of impact. He struck the quintain square on, the impact sending reverberations down his arm into his torso and down into his legs. It pushed him back against the rear of his saddle, his legs and knees gripping Adonis.

As he passed, the quintain began to swing. He leaned forward over Adonis's neck as the weighted portion swung, missing hitting him in the head or back. When he was clear, he lifted his lance and began to slow Adonis. He turned to see the quintain spinning around in a circle.

But he was not satisfied. It began to slow after two whirls, which meant he had not hit it hard enough.

He grimaced and came around to where Carlton was standing. He tried not to look at Layne.

Her smile was jubilant and full of excitement. Every time he hit the quintain, she grinned and smiled like an excited child. This was not the place for her, Griffin told himself again, but even as he did, he was glad to see her so happy. Something blossomed in his chest at her lively expression.

He tossed the lance at Carlton's feet. "What was wrong with that pass?" he demanded, adjusting his leather jerkin.

Carlton looked down at the lance, then at the quintain. "You used the stirrups."

"Aye," Griffin agreed. "I did. I will not on this next pass. What else?"

Carlton looked thoughtfully at the lance again. "The lance is still in one piece. You didn't hit it hard enough," he said quietly as if talking to himself. Then his gaze snapped to the quintain. "The quintain. It only swung around twice."

Griffin nodded. "Good. Well done." He reached down as Carlton handed the next lance up to him. He glanced once at Layne who was leaning forward in anticipation. Then, he focused on the quintain. He removed his feet from the stirrups and nudged Adonis forward with his heels. The horse charged forward.

"Let's show her how dangerous this can be," Griffin whispered to his horse. He leaned forward, couching the lance. He set his teeth, preparing for impact, aiming dead center.

He struck the quintain at full speed, the impact resounding through his arms and down his torso, shoving him back against the cantle of the saddle. The lance crumbled against the quintain, shards of wood flying out. He ducked his head in protection from the pieces of wood as well as the weighted portion of the quintain.

He tossed the destroyed lance aside as he straightened, turned and brought Adonis to a halt. The side of the quintain was gone. He had struck it with enough force to break the wooden side. It whirled around like a small tornado.

He heard a holler and glanced toward it.

Layne had leapt down from the fence and was in the field. Her face was a mask of awe and exhilaration. Her eyes were wide, her mouth open in utter astonishment.

Griffin glanced at Carlton to see a wide grin on his face. He cantered Adonis back toward Carlton.

Layne ran forward to greet him. "You smashed the quintain apart!" she said in excitement.

He dismounted, ready to chastise her for being in the field. But there was something contagious in her excitement and he held his tongue.

She rushed up to him, throwing her arms around his neck, gasping, "I've never seen anything like it!"

Startled, Griffin could only catch her around the waist.

She pulled back to look at him. There was true amazement in her large blue eyes and something else…admiration. She released him and turned back to the quintain, running her hands through her hair. "Look at it!" She spun on Carlton. "An entire side plank is gone!"

Carlton could only mutely nod agreement, a grin on his lips.

She spun to Griffin. "How did you do it?!"

Griffin stared at her. If it were Carlton, or

another knight, he wouldn't hesitate to tell them what he did. But this was Layne. He was trying to teach her to be a woman. To act like a woman. Still… the elation in her was stunning. He enjoyed the radiance blooming on her cheeks, the glow of exultation glowing around her. He hated to say anything that would diminish her joy. And yet, this was exactly what had gotten her into trouble in the first place. "It is not a woman's place to know the technicalities of the joust."

Her contagious excitement evaporated. Her face fell as the joy left it. It was almost a physical thing. Her gaze swept him, and her shoulders drooped. Her hands dropped to her side. She bowed her head.

Griffin regretted his words immediately. He glanced at Carlton.

Carlton looked at the ground with a resigned acceptance.

This only added to Griffin's guilt. And this angered him. He was doing the right thing. He was protecting her. Didn't she see how dangerous jousting was? If he had hit her with full force like that in their joust, she would have been seriously injured or killed.

Layne didn't look at him as she nodded. "Sorry," she mumbled and retreated to the fence again. But she didn't sit on the top of the fence as she had before. She ducked beneath it and retreated to a large tree close by.

Griffin watched her plop beneath it, facing away from the field of honor, without casting a look in his direction. He sighed softly. It was for the best. She shouldn't feel excited about the joust, and most assuredly, not be joyful he had destroyed the quintain. Yes. He was right telling her so. But when he remembered her radiant smile and the glowing excitement in her eyes as she looked at him, he found it difficult to justify how harsh he had been with her.

Layne plucked a blade of grass from the ground. She thought back to the last time she had been made to feel so useless. She had defeated Frances in sword to sword combat. She had been overjoyed. It had been the first time she had defeated him. She rushed to the manor, to her aunt's manor, to tell her father, knowing he would be so proud of her. That was all he cared about. Jousting, sword fighting. Tournaments. Even later when he got sick, that was what he wanted to hear about.

But when she told him of her greatest accomplishment, of beating Frances, instead of taking her into his arms and reigning praise on her, he had looked away from her. Her aunt reprimanded her for not finishing her embroidery, for wearing breeches instead of a dress. And her father had banned her from fighting with her brothers.

She ripped the blade of grass in half. She had been confused then. But not now. Now, it was clear how her father favored her brothers. Just because they were men. Women didn't have a place in the sports he loved. She loved her brothers with all her heart, but she never fit in. Not then, not now.

Colin knew. He knew how miserable she was. How lost. He had spoken to their father, convinced him to let her come with them. She overheard him telling their father they needed her to cook for them. Cook. She couldn't cook! But Colin had covered for her. He had made up an excuse so she could join them in the tournament circuit.

And she had humiliated him by jousting. She had risked everything to joust. The farm they were saving up to buy so their father had a place to live in his final days in. Their reputation.

She deserved to be sent to the dungeon. No, she deserved to be sent home. That would be even worse than the dungeon.

Jousting and swordplay had made her feel part of the family; she could participate with her brothers, talk to them about it. It was all that interested her. It was the only thing that her father liked to hear about. She didn't care about writing and reading. She didn't care about music. Her Aunt would reprimand her and tell her that she would never amount to anything. No man would ever want her if she couldn't cook, if she couldn't embroider. But she didn't care.

In the beginning, when they had first arrived at the manor home, she had tried. She had attempted to do all those things that were expected of her. She would proudly display her father's mended pants, but he wasn't interested. She had tried again and again telling him stories of the lessons of the day, of her knowledge of fashion. But her father didn't care. He would not listen, and his eyes would glaze until one of her brothers came into the room. He would listen to Colin's story for hours. But he never seemed to find the time for her stories.

She ripped another piece of grass from the ground. And now, here she was with a man who was much like her father, unable to see her for who she was. Really see her. She grabbed a lock of her hair that fell over her shoulder and swished the end of it. He looked at her and thought she should wear her hair in those horrible metal circles. She brushed at her breeches. That she should wear a velvet cotehardie. She looked at the field of honor.

Griffin rode toward the quintain again, his lance held steady, his focus unrelenting.

The problem was, if her father didn't like her for who she really was, how could she hope that the best knight she had even seen would? She tore the blade of grass in half.

And even worse, since she wasn't allowed to know about jousting and sword play and horses, how could she ever tell Griffin that someone had cut the stirrup leather? He would only scold her again and reprimand her for talking of things that were not fit for a woman.

Layne made sure to walk behind both Griffin and Carlton on the way back to the pavilion. Carlton looked over his shoulder at her, meeting her gaze. She looked away out over the sunny field.

When they reached the tent, Carlton led Adonis to the side of the tent.

Griffin turned to her.

For one moment, she locked gazes with him. Those spectacular blue eyes shone in the sunlight. Layne quickly looked away from them and moved to step around him.

"Layne," he said softly.

Was this another punishment? Was he going to reprimand her for rushing onto the field?

"I wanted to explain..."

"It doesn't matter," she whispered.

"It *does* matter." Griffin straightened, looking

down at her. "Can't you see that this is all for your benefit? I'm trying to teach you how women are expected to behave so you can marry into a good family and make your brothers proud."

Layne folded her hands before her. Her aunt had told her that numerous times. Make your family proud by marrying a man. A man who would never let her sword fight or joust. It was worse than death. "I was never good at embroidery. When I tried to sing, people would cover their ears or laugh. I can't cook. I can't read or write. I can't recite poetry. The only thing I was ever good at was sword fighting." She grinned sadly. "The only thing I was ever interested in was the joust." She looked up at him and fought down the lump in her throat. He'd saved her from the dungeon and for that she was grateful. "What kind of man would want to marry me?"

"You can change."

"I can be miserable."

He frowned. He always seemed to be scowling when he looked at her. "Layne..."

"I think my chances of marrying into a good family are long gone. So, why can't I be happy?" She turned away from him to enter the tent.

CHAPTER NINE

The sound of loud laughter woke Griffin late that night. He sat up. In the glow from the moonlight illuminating the side of the tent, he could see Carlton still asleep on his mat. He saw that Layne's mat was empty.

He stood immediately and rushed out of the tent.

The Fletcher tent was close to his. He had allowed the proximity in silence, even though it infringed on his boundaries. They were Layne's brothers. A fire burned in a small pit they had dug. The two older brothers sat close to the fire, eating something that looked fresh and smelled delicious.

Griffin spotted her immediately. Layne sat on the ground with her back to him. Her long, dark wavy hair reached to the ground. She had her arm around the youngest brother. She leaned forward, listening intently to her eldest brother Colin.

"Frances flipped him over the table and slammed him to the ground," Colin said in a hurried whisper.

"Where was Michael?" Layne asked.

Griffin stepped back into the shadows of the tent, not wanting to disturb them.

"Bringing the horses around," Frances said, taking a deep drink from his flask.

Griffin peered out between a gap in the tent flap.

"I sent him out as soon as I thought there would be trouble," Colin said in a quieter voice.

Layne looked down at Michael. He slept soundly beneath her arm. She kissed his forehead.

A longing came over Griffin as he watched her family. They were so close, each an integral part of the group. He had never felt like that with his family. He loved his father, brother and sister, but he felt like he was always competing with his older brother. And his sister, she was always too busy with her friends or her social obligations to pay him much heed. No, his family was not like hers.

"Plus, I didn't want him to see if we got our arses kicked," Colin said taking a large bite from his meat.

Frances snorted and rolled his eyes.

"We were outnumbered two to one!" Colin said around a mouthful of food.

"Yeah, by a bunch of drunk farmers," Frances clarified.

"They were not farmers!" Colin protested.

"They weren't knights," Frances countered.

"Just because the one you fought could hardly throw a punch!"

"The one?" Frances objected. "I think I handled three of them!"

Griffin smiled as the men quarreled about who took on the most men. Boys. That's what they reminded him of. Young men having a grand adventure. But why drag Layne around with them? They must have had no one to leave her with.

"Yes! Yes!" Layne said. "You both were brilliant, I'm sure."

Griffin peeked around the side of the tent to see Frances elbow Colin. Colin swatted him in the head. Layne shook her head. The silence spread easily and Griffin could hear the crackle of the fire.

"And what about you, Laynie?" Colin asked, wiping a sleeve across his mouth. "Is the old curmudgeon treating you with respect?"

Griffin ducked back into the shadows. He drew in a small insulted breath and held it.

"He isn't that old," she protested.

"He hasn't tried anything dishonorable, has he?" Frances demanded, his voice tight.

Griffin leaned closer to hear her answer.

Layne chuckled, but the sound was more of a gag than a mirthful laugh. "He wants to make a proper woman out of me."

Frances scoffed. "He can try, right Laynie?"

"What has he done?" Colin wondered.

Griffin peeked through the folds of the tent again, through the gap, to watch. Layne's back was to him, her arm still around a sleeping Michael.

Layne shrugged. "He makes me cook."

The men laughed out loud at that.

Layne threw a stick at Frances that he batted aside. "I'm surprised he's not sick to his stomach!" Frances roared.

It took all Griffin's will not to rush to her defense.

She lifted her chin. "He's strong. Really strong."

That made the men stop laughing. Good, Griffin thought smugly. He'd knock them flat in the tourney for laughing at Layne.

She leaned forward slightly. "He let me watch him practice once. He doesn't like when I do. He says that ladies should show no interest in the technicalities of the joust." Her voice mocked his as she said it.

Frances grimaced and shook his head.

"What did you learn? Does he have any weakness?" Colin asked.

Griffin stiffened. It was something he had never even considered. Was she a spy? Would she relay his fault to her brothers and betray him? Of course she would. Her loyalty was to her family.

"I didn't learn about a weakness." She pulled something out of her tunic and displayed it to her brothers. "But about a stirrup leather."

Chills shot down Griffin's spine. A stirrup leather. Where had she gotten that?

Colin took the leather from her hand, looking at it.

"I'm not supposed to have it," Layne admitted.

Colin looked at her.

Frances took the stirrup leather from Colin's hand, glancing at it. "What about it?"

"It was cut," Colin answered. "Someone's trying to sabotage him."

Layne nodded. "I have to get this back before he finds out it's missing."

Colin took the stirrup leather from Frances and handed it to Layne. "I don't want you there. If someone is trying to sabotage him, then he's in danger. And if he is, you are, too."

Layne shook her head, running her hand over

the leather strap. "I'm more worried about Griffin than me."

Griffin stayed hidden in the dark. The strap was cut? Sabotage. The word sent anger boiling through his veins. Dishonorable cur. Who could have done this? But his thoughts slid back to Layne. What was she doing with the stirrup leather? Where had she gotten it from? What did she plan to do with it? There was only one explanation. She didn't want him to find out it was sabotaged, so she had taken it. Then another terrible thought reared its ugly head in his mind. Had she cut it so her brother would win? Was Layne capable of such a dark deed...

 CHAPTER TEN

Layne collected the leftover bread to consolidate the remaining food for later. No use wasting any of it. She heard footsteps and whirled.

Frances came up behind her.

Layne grimaced. "You never could sneak up on me."

"I wasn't trying."

"What are you doing here?" Layne wondered and continued to place the leftover bread into a sack. When Frances didn't reply, Layne looked at him over her shoulder.

He shook his head in disbelief. "He's already changed you."

"What are you talking about?"

"You used to fight over cleaning up the leftovers."

Layne ignored the jeer and tied the sack closed. "It's one of my duties here. Griffin made sure I understood what my chores would be. Besides," she sat back on her heels, "he's not a pig."

Frances chuckled. "It's not me who is the pig. Maybe Michael…" Frances walked up behind her. "We need this purse, Layne," he whispered.

She stared at the dying fire pit. "I know."

"We only have this tournament and the next. If we don't win… Well, you know the plan. We need one more win."

Layne nodded. "I know the plan," she whispered. That had been part of the reason she had taken his place on the jousting field. And now, they needed even more coin to get her out of this predicament. "And when you win, I intend for you to make sure Colin still uses it to buy the farm."

Frances shook his head. "We need to get you away from Wolfe."

Layne stood. "No! Father comes first."

Frances opened his mouth to argue, but Layne grabbed his arm. "Griffin treats me well, a little too much like a pampered girl, but I can deal with that. Father… He needs a home. And so do we."

Frances closed his eyes and shook his head.

"Promise me, Frances. We will win and the coin goes to buy the farm."

He nodded and mumbled, "We have to win one more tourney. Or we won't have enough."

Layne punched him in the arm. "Are you having doubts?"

"Wolfe is a practiced knight," Frances murmured.

"Oh. So, you're afraid. That's why you let the quintain hit you."

He looked up startled. Then, his eyes narrowed.

She shrugged and turned away. "Don't worry. If I have to take your place again –"

Frances grabbed her from behind, flipped her over his hip and caught her in a headlock. "You won't be taking my place ever again. I'm the best knight and you know it."

Layne smiled and tugged half-heartedly at his arm.

"Say it. Who's the best knight?"

"Release her."

The booming voice startled them both. Frances let her go, keeping a grip on her arm so she didn't fall.

Griffin stood like an angry god staring down with stern disapproval at his subjects. His fists were clenched, his eyes icy. Hard and cold. Murderously cold.

Layne stepped in front of Frances. "It's okay, Griffin. We were just playing."

Griffin's eyes narrowed. "It is no wonder you do not know how to behave like a woman."

Layne's joy faded under Griffin's harsh words.

Frances pushed forward from behind her. "What does that mean?"

"When your own brother does not treat you as a woman, then you can't be faulted for your lack of knowledge."

Frances shoved her out of the way and lunged at Griffin.

Griffin caught him and tossed him aside like a rag doll.

"Stop!" Layne cried and grabbed Griffin's arm.

Griffin looked at her. There was something frightening in his tight jaw and his stormy blue eyes. He yanked his arm away from her.

Frances rose and Layne again rushed forward to stop him, recognizing the anger in her brother's gaze.

She placed two hands on his chest, pushing to keep him back from Griffin. "Go, Frances."

"I won't leave you with this barbarian," Frances growled.

Griffin straightened. "Unfortunately, she will remain until you and your brothers are able to pay me back."

"It's all right," Layne pleaded, pushing Frances back a step. "I'll be fine." She shoved him again.

Frances cast Layne a glance before looking back at Griffin with fury.

Layne was too familiar with that look. Frances wasn't going to give it up. "Colin!" she hollered, knowing that alone she wouldn't be able to stop him.

Colin emerged from the Fletcher tent as Frances shoved forward again.

Layne lost ground to him but pushed with all her power. "Colin!" she cried for help.

"You know nothing of women, in particular my sister," Frances ground out. "Why don't you look at your own manhood before you degrade her."

Colin leapt a log and raced to her side. He caught Frances around the shoulders. "Enough!"

"It was not my intent to degrade *her*," Griffin said.

Frances lurched forward, but Colin held him back. He struggled to pull Frances away from the camp. Finally, Frances whirled and stormed toward the Fletcher tent.

Colin cast a glance over his shoulder at Griffin and then locked eyes with Layne.

Misery welled in her eyes. Frances had always been the hot headed one, the one always first to start a fight. She knew he would pace inside their tent with determined strides, muttering all sorts of vengeful plans against those who had wronged him.

Colin turned and hurried after Frances. Colin would see to him. He had a way of cooling Frances's temper.

Layne watched them go until they disappeared into the Fletcher tent. She whirled on Griffin. "You had no right!"

Griffin straightened.

"You can ridicule me all you want in private. But not in front of my family. Frances is not responsible for the way I act."

"Not responsible?" Griffin sputtered. "As your elder brother, he is very much responsible."

Layne stepped up to him, glaring. "He can't control me. Anymore then you can." Her voice thickened. "I will not tolerate you belittling my brother."

Griffin frowned as he stared at the fierce dedication in her eyes. He had wounded her in defending her. When he had returned for his sword, the first thing he saw had been a man with his arm around her neck. He had sprinted the rest of the way, thinking she was in trouble. A rock had settled in the pit of his stomach as he raced towards her. What if he didn't reach her time?

As he neared, he realized it was her brother and his fear dissolved into rage. He would never treat a woman like Layne's brother had, let alone his own sister!

Facing Layne's anger and humiliation now, he

realized he had been wrong and rash. He didn't know what to say to her. He was trying to set an example for her, but he was failing.

She whirled. "Besides, I could have beaten him."

He stepped closer. "And how could you have possibly done that?"

She straightened. "I would have pinched his ears and made him squeal. He hates when I do that."

Griffin saw her smile, but he kept his mouth even. "So this tussle you had with your brother was a game?"

She nodded. "Of course." She looked at him with an odd glance. "Didn't you ever play games with your sister?"

Griffin nodded. "Chess. Dice games. But I never put her in such an undignified position as a headlock when she beat me at dice, I dare say.

She stared at him for a long moment. "Where is your sister now?"

"At home." Waiting for father to find the right husband for her, he thought. But he chose not to share that fact for the moment.

"Weren't you close to her?"

Griffin thought about Gwen. It was the first time in a long time he had thought of her. His younger sister had idolized their older brother, Richard, but she had barely given him a second glance. He was sure she loved him. He was just different than Richard. Not as accommodating.

His silence was enough answer for her. She nodded. "I wouldn't have gone with you, either." And she turned away and ducked into the tent.

His eyebrows rose in surprise. He had not asked Gwen to accompany him. It wouldn't have been proper. She never would have come with him. Her life was in the castle, not wrestling at tournaments with her brother.

He bent to pick up his sword and caught his reflection in the blade. No, he had never been close to his family. Not to Gwen and not to his brother. Richard was the charmer, the fun one to be around. He had always been the responsible one, not Richard. Still, it had never been enough for his father. He had never been good enough for his father.

# CHAPTER ELEVEN

𝕷ayne leaned against the fence, watching the entrance to the jousting field. Her brothers stood with her. Colin stood beside Frances who was next to her, and Michael hung over a rail on her other side.

The sun was hot and bright, and she shielded her eyes as she stared at the entrance. She could barely control herself. Her foot nervously bounced and jiggled her leg. She continued to drum her fingers on the wooden fence. Something clenched tight in her gut and it took her a moment to realize she was nervous for Griffin. She shouldn't be. Not after his performance with the quintain the other night. She grinned at the memory of his show of power and skill. He was skilled and stunning and... magnificent.

Carlton waited inside the field, near Griffin's lances on his side of the field.

His opponent rode in. The black and red cross of his heraldry was emblazoned on his horse's skirt. De la Noue should pose no problem for Griffin. Layne had seen him joust before. He was an arrogant lord who enjoyed the theatrics of participating in the jousts much more so than the physical contest. He believed himself better than he actually was, and his arrogant boasting knew no bounds. True to form, he started mocking Griffin as soon as he reached his side of the field. "Looks like a good day to skin a Wolfe!"

Smatters of applause burst out around the crowd.

De la Noue rode around the field, bowing his head to the women who waved their favors at him.

Layne stood on the tips of her toes, swiveling her gaze back to the entrance of the field. Her fingers wrapped tightly around the top wooden plank of the fence in anticipation of Griffin's arrival.

The energy in the crowd seemed to grow in expectation.

Griffin charged in on his white steed to wild cheers and applauses. Griffin was a favorite and most of the spectators were rooting for him. He didn't pause or acknowledge anyone as he came to his side of the field where Carlton stood. Carlton handed Griffin his lance.

The two combatants settled their lances into position at their hips. Layne watched and waited. A trumpet sounded signaling the beginning of the joust!

Griffin reined his horse around and charged forward, lowering the lance.

Layne chewed delicately on her lower lip. Perfect form. Lance positioned correctly. She swiveled to de la Noue. His mastery of his horse was off. The horse balked once before he got him under control. Finally, he started forward, his lance held forward. Too far forward.

Layne tensed, preparing for the impact. De la Noue didn't have a chance.

But in the last moment, Griffin raised his lance. De la Noue followed suit and the riders passed without striking. The crowd groaned and smatterings of discontented hisses erupted.

Layne stepped up on the lower plank of wood, so she was leaning over the fence. Tingles raced along the nape of her neck. Something was wrong.

Griffin rode around to his side of the field where Carlton stood. He spoke to Carlton and then looked across the field at de la Noue. He held the lance upright and Adonis danced beneath him.

Trepidation spread through Layne. "Something's wrong."

Frances grunted. "The horse just balked. Nothing is wrong."

Layne shook her head. "Look. His feet are not in the stirrups."

Colin leaned forward so his arms were over the top plank of the fence.

"How can he possibly unhorse de la Noue without using the stirrups?" Frances demanded, his arms crossed over his chest.

"He doesn't need the stirrups for the impact," Colin said.

Anxiety and nervousness filled Layne. The voices of her brothers became distant as she focused on Griffin. What had happened?

Griffin turned Adonis and spurred him with his heels. Adonis reared slightly and began racing down the field.

De la Noue charged down the field toward Griffin. His lance was steady, and he seemed more confident this time.

Layne's fingers curved against the wood and she

leaned forward, willing Griffin's victory.

The two horses galloped full speed down the field, dust rising in their wake. The crowd quieted as Griffin lowered his lance.

The impact was horrendous. A loud thud. Griffin's lance struck de la Noue hard, sending him back and up over the rear of the horse. He was suspended for just a moment before falling to the ground on his bottom.

De la Noue's lance struck Griffin hard and he was tossed backwards, over the end of the horse.

Layne gasped as he struck the earth. A cloud of dust rose about him. Visions of her joust with Griffin came back to her. He could be hurt! She moved instantly to duck beneath the fence.

Frances grabbed her arm. "What are you doing?"

Layne faltered.

Frances shook her. "You can't go onto the field of honor!"

Layne swiveled her gaze from Griffin to Frances. Over his shoulder, she saw Colin glaring at her.

"He might be hurt."

"Good," Frances said.

Layne's chest tightened in dread.

"Nay," Michael cried, pointing into the field. "He's getting up!"

Griffin pushed himself to a sitting position. He looked around the field and stood to his feet, calling for his sword. Carlton raced out, holding his weapon and handed it to Griffin. Griffin approached de la Noue who lay on his back and had not moved. He nudged de la Noue with his toe.

De la Noue lay still.

The crowd was silent as if holding its collective breath.

Griffin straightened, holding his sword before him. Again, he shoved de la Noue with his boot.

De la Noue moved, lifting his head.

Griffin put the sword tip beneath his neck. "Yield," he ordered.

De la Noue lifted his hands in surrender.

Griffin lowered his weapon. He whistled and Adonis cantered over to him. As he sheathed his sword and mounted, the crowd roused, and cheers began. A chant started to build. "Wolfe, Wolfe!"

Layne scowled. Colin shook his head. Frances muttered a curse.

Griffin held his right arm against his side, almost imperceptibly. If she hadn't spent the last days with him, she would never have noticed it. He *was* hurt!

He rode out of the field amidst cheers and Carlton jogged after him.

Layne whirled and dashed away from the field, running toward Griffin's tent. He is hurt, her mind repeated. Just like my joust. Anguish filled her. Was this her fault? Was this…?

"Layne!" Colin called.

But she didn't stop, she couldn't. Griffin was hurt. She leapt a small ravine and sprinted across a field. Her breathing was loud in her ears; her worry ate away at the corners of her mind. The noise of the crowd grew distant as she moved closer to the tents.

She didn't hear the horses thundering behind her until they were almost on her. She whirled and cringed as two horses rode by so close the riders could touch her. One of the horses bumped into her, sending her sliding to the ground. She landed amidst the pebbles and grass in the field.

She looked up to see horse hooves bearing down on her. She rolled out of their way and recognized one of the riders as he moved past, the sharp hooves of his horse only inches from her head. It was Simon Wellington, Daunger's squire. She leapt to her feet and raced toward the cover the trees. If she could reach the trees, Simon and the other rider would have to come after her on foot. But as she ran, she realized she wouldn't make the trees. They were too far away. She made a sharp turn just as the horses behind her roared past, unable to make the turn as quickly as she.

Another horse and rider stopped a few feet before her.

She came to a halt, her feet skidding in the grass.

Osmont sat on his steed, glaring at her. "Imagine my delight when I saw you running alone through the field. No one is here to protect you now. You shall pay for dishonoring the field of honor."

She barely had time to turn when something slammed into the back of her head, sending her to the ground. For a long moment, she lay on the ground looking at the clouds through the tall blades of wild grass. Her world spun, swirling around the pinpoint of light in the sky as darkness hedged the edges of her vision.

She heard voices but couldn't understand the words. She saw boots come toward her through the grass. More talking. She could barely keep her eyes open. A thrumming sounded in her head.

And then, she heard a voice. A familiar voice. A boy's voice. No. Her head ached. She tried to lift it.

Someone knelt beside her. Calling her name. Michael. He bent down to look into her eyes. Worry furrowed his brow as he shook her shoulder.

Concern willed her fading vision away. She mumbled something, or at least she thought she did. "Run, Michael." She pushed her palms against the dirt, preparing to lift herself up.

Michael stood. "She is hurt!" he proclaimed. "You hurt my sister!"

"Out of the way, boy," a voice ordered. "She needs to learn her place."

Michael! Michael! her mind screamed. Layne pushed over and lifted herself to her knees. She stared down at her fingers curled into the grass. "Michael," she gasped. The world tilted, and she closed her eyes for a moment, willing the spinning to stop. She had to help Michael.

"It's all right, Laynie," Michael whispered. "I won't let them hurt you."

When Layne opened her eyes, tears blurred her vision. Drops of crimson splashed the back of her hand. No, it wasn't tears. It was blood. Where was it coming from? "Michael," she called again, firmly. "Go. Go and get Griffin. Run. Run."

"No. I won't leave you."

"Get out of the way, boy."

And suddenly Michael was shoved out of her vision. Layne looked up to see Osmont coming toward her. She lifted her hand, but his kick connected with her side, spinning her onto her back.

"No! Leave her alone!" Michael stood in front of her again, his arms splayed.

Layne was surprised at how blue the sky was. How could it be that blue when it was raining blood? She looked at Michael. "Please," she whispered. But her voice was weak. Beyond Michael, she could see two more figures. Simon's face was twisted with disgust and pleasure. She didn't know the other man. Why would he want to hurt her? Her head hurt, pounding like a horribly loud drum. She moved her hand, clutching her fingers around the grass at her side. It was smooth and she could almost feel each individual stalk.

"Boy, I won't tell you again."

Layne grit her teeth. Michael. She turned onto her side, bumping into his leg. She grimaced as the earth moved, rolling beneath her. She clenched her teeth. She wouldn't let Michael do this alone. She wouldn't let them hurt Michael.

Michael looked over his shoulder. He locked eyes with her for a long moment.

Layne read desperation and then resolve in his young eyes. No. Oh God, no. She knew that look. When Frances was picking on him and Michael was going to do something rash, something stupid like attack him, he wore that same look. She pushed herself to a sitting position and reached for him. "No, Michael."

Michael either didn't hear her or didn't listen to her. He drew his dagger. "Stay away from her or I'll cut you all down."

Her fingers closed too late over empty air as Michael lunged forward, swinging his tiny dagger.

Osmont cackled in laughter and stepped forward, reaching for Michael. "Boys shouldn't play with men's toys."

Michael was quick and ducked out of reach, swiping his dagger. He cut Osmont's arm.

Osmont pulled back, clutching his arm. He looked down at his wrist where a line of red had appeared. He gritted his teeth in disbelief. "You insolent cur!" He yanked his sword free of its sheath and raised it.

Michael put up his dagger.

Layne lunged forward and her fingers wrapped around Michael's tunic as Osmont brought his sword down.

"Nooo!" Layne screamed.

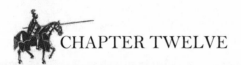# CHAPTER TWELVE

Griffin's jaw clenched as Carlton dabbed at his wound. It was the same cut he had received from Layne during their joust. It had reopened. It wasn't serious, but it was a painful nuisance. He was so furious that his hands clenched tight on his thighs. Unhorsed! For a second time! By a knight he considered to be far inferior.

Something made the skin at the nape of his neck prickle. He rose away from Carlton's ministrations and moved to the flap, pushing it out of the way to gaze into the forest around their camp. The sun dipped behind a cloud in that instant. Silence stretched across the camp.

Unhorsed for a second time. It was unthinkable.

Adonis's ears flicked in his direction and Griffin walked over to his steed. He patted him gently. The horse nickered nervously. Griffin wondered if the horse was feeling his own unease or if he heard something else.

"Nooo!" The echo rent the air.

Layne! Griffin swung himself onto Adonis, spurring him. Panic tightened his chest. Where was she?

Adonis rode forward, toward where Griffin believed the cry had come from.

"Michael!"

He swung his head to the side, toward the clearing beside the tents in front of the field of honor. He jerked the reins to the side and spurred Adonis between the trees.

It wasn't fast enough. His heart beat with dread and foreboding. It would never be fast enough. Layne's anguish-filled cry tore through his soul.

As Adonis burst from the trees into the clearing, Griffin took in the sight. Michael sat on the ground, his arm against his chest. Layne smothered him like a blanket and Osmont loomed over the two of them, his sword stained with blood.

Layne whirled to face Osmont as Griffin charged closer. Her lips were curled back in a feral snarl, baring her teeth. She grabbed something from the ground.

Adonis reached them and Griffin slid to the ground between Osmont and Layne.

At first, her gaze was wild and blank and centered on Osmont. But when Griffin went to her, blocking her view of Osmont, and took her head into his hands to force her to look at him, she focused on him.

Tears rose in her clear blue eyes and her lower lip pouted. "Michael," she gasped.

Griffin turned to the boy who had not moved from the ground. He was hunched over, his complexion so pale that at first Griffin thought him to be dead. He dropped his hands from Layne and turned to Michael, but something caught his attention. Staining his own hand was dark red liquid. He looked back at Layne as she dropped to her knees at Michael's side. Blood caked her hair on one side of her head, running over her tunic.

Rage erupted inside of Griffin. "Layne," he called through a tight voice. When she looked at him, Griffin realized the blow must have come from the back. He snarled, caught between concern and overwhelming fury. "Are you all right?" He held up his hand to show her the blood.

She nodded; the movement of her head barely perceptible. But it was enough for him. He spun on Osmont.

Osmont spit on the ground, sheathing his weapon. "The boy cut me. I had every right –"

Griffin lunged at Osmont, catching his tunic in a clenched fist. He raised his other hand and delivered a solid blow with so much power the knight was launched backward. But Griffin held him firmly and pulled him back for another blow. And another. His anger spewed forth like molten lava fury. He hit him again.

Osmont raised his hands, trying to deflect the blows. Griffin punched him in the stomach. When Osmont lowered his hands to protect his torso, he hit his face again. Osmont tried to pull free, but Griffin's fingers tightened around his tunic. He shoved his face close to Osmont's. "I told you she is under my protection," he growled savagely before landing another blow square in Osmont's face. His nose crunched and Osmont let out a wail of pain.

Hands grabbed at Griffin, pulling him off of Osmont.

Griffin lunged forward to attack again as the hands held him back and that was when Osmont threw the only blow that landed to Griffin's jaw.

The hands pulled him back.

"Enough, Wolfe," a voice called.

All Griffin wanted was to smash Osmont's face in. He dared to hurt Layne! Layne. He glanced at her as the hands pulled him back from Osmont.

She sat on the ground beside Michael, her large eyes staring, her lovely lips parted in shock.

Some semblance of rationality returned beneath the blazing inferno of his rage; he saw a crowd had formed around them. Layne's brothers, Colin and Frances, held him back from Osmont, along with three other knights.

Griffin yanked his arms free from their hold and straightened. His calm demeanor managed to return despite the churning fury in his gut. He looked at Osmont's bloodied and bruised face. It wasn't enough. "Stay away from her," he announced and turned, presenting his back to Osmont. He wished he would attack him. He hoped he would jump him. He'd like nothing better than to continue his assault.

Layne sat beside Michael, her arm around her brother's shoulders, but her eyes were on Griffin. Worry filled them and Griffin didn't know if it was for him or her brother.

"You're out of your bloody mind! She needs to be punished!" Osmont declared. He wiped angrily at his bloody and battered nose. "It should be a warning to other commoners. No women dares dress as a knight and comes away clean."

Griffin whirled on Osmont, his teeth clenched, his eyes narrowed. "She paid her dues. You are not to declare her punishment!"

"You're growing soft, Wolfe," Osmont growled.

Griffin took a step toward him and Osmont cringed away. "Hurt her again and I will kill you."

A murmur spread through the crowd of

onlookers.

"Keep it on the field," Colin advised.

"This woman is under my protection!" Griffin announced. "No man shall harm her."

Colin and Frances exchanged glances of surprise.

Griffin walked over to Layne and Michael. Colin and Frances followed.

Osmont grumbled and backed away.

Griffin stood over them. Michael held his right hand crushed tightly beneath his left arm. Blood stained the side of his tunic.

Colin gingerly lifted Michael's left arm to inspect the wound. As soon as he did, blood spurted from the injury. Osmont had cut off two of Michael's fingers.

Layne glanced up at Griffin. She pressed her lips together tightly so as not to cry or gasp.

Griffin laid a hand on her shoulder for support.

"It should be cauterized," Frances said.

"Let's get back to the tent," Colin advised. "Frances, go for a physician."

Immediately, Frances rose and dashed off.

"Keep him warm," Griffin advised.

Colin nodded. He glanced at Layne. "Can you make it back?"

"I'll make sure she gets to the pavilion," Griffin said.

Colin lifted his tunic over his head and pressed it to Michael's hand, effectively shielding it from the boy's view and slowing the loss of blood. He put his hand around Michael's shoulders and helped him to stand. Layne stood, supporting Michael on the opposite side. The boy wobbled, but Colin held him firmly. Slowly, they made their way toward the tent.

Griffin watched them for a moment, then looked at Layne. His gaze swept her. She looked all right, but head wounds were tricky. He had seen a man get bashed in the head and seem fine and then be dead hours later. His stomach clenched tight.

The crowd around them began to disperse. Osmont was gone.

Griffin put a hand on her arm. Just the touch soothed his concern. "Layne?"

She looked at him and launched herself into his arms, letting the torrent of her sorrow out. Her body shook with sobs as he held her. "It was my fault," she whispered. "I didn't listen. I didn't listen."

The agony in her voice twisted his heart and he tightened his hold on her. "Your brother is a fighter. He'll be fine."

Her hands balled to fists in his tunic and her tiny body trembled.

Griffin lifted her in his arms. He was concerned with her head wound and wanted a physician to look at it immediately, but right then it seemed more important to hold her.

Layne sat on Frances's mat, watching the physician tend Michael's hand. She was so proud of her brother for defending her. He had acted as bravely and honorably as any knight she had ever seen.

Michael stared at his wounded hand, blankets draped around his hunched shoulders. He did not look at her and that worried Layne above all else. Osmont had taken one and half of his fingers with his savage blow.

Colin stood to one side of Michael, Frances to the other, watching the physician work.

It must have hurt like the devil, but Michael had only cried out when they cauterized his wound. Now, his body stiffened as the physicians turned his hand, inspecting, but he was so brave that Layne felt proud of him.

Griffin stood in the tent opening, his arms crossed. He had carried her across the field to her brother's tent, which Layne was grateful for. Now, he watched her with an intensity that would have made her cheeks blush if she wasn't so worried about Michael.

Another physician gingerly moved her hair aside to look at and treat her own wound. Her head pounded like a castle wall had fallen on it, but she said nothing. It couldn't be as painful as Michael's wound.

The physician finished cleaning her injury at which point Griffin strolled in to look at it.

"The blow caught her here." The physician pointed to an area at the back of her head. "I'll need to stitch it. As you know, she'll need to be watched for other symptoms. A leech might be wise."

Griffin grunted softly. He stood beside her, his hand on her shoulder, as the physician stitched her head. Flashes of white light filled her vision as the physician pushed the needle into her skin. She closed her eyes tightly. She wavered once, but Griffin held her firmly. She was glad he was there and concentrated on his grip on her. Warm, commanding. She forced herself quiet, keeping the groans and cries inside, keeping her mouth shut against the pain. The echoes of Michael's cries when they cauterized his hand still rang in her mind.

When the physician was finished, Michael was

asleep on the mat. Colin and Frances stepped out of the tent to speak with the physician.

Griffin sat beside her when the physicians left the tent. "How do you feel?"

"Miserable," she whispered. Her head was throbbing, and it felt like a bubble. She shook her head and leaned her forehead against his strong shoulder. Even that little movement hurt.

He reached over and took one of her hands into his. He inspected her palm.

She followed his gaze and was surprised to see cuts and scrapes on her palms.

He bent and picked up a clean cloth. He dipped it into a basin of clean water and gently ran it over her skin.

It burned and she winced.

"What happened?" he asked.

She looked back at Michael sleeping on his mat. A lock of brown hair fell across his forehead. "I was running back to our tent."

"Alone?"

Layne nodded. "I thought you were hurt. I couldn't wait... I didn't want..." She looked at him.

He paused in cleaning her hands to meet her stare.

How could just a look from him instill such calm? She sighed. "I saw the way you held your arm against your side. I know you were hurt."

He looked back at her hand. "Where were your brothers?"

"Watching the joust. They probably sent Michael after me."

Griffin's jaw clenched and released as he ran the cloth over her cuts.

"I was running toward our tent. Two of the riders came upon me from behind. I saw Simon."

"Simon?" Griffin's hand tightened around her wrist.

"I think there might have been at least one other rider." She scowled as she tried to remember. Pain flared in her head and she rubbed her forehead. "But I can't..."

"Just relax. You can think of it later," he said with a tight voice. He placed her hand in her lap and picked up the other one.

She studied him for a moment. His hard jaw, his thinned lips. "I'm sorry." She looked at Michael.

"This is not your fault," Griffin said with conviction. "It is those men who deem to take punishment into their own hands. Striking a woman is unforgivable and will not be tolerated."

Carlton burst into the tent.

Griffin put a finger to his lips and indicated the sleeping Michael.

Carlton nodded and stepped up to him. "You are jousting Osmont on the morrow!"

CHAPTER THIRTEEN

Unable to sleep, Layne lay on her mat in Griffin's tent, staring at the top of the pavilion. Muted light illuminated the triangle at the top. Something was bothering her even more than the fact that Griffin was going to face Osmont and more than the painful throbbing of her head. The joust against de la Noue. It was just like her joust with Griffin. He had been unhorsed again. She should have checked his equipment. Carlton didn't know to look for sabotage.

Her head pounded and the left side of her face felt heavy and numb. She could only rest if she tilted her head to the right, away from the injury. But that made her stare at Griffin. One long, muscled leg lay out of the covers, over the ground. One arm lay over his eyes as if covering his face in embarrassment of the unhorsing. She knew that if she had not been injured, he would have been out practicing.

She must have dozed in and out of sleep. Images of Michael's raised hand with his dagger flashed in her mind and Osmont's face looming over her materialized.

Every time she woke, she thought of Griffin's joust. The end result had been just like hers. Had Carlton overlooked something?

She swung her legs from the mat and stood. The pavilion swayed for a moment and Layne thought of sitting back down. She touched her throbbing head, covering the wound with her hand as if that would make the pain go away. The sensation passed and she lowered her hand. She glanced at Griffin and then Carlton before heading for the opening.

The air was cool, the night fresh against her cheeks. She was careful as she made her way to Adonis, who whinnied and pawed the ground as if calling to her.

She walked over to him and he bowed his head. She gently stroked his nose and a grin came to her lips. He threw his head back and Layne smiled full out. She walked over to the saddle on the ground near the tent. "Shh," she whispered. "Don't get me into trouble."

She bent down to inspect it. The world shifted and she had to sit down beside the saddle. She closed her eyes, waiting for the spinning to stop. When it did, she looked at the saddle, running her hand over the hard leather that held Griffin's bottom. The saddle was so important. If she had been the saboteur, this would be one of the objects she would consider sabotaging. The cantle at the back of the saddle and pommelto at the front looked fine. But they had to. That would be too noticeable.

She recalled that during his joust with de la Noue, something had been wrong. Griffin hadn't used the stirrups. Layne picked up the stirrup leather and examined it, first one side, then the other. It would be too suspicious if the stirrup leather failed again. So, it wasn't surprising to her that nothing was wrong with either one.

She put her hand to her head and thought back to the joust. Griffin had taken his feet from the stirrups. Why?

"What are you doing?"

Layne spun to find Griffin standing in the tent opening. She quickly stood and teetered as the spiraling world encompassed her.

Griffin steadied her with a hand to her elbow.

Panic flared within her. What could she tell him? "I was warm. The fresh air is cool."

His eyes narrowed slightly, but he placed cool fingers against her forehead. "Sit," he said. "I didn't mean to disturb you."

Gratefully, she gingerly returned to her seated position.

He stood beside her, his arms crossed over his chest, as he regarded her through cool blue eyes. "You should have woken me. I don't want you alone anywhere anymore."

Layne shook her head stubbornly. "I didn't want to wake you. You joust against Osmont today and I want you to win."

His jaw clenched. "As do I. But that is not a reason to put you in further danger."

Layne turned her head to look up at him. His arms were akimbo, his gaze on the Fletcher tent in the distance. He wore no shirt and she perused his strong torso. Every plane, every curve of muscle rippled with power. He was glorious. When he turned those blue eyes to her, she inhaled sharply and quickly turned away. She cleared her throat. "Your joust with de la Noue…"

He straightened.

"I saw you take your feet from the stirrups. Why did you do this?"

"An equipment malfunction." He shrugged. "I have trained with Adonis for such mishaps."

She nodded and softly bit her lower lip. "Yes. It happens." She lifted her gaze to him and swallowed. "Was it a stirrup leather like what happened in our joust?"

His frown deepened.

"It's just that… In our joust you listed to one side. I thought that maybe that was the reason and –"

"No. One of the stirrups did not break."

Layne scowled and looked back at the saddle. "Then why --?"

"It was the cinch that broke."

She almost gasped with the revelation. She wished she could inspect the cinch to see if it was cut as the stirrup had been. But she dared not push her luck. "That's a strange coincidence. Don't you think? The only times you were unhorsed was when something broke."

"No. That is not true. There have been times when the stirrups broke in the past. Equipment fails. You try to prepare for that possibility, but it is always an unknown factor in jousting. I attribute yesterday's unhorsing to lack of practice and --" He looked pointedly at her. "Distraction."

Still, Layne scowled. Yes, she was probably distracting to him. But how could she make him understand that it was sabotage? She chewed her lower lip. "Carlton has been distracted lately, also. Perhaps he has not been as diligent checking the equipment."

Griffin's eyes narrowed. "What are you saying?"

She had to be careful not to insult him or Carlton.

She needed to lead him in the right direction. He had ordered her to stay away from his horse and the weapons. "I just think that you should check everything. Make sure..." She looked up at him, keeping her suspicions guarded. "...the equipment is working properly."

Griffin was quiet for a long moment as his gaze swept her face. "Carlton is quite adept at checking the equipment. He has not failed me in the past and I suspect he won't in the future."

"If you are distracted enough to be unhorsed, perhaps Carlton was distracted enough to miss something when he checked the cinch."

"Again, I ask what you are implying."

She tightened her hands around each other as if praying. She should tell him what she found and what she guessed, even if he was angry with her. It was better he knew the truth. She could deal with his anger. She just didn't want him hurt. If he knew the truth, he could at least guard himself, even if he hated her for disobeying him. It was the honorable thing to do. "Many knights would do anything to be the best, to win a tournament."

"Yes."

"Not all knights are honorable."

"Again, I agree with you."

How to word this? How to make him see? "De la Noue is not very skilled. He tends to be overconfident and boast about his skill."

Griffin nodded. "Yes."

"Then you should have beat him. Easily. And everyone knows it."

A scowl furrowed Griffin's brow. "Are you trying to insult me?"

"No!" She rose to her feet and forced the subtle spinning away to concentrate. He had to know! Her hands clenched at her sides. "I'm trying to protect you. I don't like to see you hurt. You can't explain this away on coincidence. You should have beaten de la Noue. You should have beaten me!" She reached inside her tunic and took out the stirrup leather, shoving it toward him. "Your equipment was tampered with! You should have looked closer at that stirrup leather! It was cut. And if you check the cinch, I'm sure you'll find the same thing. Someone cut them so you would lose."

CHAPTER FOURTEEN

⚓ingles shot along the nape of Griffin's neck. He couldn't move. He couldn't quite believe someone would dare sneak into his camp and damage his equipment. Or rather, he didn't want to believe it. He took the offered stirrup leather but did not even bother to look at it. His hot gaze bore into her. Why would she tell him? Was she trying to throw him off of her trail? Confuse him? Had she cut the strap to aid her brother's victory? But he wasn't facing one of her brothers when the cinch had been cut. He had been jousting de la Noue.

He brushed past her to where the saddle lay on the ground. He bent to it, picked it up and turned it over.

Layne joined him, standing just behind him. She watched him over his shoulder.

Griffin ran his hand along the cinch to the spot where the break had occurred. It had been lucky he was able to hold onto Adonis. He could have been knocked off. He could have been killed. Did someone want more than just to sabotage him?

He lifted the broken cinch before him until it was

117

silhouetted by the moon. As Layne had surmised, as he had feared, the beginning of the tear was flat and even. Cut.

There was no doubt in his mind. Someone had sabotaged him. Whoever had done this was dangerous. They would stop at nothing to have him lose. Not even if it meant his life.

"Cut?" Layne asked.

Griffin nodded. "Did you see someone cut it?"

"No."

He stood up before her. He couldn't bring himself to believe that she had cut the cinch. She was not cold hearted enough. And maybe he didn't want to believe that she could be capable of something so dishonorable. He looked down at the stirrup leather in his hand. "Why didn't you tell me about the stirrup leather?"

She swallowed, her skin a pale white in the moonlight. "You told me to stay away from Adonis... it was Carlton's responsibility. I knew you wouldn't be pleased." She looked down at the ground with a sigh and added, "I just thought you should know. Even if you got angry with me."

Griffin's gaze swept her face. He knew he should be angry with her. She had not followed simple orders. But he couldn't. She had proven herself loyal. She had told him the truth. He was amazed she had found the cuts when Carlton had not. Her eye for detail was remarkable. She was even able to pick out style flaws in the practicing knights. She was very good at it. He should trust her more. She had earned it. She was intelligent and brave. He knew without a doubt that she was not the one sabotaging him.

There was still only one thing bothering him

where Layne was concerned. How could he keep her safe?

"I just wanted you to know," she whispered. "Before something happened."

He sighed softly. What was he to do with her? She had directly defied him. On a suspicion that could bring harm to him. She wasn't doing it for her own sake, but for his. Warmth blossomed in his chest as he stared down at her. She knew what she had done would get her in trouble. She knew she had gone against his orders. But she had done it anyway and admitted to him what she had found. That took courage. "Why did you tell me?" A delicate scowl of confusion darkened her brow. He was as confused as she was. "You could have kept the secret and gotten away with it."

"Someone is trying to sabotage you. It is dishonorable. You needed to know before harm could befall you."

God's blood! She was gorgeous. Honorable, truthful, a little mischievous and just downright tempting. How was a man to resist?

"I don't want you to be hurt."

As if she could protect him. She was making herself more and more irresistible. He wanted to take her into his arms. He wanted to sample her lips. But she was under his protection. He was trying to show her how a woman acted. He could come up with a million reasons not to kiss her and just one to kiss her.

Because he wanted to.

He nodded and took a step away from her. "You must promise me, Layne. You are not to become involved in this."

"But –"

"No," he said firmly, his hand tightening around

the stirrup leather. "If there is someone trying to sabotage me, he would not hesitate to harm you if you interfered."

Her scowl grew fierce and he was reminded of a lioness he had once seen at court.

"I won't stand by and watch you get hurt."

How he loved her combative nature, how she would fight for those she cared about. Cared about. Did that include him? She cared for him? God's blood! He grabbed her arm and pulled her against him. "Why must you throw yourself into danger?"

Her gaze moved over his face like a heated caress. Her soft, pliable body pressed against his. "For you."

With a growl, he gave in, unable to resist her. He pressed his lips to hers, hungry for her touch, ravenous for her mouth. She parted her lips for his exploration. His desperate kiss gave way to a gentle longing. He pulled her closer to him, not able to get enough of her. For him. She did it for him. He ran his hands up into her hair.

She winced and a groan escaped her lips as his fingers brushed too close to the cloth about her head.

Immediately, he pulled back. He was about to apologize for being such an oaf and putting his needs before hers.

"I'm sorry," she whispered, refusing to relinquish him from her embrace.

A slow smile spread over his lips. Must she always beat him? He kissed her lips quickly and stepped back. "You need to rest."

A groan of disappointment escaped her lips. That was a groan he could tolerate, better then hearing her in pain. He placed an arm about her shoulders to guide her back into the pavilion.

"As do I," he added. He knew she would relent and put his needs first. She didn't resist then but allowed him to lead her into the tent. "I battle Osmont on the morrow."

The sun hid behind large white clouds as if afraid to witness the spectacle below.

Griffin stared down the field of honor at Osmont. His visor was up and he watched with an unsettling calm while Osmont lifted his hands to get the crowd to cheer for him. Griffin heard the cheers and the chants of Osmont's name, but he paid them no heed.

The commander at arms had just finished announcing the start of the joust and he was walking out of the field.

Griffin waited patiently. A strange calm settled over him.

Osmont turned a sneer to Griffin and pointed down the field at him.

The only image Griffin could see was Osmont hitting Layne in the head with his sword. He quickly pushed the thought from his mind and replaced it with a flash of Osmont flying from his horse as his lance struck him hard in the stomach.

Carlton handed the lance to Griffin. Griffin lowered his visor and took the lance, holding it raised for a long moment. He glared down the list at Osmont. There would be no doubt of the consequences of his actions. He would not win this joust. He spurred Adonis. Adonis needed little encouragement. His horse seemed almost as hungry for this joust as he was. Griffin lowered the lance. He would need only one pass. He planned to take Osmont out so quickly there was no doubt.

Adonis thundered down the field of honor. Griffin's body moved with his steed, one with the animal. His grip tightened in preparation for the impact. One pass. One pass.

He leaned forward slightly, concentrating.

He felt the glancing blow. Osmont was not going to make this easy.

It all happened in slow motion. Griffin instinctively corrected for the blow he was taking and lunged forward with his own lance, throwing Osmont's aim off.

Griffin's lance struck perfectly. Osmont's shoulder jerked back. He spun around with so much force, he was launched from the saddle. A perfect strike.

Griffin released the lance. As he rode by, Osmont seemed to be suspended, twisted in mid-air for a moment. Adonis raced to the end of the field. Griffin turned in his saddle. Osmont lay on the dusty ground as Griffin rode back to his side of the field.

Osmont flopped in the dirt like a turtle before he gained enough momentum to sit up.

Griffin lifted his face visor. It wasn't enough. Not enough of a punishment. He slid from Adonis, watching Osmont, silently willing the fallen knight to call for his weapon. His pride would be wounded. He had lost in one pass. The arrogant, pompous knight who had promised victory and swift retribution would call for his sword, Griffin was sure.

Osmont climbed to one knee. His squire appeared at his side, trying to help him to his feet. Osmont pushed the young man away and shouted,

"Sword, boy!" The young man sprinted away to his side of the field.

Satisfaction filled Griffin. Carlton was at his side, handing him his weapon with a resigned sigh. Griffin's hand tightened around the pommel of his sword.

Osmont whipped his sword from his squire's hand and held it pointed at Griffin.

Griffin didn't approach. He stood with the tip of his sword pointed down, waiting.

With a howl of rage, Osmont lifted his sword and charged at Griffin.

Griffin swung, deflecting his strike. The clanging of the swords rang through the silent field. He lifted his sword to meet the next swing of Osmont's weapon. A sharp shearing noise sounded as the swords slid against each other.

Osmont growled and arced another blow. Griffin easily averted it. Let him tire himself, Griffin thought. It was the best way to defeat him. As Osmont's sword lifted, it caught the sunlight and reflected the light of its silver blade.

Griffin wondered for a brief moment if this was the sword that hit Layne. Layne. Her image flashed to his mind. Blood dripping from her wound, disoriented but standing bravely before her brother. He grit his teeth. His sword came alive in his hands, crashing against Osmont's blade with stunning force. He swung again, clashing the blades together.

Osmont stumbled back under the barrage.

Griffin lunged, hitting him in the side. As his sword bounced off Osmont's armor, Osmont tumbled to the ground. Griffin stomped his booted foot on Osmont's sword arm, pinning it to the ground. With a cry, Griffin raised his sword above his head.

Osmont lifted his free arm to protect himself.

Time stopped. Griffin with his sword raised above his head for the final blow. Osmont cowering and trying to protect himself with a raised arm, fear glimmering in his dark eyes.

Griffin bent and grabbed Osmont's breast plate, pulling him slightly off the ground. He pushed his face close to Osmont's. "Yield."

Osmont's upper lip trembled in hatred.

"There is nothing I would like more than to run my blade across your neck," Griffin warned. "Yield or you are a dead man."

"I yield," Osmont snapped in contempt.

"Louder. They didn't hear you."

"I yield!" Osmont shouted.

Griffin straightened. He stared down at Osmont for a long moment. He wanted with every fiber to run him through. But the rules of the joust were clear. Griffin had not only won, he had defeated him soundly.

He removed his foot from Osmont's arm and turned to walk away.

The crowd exploded in a cacophony of wild applause and cheers.

Carlton met him halfway across the field, leading Adonis to him.

Griffin took the reins. His blood pounded through his veins; his teeth clenched tight. He had never known such anger.

Carlton grinned proudly at him.

Even his squire's happiness could not ease his fury. He still wanted to run Osmont through. It wasn't enough. He headed toward the exit. Sweat dripped down his forehead. He removed his helmet, tucking it beneath his arm. He instantly spotted her at the gate.

Layne stood at the fence, Colin and Frances behind her. She smiled with joy and delight. Radiance lit her face. And just like that, his anger was gone, evaporated like the morning dew beneath the hot sun.

Just like that, it was done. One pass. Layne glanced at her brothers. Colin was staring open mouthed. Frances was scowling in disbelief.

She looked back at Griffin as he exited the field of honor. He stared back at her. Tingles raced all the way through her body like a delightful summer breeze. She could barely contain the pride she felt. Griffin was magnificent. One mighty pass. And he had defeated Osmont soundly in hand-to-hand combat. She looked again at her brothers. Colin shook his head. Frances closed his eyes. Slowly, Layne's smile faded as the implications swept through her. How could her brothers possibly beat someone like that?

Frances looked at her. "You have to find some way for us to beat him."

At many levels, this upset her. It was dishonorable. They should be able to defeat him based on their own skills, not through trickery or some hidden secret. But there was also something else. Layne couldn't betray Griffin like that, not even if she knew a trick that would help her brothers win.

"No," Colin said before she could answer. "You can't ask that of her. It's our duty to find some way to defeat him."

"Did you see that?" Frances asked, sweeping his hand out to the field toward Osmont who stormed off of the field. The defeated knight was followed by his squire who hurried to keep up with him. "How can we hope to defeat him?"

"We'll find a way," Colin said. "We'll practice more."

Layne nodded in agreement, but she wasn't sure if all the practice in the world would be enough to defeat Griffin Wolfe.

Layne walked back to Griffin's tent with her brothers. It was a somber mood. And she knew she should feel the same. But inside, she was overjoyed at the competent, strong way Griffin had unhorsed Osmont. She felt a personal victory. In one pass, her mind continued to repeat.

Carlton sat near the front of the tent, polishing Griffin's armor. He looked up. Layne stopped before him as her brothers moved to their own tent. Colin was jousting later and they had to prepare.

Layne stared Carlton in the eye. Slowly, Carlton's lips turned up in a grin and his eyes danced with exhilaration.

Layne knelt before him, grabbing his arms in elation, unable to keep the unabashed joy from her smile. "One pass!" she whispered in excitement.

Carlton nodded. He shrugged, trying to suppress the excitement in his voice. "He thought Osmont deserved no less for what he did to you."

Pride and warmth blossomed in her heart. Layne leaned forward. "It wasn't anything less." She smiled. "Is he inside?"

Carlton nodded and looked back down at his work. She patted his shoulder and rose, entering the tent.

Griffin whirled. He wore no shirt, only breeches that hugged his legs and hips.

For a moment, Layne could not move. Her mouth went dry and she could only stare. His torso was chiseled perfection. Gleaming with a light sheen of perspiration, his muscles shone in the sun shining in from the open flap. He put his hands on his hips. "You should have been resting."

She tried to form the words, but nothing came to mind. She nodded. Lord, how she wanted to touch him, to run her hands over the smooth expanse of his chest.

"You have nothing to say?"

She swallowed hard. Magnificent. Spectacular. Wonderful. All of these words came to her mind, but they had nothing to do with the joust.

"Speechless?" he asked, dropping his hands. "Yes, I suppose I would be, too." He shook his head. "I made squire errors."

Her mouth dropped in shock and she stepped forward, shaking her head. "No!" she protested.

He looked up, meeting her eyes.

The blue of his orbs left her reeling. "No," she whispered. "You were wonderful. There were no mistakes. You were perfect."

His brows lowered in disagreement. His gaze swept her face. "There is no such thing as perfect."

"You gave Osmont a thorough thrashing, but I suspect you know that." She stepped into the tent and the flap swooshed closed behind her.

"It wasn't enough," he whispered. "It took all of my training to keep my anger at bay. Osmont wasn't so fortunate. He doesn't have the will I do."

She stepped closer. "Or the strength." Her gaze

moved over his torso and then back up to his eyes. "You are perfect." A heated blush flushed through her body and she looked down. "You did wonderfully in the joust. I couldn't be more proud."

"You couldn't?"

It was the way he said it that intrigued her. With shocked innocence. She glanced up at him. "Well..." She smiled in embarrassment. It wasn't her place to be proud of him. "What I meant to say... Is that I don't think you made any mistakes."

"Then you are not as observant as you say you are." He crossed his arms. "What did your brothers think?"

Seriousness returned, erasing the joy. Layne glanced back over her shoulder at the tent flap. "I don't think they felt the same way."

"I should hope not. There's a good chance I will joust against one of them on the morrow. That is, if they win their jousts today."

How could they hope to beat him? And who would she root for?

CHAPTER FIFTEEN

Layne sat beside Michael as he lay on his mat. His morning meal of apples and bread lay untouched on the floor where she placed it. "You should eat, Michael. To get your strength up."

"For what?"

"For what? Frances and Colin still need their squire. The weapons need to be sharpened and cleaned –"

"How am I to do that?" He waved his bandaged hand in the air.

Layne sat back. "It will heal."

"Am I to re-grow my fingers? Is that what will happen?" He turned away from her, facing the side of the tent.

A wave of sympathy crested over her. This was her fault. He had been defending her. She touched the side of her head where a welt had formed around the gash. She hated the bandage and removed it, letting the air heal it. She looked at Michael's slumped back. She could have easily fallen into the same sorrow as

Michael. He had lost his fingers. But she needed to be strong, to set an example, for Michael. She couldn't let him feel sorry for himself. That was a dangerous path. She needed him to have purpose, to be strong. "You still have three fingers."

"Leave me alone."

"You're looking at this all wrong. Who else could boast of such an injury and lived? Not even Frances and Colin. You fought off a knight's sword with naught but a dagger."

Michael crossed his arms and refused to turn to her.

"Think of the stories you could tell. How you came to my rescue. How you faced a knight on horseback with only a dagger." She tickled him, but he jerked away. Layne sat back with a sigh. "So that's it? You're going to give up? I suppose I can't blame you. Losing two fingers is almost like losing an arm. Losing two fingers is almost like losing a leg. I suppose those people who lose those are as good as dead."

Michael whirled on her, his eyes brimming with tears, anger in his voice. "You don't know what it's like!"

"No, I don't. But I tell you I wouldn't let that foul Osmont get away with this. I'd be up practicing until I could thrash him. I wouldn't be laying around and letting others feel sorry for me."

He clenched his teeth and glared at her. "I wish I had never saved you!"

His words stung, but she ignored them to curl her fingers into a tight fist. "You're a Fletcher. You're a fighter, damn it. Fight!"

"I'm going to tell Colin you said an unlady-like word."

She crossed her arms over her chest and lifted her chin. "You'll have to get out of bed to do that."

"I hate you, Layne!"

"Here, now," Griffin said, ducking beneath the tent flap. "Knights of the realm do not speak thus to any lady."

"She's no lady," Michael snapped. "She's a pain in my arse."

Layne knew he was angry, and she was glad. Better for him to be angry than sad and pitiable.

"Michael!" Griffin reprimanded. "How do you expect her to treat you as a knight if you don't act like one?"

Michael glowered at her.

At least he is sitting up, Layne thought, answering his fierce stare with one of her own.

Griffin picked up a dagger at the side of the bed. He inspected it, running a finger over the blade. "When I was a lad, my father insisted I treat even the servant women with decorum and respect. He always said that if I didn't act like a knight, I could never truly become one."

"Obviously, you ain't got a sister like her!"

"Oh, on the contrary. I do," Griffin said. He held the dagger to his eye, looking down the blade. "Although, she is not as adept with a weapon as Layne, she uses many of the same tactics to achieve her goals." Griffin glanced at Layne.

"Tactics?" Michael echoed in confusion.

"Gwen is proficient at fake tears and pouty expressions."

"Hey!" Layne objected. "I can't fake cry."

Griffin chuckled and picked up a whetstone. He shrugged casually. "Perhaps not, but there are other

131

tactics you use. Innocent looks. Arguing."

"You argue, too!" Layne protested.

Griffin ran the stone across the side of the blade. "How many times do you think Layne will have to ask you to eat?"

Michael glanced at the food. He pushed it away with his booted foot. "Many," he said stubbornly and defiantly.

"Ah, good lad," Griffin said. "Resist until the end." He ran the stone along the other side of the blade. "But now, man to man, how many times would I have to ask?"

Michael looked at him. "Only once. But you are a knight. She is a –"

"Lady," Griffin corrected.

Layne narrowed her eyes.

Michael grudgingly growled, "Lady."

Griffin drew the trencher closer to the mat. "Eat," he commanded Michael. "To be strong."

Michael glared at the food for a long moment and then finally reached out to rip a piece from the bread and gingerly took a bite of it.

Griffin met Layne's stare and shared a conspirator's grin with her.

Warmth flooded through Layne. He had achieved what she could not. With her own brother. She should be insulted. But she wasn't. Not at all. She was grateful.

Carlton stuck his head into the tent. "Frances lost."

Layne slowly turned the roasting stick over the

fire outside of Griffin's tent, cooking the duck that was skewered on it. She glanced at the Fletcher tent. It was strangely quiet, although she knew Frances and Michael were inside. Frances was furious he had lost. He was always hard on himself when he lost a competition, but even more so now when so much depended on him. Colin sat outside of the tent, sharpening his sword.

Even more depended on Colin now. They needed to win one more tournament to have enough coin for the farm. A home of their own. It's what they all wanted. She knew that Colin would be torn whether to buy the farm or keep the money to pay to Griffin for her freedom. She was determined to make that an easy choice for her brother. She could survive much more time with Griffin, much more time than her ill father had left in the world.

Colin ran the whetstone across his blade. He was always so calm, so even tempered. She wondered how he did it. He knew the risks. He knew what they had to do. She admired Colin. She wished she could be more like him. If she was, she would never be in this situation. She would not have taken Frances's place and jousted. She slowly turned the stick.

Griffin had let her stay with her brothers while he and Carlton went to practice.

"Ahh," a voice called, and she turned to find a tall man approaching her.

She slowly rose, glancing at Colin who had paused in his work to watch her.

The man stopped; his hands raised. "I'm sorry. I didn't mean to frighten you." He bowed slightly. "Ethan Farindale."

"Griffin is not here."

Ethan nodded. His sharp eyes took in

everything, his surroundings, the duck she was roasting and her brother who watched him. He lifted a hand to Colin in greeting before looking back at Layne. "Where is my friend?"

"Practicing."

"With the jousting he did today, I'm not sure he needs to practice."

She had to agree with Ethan on that. "Should I tell him you stopped by?"

Ethan's gaze swept her. He glanced at her brother. "Perhaps I can wait for him."

Layne shrugged and knelt down to turn the stick the roasting duck was cooking on, easing it over so it cooked evenly.

"I didn't get your name," Ethan said to her.

"I suspect you know my name."

His lips curved up into a sideways grin. "I do, indeed. Fletcher. Layne Fletcher. The only one to ever have unhorsed Griffin. Well, until de la Noue, that is. But you will always be the first."

Layne watched the duck, trying to remain impassive at his statement. Yes. She would always be the first, but she knew what had happened. She knew why Griffin fell. A tingle shot up her spine and she shifted her gaze to Ethan. She wondered if he did.

Ethan's gaze moved over her, assessing her. "Why do you wear men's clothing?"

"It makes riding easier."

Ethan chuckled softly. "That's true. Perhaps that is why knights do not wear dresses."

"Would you like me to tell Griffin that you stopped by?" Layne asked, turning the spit.

Ethan smiled. "Are you trying to get rid of me?"

Layne shifted her gaze to him. "I'm just

wondering what you want."

"Ha!" Ethan exploded. "You don't find me good company? You are not intrigued by my dashing good looks?"

A strand of dark hair fell into his blue eyes as he leaned forward, putting his arms on his crossed legs. His looks were indeed the type that maidens would fall for. One flash of his smile and he could have any woman at his mercy. Any woman except her. There was something she didn't trust about Ethan. "Should I be?"

Ethan chuckled, but the full-fledged radiance of his smile didn't fade. "I suppose not. You're not like all the other women."

"I'll take that as a compliment." She looked at him through narrowed eyes. "There is something I would like to know."

"Really?" He leaned forward and his look turned downright wolfish.

"How long have you known Griffin?"

Ethan sat back, blowing one of the dark strands from his eyes in disappointment.

Layne had a moment of satisfaction deflating his self-worth.

"It was shortly after he left home. I met him just before his first joust. I saved him from a group of ruffians. He never would have made it if it wasn't for me." He looked at her. "Are you impressed?"

She turned the spit. "Somehow I don't think that's the truth."

"I have a question for you."

"Another one?"

Ethan rumbled with laughter, but his humor slowly faded. He cast a glance at Colin who had sat back down. "Why would your brother trust you to Griffin's care after you humiliated him?"

That familiar stab of guilt wound in Layne's heart. Humiliated? "You mean because he was unhorsed."

"By a woman."

Layne ground her teeth. "I thought it was very honorable what Griffin did. Colin needed his help and Griffin offered his protection." She looked at Ethan. "Besides, there is no humiliation in being unhorsed during a joust. No one can win all the time."

"Well said, m'lady!" Griffin called, reining in Adonis and dismounting all in one movement. He walked toward Ethan with a menacing gate.

Layne stood.

Ethan jumped to his feet.

Griffin stalked forward until he was directly before him. "Have you something to say to me, old friend?"

Ethan stammered, "I... I... I thought you were practicing."

Griffin's ice blue eyes were chilly. "You did not think I would be that long, did you?"

Something passed between the two men and Ethan bowed his head. He ran a hand through his hair. "Of course not," Ethan said.

"Why did you come?" Griffin demanded.

Ethan cast a glance at Layne and then back at Griffin. "I heard tell she was the one who unhorsed you. I wanted to see for myself."

Griffin's jaw clenched. "She is. Have you something to say about that?"

Ethan's brows rose in surprise. Then a slow grin curved his lips. "No."

Layne felt a twinge of remorse and pain for

Griffin. How many times would he have to defend himself, his reputation?

"No." Ethan backed away from Griffin. "I guess… I'll be going."

Griffin grabbed his tunic front and pulled him close. "Stay away from her, Ethan. Do you understand?"

Again, Ethan's eyebrows rose in surprise.

"She is under my protection."

Ethan nodded. "I've heard."

Griffin released him.

Ethan's lips tightened in what looked like regret, before he moved off toward the cluster of tents in the distance.

Layne looked at Griffin. He watched Ethan with a cold gaze and tight jaw. "Do not be deceived by his charm. He is untrustworthy."

"That's what I thought."

Griffin glanced at her in surprise. His lips curled up at the ends. His eyes were so blue, staring at her with such focus, such acceptance. Her mouth went dry, but she couldn't look away. She didn't want to look away. A slight wind rustled past, tossing a lock of his blond hair before his face.

Layne dipped her head in embarrassment and found a grin lighting her face.

Carlton ran up to them. He took Adonis's reins and started to lead him to the side of the tent. The moment was lost.

Layne stepped into the Fletcher tent.

Michael looked up. "What do you want?"

Layne grimaced. She wished she hadn't been so

harsh with him, but at least now he was sitting up. She was not going to apologize to him. She didn't want him to feel sorry for himself. "Colin is preparing to joust." She stood in the doorway, hesitant.

Michael shrugged.

"You know how important it is that he win this purse. Now that Frances is out –"

"I know."

Layne stared at him. He wouldn't look at her. He cradled his bandaged hand beneath his other arm; his shoulders drooped. "I need your help."

He grunted. "For what?"

Layne took a deep breath. She glanced out the tent flap. Colin and Frances were at the field of honor. Carlton and Griffin were at their tent.

"I learned why I was able to unhorse Griffin."

"So what?" Michael snapped. "So you were able to defeat him."

"Michael," she said sternly, drawing his gaze. "Someone is trying to sabotage him."

His brows furrowed and then distaste twisted his mouth. His eyes narrowed in doubt. "How do you know?"

"When he lost to de la Noue, his cinch was cut. Not torn. And when he jousted with me, the stirrup leather was cut."

Michael looked down at the ground again. "Did you tell him?"

"I did."

Michael shrugged. "What do you want me to do about it?"

"Griffin, Carlton and I are going to the joust to watch Colin. I just want you to sit outside and watch his tent. Make sure no one comes around."

Michael scowled and looked down at his wounded hand.

Layne knew he'd rather go see the joust. "Or you could go to the joust and I'll talk Carlton into staying. I just thought that maybe you'd like to help." She turned to exit the tent.

"Wait," Michael called.

Layne paused.

Michael frowned his pouty expression, staring at the ground. "You could be wrong. You know you're wrong sometimes. You don't know everything."

"Yes, I could be wrong. And I want to be. But he's been unhorsed twice now. Against me and de la Noue. He shouldn't have been unhorsed against us. Not against us. We're not as good as he is."

Michael was quiet for a moment as he considered her words. "I'll watch." He stood. He brushed past Layne. "I'm not doing this for you."

She pressed her lips together. She knew he wasn't. He was doing it for Griffin or maybe to prove her wrong. It didn't matter why, only that he was doing it. "Thank you," she whispered.

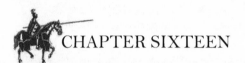# CHAPTER SIXTEEN

 riffin stood beside Layne, his gaze moving over the field of honor and through the spectators as if he were searching for something. In truth, he was calculating where the knights were positioned. They posed the most threat to Layne, and while Griffin was sure they wouldn't act in a crowd, he had to be cautious. Carlton leaned on the fence beside him.

Colin rode Angel back and forth on his side of the field, preparing for the joust. Frances acted as his squire for the match. Colin moved Angel over to Frances and spoke quietly to him.

Griffin's gaze shifted to Talvace, Colin's opponent. He wore no helmet yet and his dark hair hung to his shoulders. Fool, Griffin thought. It would get in his way when he jousted. It should be tied back. Still, he was good, a competitor not to be taken lightly. But so was Colin. It should be a great match. His gaze slid to Layne.

She stood on the first wrung of the fence, her hands on the top plank. She tapped her foot constantly, nervously. A slight breeze blew her hair back from her face, giving him a glimpse of the healing wound on the back of her head. His jaw tightened. Instinctively, he scanned the field and the spectators. It took a moment, but he finally found Osmont. He was on Talvace's side, at the other end of the field from them, laughing at something one of his companions said. Of course he was on Talvace's side. Any side other than the Fletcher's.

"You shouldn't scowl at him."

Griffin swiveled his head to find Layne grinning at him. She was eye-level with him, and her beautiful blue eyes sparkled in the sunlight.

"People will know of your displeasure."

Griffin looked back at Osmont. "It is only important that he know of my displeasure."

"I think he knows."

At the sound of the horses thudding through the dusty earth, they looked back at the field of honor. The match had begun. The knights lowered their lances and closed in on each other. Talvace missed Colin completely, but Colin landed a blow to his shoulder.

"Not hard enough," Carlton said.

Layne glared at him. "His horse slipped."

Carlton looked at Griffin, who nodded in agreement. Only a trained eye would have seen it. It didn't surprise Griffin that Layne had spotted it. She was good.

As Colin rounded and rode past them toward Frances, Layne pushed herself upright and cheered and clapped.

Griffin got the feeling she was being reserved.

Colin took his fresh lance from Frances.

Talvace was offered a lance, but shook his head, pointing to another. His squire offered up the lance

Talvace had indicated.

Colin set off first, giving him the advantage.

Layne leaned over the fence, her hands together, the tips against her lips as if she were praying.

Griffin narrowed his eyes. The lance Talvace held didn't move at all as the horse galloped down the list. Usually there was a little play that the rider had to contend with. Either he had a tremendous grip on the lance or…

Griffin straightened in dread.

The brutal impact struck a blow to Colin's side, launching him back and off of his steed. Colin's lance struck Talvace's stomach but slid off his armor; Talvace remained firmly in the saddle.

Layne stood up on the plank of wood, her hands in her hair, her face twisted into one of disbelief and concern.

Griffin stared as well, but he was not looking at Colin. The lance Talvace used lay on the ground, unbroken.

From the other side of the field, a cheer went up as Talvace threw his hands in the air in victory.

Frances ran out to Colin who lay on the ground, unmoving.

Layne leaned forward, over the fence as if she wished she could go to Colin.

Griffin grabbed her arm, partly in comfort, partly to prevent her from leaping the fence and racing out onto the field. He leaned over to Carlton. "Go and feign checking on Colin." He spoke quieter. "But check Talvace's lance."

Carlton nodded and ducked beneath the fence to run onto the field.

Colin lay still on the ground. Prickles of

apprehension raced along Griffin's shoulders. He looked at Osmont, who was lifting his hands in victory, pumping them in the air. Talvace rode before the fence, back and forth, waving to the cheering crowd.

Carlton slid to his knees beside the lance. His hands ran over it, inspecting. He knocked on it.

Talvace's squire, a blonde boy, raced to Carlton. He tried to pull the lance away from his study, but Carlton seized it and knocked on it, again. The blonde squire shoved Carlton, taking possession of the lance

Carlton sat back and for a moment Griffin thought he was giving up. But then he stood as the squire lifted the lance and began to carry it from the field.

"Foul!" Carlton screamed, pointing at the retreating squire.

The squire faltered. He glanced back at Carlton; his eyes wide with fear.

"Foul!" Carlton repeated, lifting his voice above the celebration and cheers of victory.

The crowd began to calm and quiet.

"Foul!" Carlton cried again, poking a finger at Talvace's squire.

Layne straightened.

Griffin leaned toward her. "That lance didn't move as he jousted. In this tournament, a lance like that is prohibited."

Layne gasped. "It's solid."

Griffin nodded. "That's what they'll find out when they test it."

Three nobles dressed in black robes appeared from beside the grandstand and walked toward the squire, across the field. The poor young man looked at Talvace and then at the nobles in indecision.

Griffin kept his hand firmly on Layne's arm. He didn't want any reason for this victory to be upheld.

Two of the nobles took the lance from the squire.

Talvace didn't look so smug anymore. And Osmont had stopped his celebration. But why would he do it? It was an even match. Talvace had every chance of beating Colin fairly. Griffin's gaze settled on Osmont and his eyes narrowed. He had a suspicion why.

Carlton walked over to Colin as Frances was helping him sit up. Colin held his hand to his side, but he appeared to be all right. They glanced at Carlton who spoke and then looked down the field at the black robed nobles near Talvace's squire.

A tall thin noble straightened as his two companions held the lance. Griffin knew him as Lord Bartlett. He was one of the judges for the Norfolk Tournament. He pointed to Talvace. "Disqualified!" he proclaimed. "Sir Colin is the winner!"

Layne didn't rejoice. She scowled. "They did that to hurt him."

Griffin shook his head. "Not him. You."

Layne glanced at him in surprise.

"I'm sure Osmont is behind this," Griffin said, staring across the field at the dark-haired knight who was speaking with Talvace. "Punishing your brothers for what you did."

The final joust of the Norfolk Tournament was scheduled for later that day. But before that closing event, there was still another joust that had to take place; the winner of that match would be the man who would joust against Griffin. It was between Colin and Sir

Geoffrey Williams. Layne sat in a corner of the tent, pulling a thread through a tear in Carlton's breeches to stitch it up. She sat in the far corner, facing the tent entrance. Her knees were bent, and she concentrated on the stitching. She pulled the needle through the fabric.

They had given Colin a reprieve of a few hours to tend his injury. It wasn't bad. He had only been bruised. Layne scowled, poking the needle through the fabric. It shouldn't have happened. He should have faced Talvace in a fair competition. Why would they want to injure him? Because of her. Her scowl grew. Colin had to win. But even as she thought this, doubt festered in her mind. What if his bruise hindered his performance?

She pulled the needle through the fabric, but it caught. She tugged at it and the thread snapped off the needle.

What if Colin lost? She sighed and bent her head to her knees? Only in privacy could she admit her fears. His chances of winning at the upcoming Woodstock tourney would be even less than here at Norfolk. It was a larger purse and many more knights would participate.

"Layne?"

She lifted her head to see Griffin entering the tent. His entire form took up the space in the opening. His blonde hair hung in waves to his shoulders. The sunlight shining in from behind him accentuated his strong arms, casting a golden hue over his shoulders. Her breathing hitched unexpectedly.

"Carlton told me you wanted to wash clothing. He is busy with my armor. I will escort you to the stream."

Layne nodded. She tied off the string with a

knot, folded the breeches and put them in the dirty pile. She lifted the clothes into her arms.

Griffin did not move as she approached. "Is your head bothering you?"

She shook her head. "No. It's healing. Tender to the touch, but all right."

Griffin's gaze swept her face. "Then what is it? What troubles you?"

Her eyebrows rose in surprise. Was she that transparent to him? "I..." She wanted to tell him. She wanted to tell him how important it was for them to win. She sighed softly and looked down. He was well off. He did not lack for weapons or a fine horse. Just another thing that separated them. He wouldn't understand. "No. I'm fine."

For a long moment, he stood before her, gazing at her. She couldn't meet his stare. Finally, he stepped aside, and she walked out of the tent, moving down the slight rise toward the stream. She heard his footsteps as he followed. She ducked beneath a branch and entered the forest.

He caught up with her then. "You are worried about your brother."

Layne shrugged. "Of course. After the last joust, can you blame me?"

He shook his head.

"And for you. Carlton is checking your equipment?"

Griffin lifted his head to the forest ceiling where branches merged above their heads. "He is, but you should not concern yourself with that."

"How can I not?"

He turned his piercing gaze to her.

She stopped and faced him, pushing the clothing

down so she could speak. "I have to worry about it. I have to worry about you. Someone does."

He took the clothing from her arms. "I have no need for someone to worry about me." He continued through the forest.

Layne hurried after him, surprised that he had taken the clothing and now carried them for her. "Everyone should have someone to worry about them. What about your sister?"

He laughed; his rolling deep chuckle edged with bitterness. "She is too worried about fashion and her next new dress."

Pity twisted inside of her. She had her brothers and they all worried for each other. She couldn't imagine not having someone to be concerned about her. She nodded and lifted her chin. "Then I will worry about you."

He glanced back at her.

She smiled at him.

"And if I don't want you to worry about me?"

"I'm afraid you can't stop me."

He stopped and she almost bumped into him but brought herself up short. "No one has been concerned for my welfare since I was a child. My father was too busy tending to the castle and lands. My brother had more concern for his sword than he did for me. No. I am the only one who looks out for myself."

Layne's gaze swept him. "Not anymore." She raced past him and dashed to the stream. "I won."

"I didn't know we were racing."

"It's always a competition between my brothers and I. For just about everything we do."

"Is that why you feel the need to sword fight and joust?" He set the clothing on the ground.

Layne considered his words. "My father liked to sword fight and joust. I suppose I thought if I liked it, that would bring us closer."

"Did it?"

Layne knelt at the shore and picked up a shirt. "No." She dunked the clothing beneath the water. "He was much of the same mindset as you are. It is a man's game with no place for a woman." She could feel Griffin scrutinizing her. She felt she was on display. This was something she didn't want Griffin to see, a longing inside of her that she wanted kept private. "It really didn't matter what I did. My father was more interested in my brothers than me."

"Where is he now?"

"Edinfield Manor awaiting our return." She took the soap and scrubbed the tunic. Then she dunked it into the water. "We will return after the Woodstock Tourney." She froze and glanced at him. "Well, at least my brothers will."

"They will not have enough coin to pay me."

Layne looked down at the tunic in her hands. Griffin's tunic. "Not if they don't win a tournament. And even then, they might not." She wanted Colin to buy the farm for their family, not pay for her release. She closed her eyes. She had really messed things up. "You might be stuck with me longer than you think."

"You think that is a punishment for me?"

His words caught her off guard. "I think I am a chore for you. I think I distract you. I think --"

He knelt beside her and put a finger to her lips. "You think too much." He brushed a lock of her hair back from her cheek. "You are a pleasant surprise for me. I was not expecting you."

"Is that good or bad?"

148

His gaze swept her face, tenderly, a warm smile on his lips. "Good. You are like a breath of fresh air when the world had gone sour."

His words shocked her, and her blood began to simmer with the promise of those words. Slowly, doubt clouded her mind and a scowl etched into her forehead. She turned from him to continue washing. "Then why would you try to change me?"

"I don't want to change you," he said softly, his voice velvet and gentle. "I did in the beginning. I wanted you to be like other women."

Layne scrubbed the fabric harder with the soap, her heart dropping. Just like her father. Just like her aunt. They had always wanted her to fit the mold of a lady, to be like the other young ladies. But she never could.

"Only now do I realize what a mistake that is."

Surprised, she snapped her gaze to him. Confused, she could only stare. She must have misheard him. He couldn't have said those words. Because she wanted him to say them. With all her heart, with all her being, she wanted him to say those words. She wanted him to love her just like she was. Love her? She froze, stunned by the thought.

"You are a wonder. You can see mistakes that most men would miss. In style, in weapons. In people. And you caught the sabotage. Even Carlton missed that."

Was she dreaming? Was Griffin actually complimenting her on her jousting and weapons skills? Her mouth dropped slightly.

He sat back, leaning on his arms. "You must think I am mad. I think I'm mad. And don't think this lets you off the hook. I still think you are in danger.

From Osmont. From whoever is trying to sabotage me. I won't allow you to place yourself into any more danger."

Layne's heart pounded in her chest. It was the closest thing to concern he had ever expressed to her. "Do you mean it? Truly mean it?"

"Do I mean you will stay out of danger? Absolutely!"

Layne rolled her eyes. "No. Not that."

Griffin's smile was relaxed and gentle and full of warmth. "I mean that you are perfect the way you are. Except, I would see you in a dress now and then."

She smiled. "If the occasion arises, I promise I will don a dress."

He gently laid his hand on her cheek. "You shouldn't worry what others think and say."

"I don't," she agreed. His palm was hot against her skin and she couldn't help staring at his lips. "Only what you think and say."

His eyes glinted in happiness and he eased her head toward his lips, running his tongue across her top lip before entering her mouth hungrily. Tingles danced through her body. She would never grow tired of feeling his lips on hers, of having him kiss her. She reached around behind him, wrapping her hands behind the nape of his neck.

He braced himself with one arm and pulled her close with the other, curving his arm around her waist.

She angled her head to give him better access to her mouth. He tasted of warm ale, heady duck and a tinge of honey. There was a tenderness that belied his strength. He pulled her closer, more demanding, holding her tighter as if he was afraid to let her go. Her senses reeled as the kiss deepened. She clutched his shoulders.

"Ooooh! I'm telling."

The voice was like a douse of cold water. Layne pushed herself from Griffin, her face coloring.

Michael stood near a tree between the tent and them.

"Michael!" Layne exclaimed, rising.

"You were kissing him," Michael sang in sing-song fashion and turned to rush back to the tent. "I'm telling Colin."

"Michael." Griffin's voice demanded obedience. "Come here, boy."

Michael froze and then slowly, obediently, turned and approached him with his head down.

"Look at me."

Michael lifted his gaze and there was a furious scowl on his brow.

"Do you have something to say to me?" Griffin demanded.

"You shouldn't be kissing my sister unless you intend to marry her," Michael stated.

As embarrassed as Layne was, she had to admire Michael's bravery. Even after he was injured, he still had the demeanor of a great man.

"You are correct," Griffin said.

Michael's eyes widened. "You're going to marry Layne?"

"Perchance," Griffin said.

This caught Layne off guard. They had never said anything about marriage. But she couldn't help the strange flutter that settled in her stomach at the thought of marrying Griffin.

"Then you shouldn't be kissing my sister until you are certain."

Griffin nodded in agreement. "You are correct. I am very fond of Layne." He glanced at her and a gentle smile came to his lips. "Very fond."

Joy ignited inside Layne. Joy and something else. She wanted to kiss him, to hold him, to touch him.

"But there are things that Layne and I have to work out privately. The jousts must come first." He put a hand on Michael's shoulder. "As a young squire, you know that."

Michael scowled again and kicked at a pebble on the ground. "Maybe."

"This matter will remain a secret. You will not tell Colin. Yet."

"But he should know."

"And I will tell him when the moment is right." Griffin gently shook Michael's shoulder. "Agreed?"

Michael nodded. "Agreed."

"Man to man."

Michael nodded again, a lock of his brown hair falling into his eyes. "Man to man."

"Good boy." Griffin ruffled his hair. He glanced at Layne.

She was shocked that Michael had agreed to keep the incident from Colin. But she was again amazed at the way Griffin had handled her brother, amazed and proud.

"Let us head back. We have a joust coming up."

"I still don't see why we couldn't go," Layne complained.

Griffin sat on the straw mat, watching her pace the tent. "Carlton will tell us who is the victor."

"I could have seen for myself if..." She whirled on him; the look on her face was like that of a trapped animal desperate for freedom beyond its cage. "Why couldn't we go?"

"It's best not to keep you in the forefront of Osmont's mind. Let him think of other things. A fair joust, for one."

"Osmont wasn't jousting."

"But he's there," Griffin said softly. "Layne. You being there or not being there is not going to affect the outcome. Relax."

She frowned and paced again. Back and forth. There certainly wasn't enough room to move, let alone get the pent-up frustration out. "I don't like Colin out there without protection."

"And you think you can protect him?"

Layne stopped to stare at the ground. "Even you said that I have a good eye. Maybe I could see something everyone missed. Maybe ---"

"Maybe you would run out onto the field again."

She rolled her eyes and looked up at the top of the pavilion. "I was not going to run out onto the field."

"Because I had your arm." Layne opened her mouth to protest, but Griffin continued, "You react with your heart, especially where it involves the ones you love. If you could control that initial reaction you would be a very dangerous opponent."

Did he mean -? Could he actually mean -? "You mean on the field of honor?"

He stared at her for a long moment, a play of emotions moving through his eyes.

Her heart soared with hope, longing to hear the words of praise on his lips. Anticipation thrummed in her veins.

He looked down at the ground. Several pairs of torn breeches and a pile of tunics with various tears and rips in them lay scattered nearby. "Do you not have chores to do?"

There was a moment of silence in which her hope disintegrated. Of course he would never mean the field of honor. Not with her. No matter how good she was. She didn't belong on the field of honor. She looked at the clothing. "You meant as a mender of clothing," she said with rich sarcasm. "Yes. Those other menders are very dangerous, too. I'm just terrified of them." She scooped the clothing up in her arms.

"Where are you going?"

She glanced at him around the clothes. Her hair fell forward and she had to brush it back from her eyes. "I'm going outside to mend. You'd best accompany me. Those frightful menders might be there. I might need protection." She ducked out of the tent.

"Layne!"

She looked over the slight rise toward the field of honor to see Carlton rushing toward them. Her heart twisted with dread and excitement. Eagerness rushed through her veins. Colin had to win. He had to!

"He lost. Colin was unhorsed."

Lost. Her heart plummeted. That meant the Fletchers were out of the joust. The purse was no longer theirs to win. That meant only one thing. One of them had to win the Woodstock Tourney.

 CHAPTER SEVENTEEN

Layne sat in the tent with her brothers. She watched them somberly as they all packed up to leave. No one said a word.

Griffin and Carlton were at the field of honor jousting their last joust. There was no doubt they would win.

Colin stared at a flask of ale he was packing.

Layne grimaced. She knew he was disappointed. "Colin ---"

"Don't," Colin ordered. "I was expecting to be jousting out there against Wolfe."

"Sometimes even the best are unhorsed," she told him gently. "This is not a perfect art. Things go wrong."

"Nothing went wrong!"

"Obviously something went wrong if you were unhorsed. Did you check ---?"

"Everything," Colin insisted. "There was no sign of tampering."

He sounded disappointed. She wished she had

155

been there to see what happened, what went wrong. "Then we'll just have to win next time. At Woodstock."

"You don't understand," Colin said. He leaned toward her. "We *have* to win at Woodstock. Or we won't have enough for the farm. Father... we... won't have a home for the winter. We need that purse."

Layne shrugged. "Then we will win."

"It's as simple as that?" Frances mocked.

"Yes," Layne insisted. "If I could knock Griffin from the horse, then so can either of you."

"You said someone cut his stirrup leather," Colin said, looking down at the flask in his hand.

"It doesn't matter. You can do it. You just need to practice. A lot. I'll sneak out later and meet you at the field of honor." Colin looked at her and was about to protest, but she continued, "We'll practice every moment we can. Every second we get. We *will* beat them. All of them."

A grin curled Colin's lips and he looked at the flask. "All right then. We'll practice."

"Of course, if you weren't so lazy, you all would have been practicing already."

"Really?" Frances demanded, rising and approaching her with a menacing gait.

"Is that so?" Colin demanded, tossing the flask at her.

She ducked and the flask sailed over her head, but Frances grabbed her around the waist, pulling her to the ground. He began to tickle her. She tried to fend off his hands, but peals of laughter issued from her.

"That is not how a lady is treated."

Frances and Layne looked up to see Michael standing over them, a severe scowl on his brow.

"No?" Frances asked.

"You do not throw a lady to the ground and lay on top of her to tickle her."

Layne shrugged. "He's right, you know."

Frances guffawed. "If I see one, I'll be sure to treat her properly."

Layne punched his arm.

A predatory look came over Frances's face, dancing in his eyes as he slowly pushed himself from on top of Layne and approached Michael. "But there's no rule against attacking your brother!" He leapt at Michael.

"Frances!" Colin called, sparing Michael who had turned to run. "Let's pack up so we can leave first thing in the morning. That way we can practice later and ---"

A loud cheer came from the field of honor.

Layne led the way out of the tent, followed by the other three. She stared in the direction of the field. Nervousness churned her stomach. Then relief and a surge of happiness and pride settled her unease as cheers filled the air.

"Wolfe! Wolfe! Wolfe!"

"He won," Frances whispered.

Her lips curled into a smile. "Yes, he did."

"How am I supposed to beat him?" Frances queried, running a hand through his dark hair.

"Stop it," Colin ordered harshly.

"He's amazing," Layne whispered, remembering how expertly he jousted. But it wasn't quiet enough. All of her brothers turned to her in disbelief. "He deserved to win this tournament!" she exclaimed. "You can't deny that."

Colin grit his teeth. He leaned in close to her.

"We better think of something before the next tournament or all of us, Father included, are out on the street. And winter is coming."

Winter. That cold biting monster was a death sentence with no home to shelter them. She looked at Michael. For all of them.

From across the field, she saw Griffin riding Adonis, coming toward his tent. Just the sight of him in full plate mail gave her a breathless anticipation. He was magnificent. Strong, confident and talented. The feel of his hot lips as they claimed hers burst to the forefront of her mind and she blushed. She looked down, hoping her brothers would not notice.

When he drew close to her, he said, "I go to the castle for the celebratory feast. You go help your brothers and Carlton pack."

Disappointment flooded through her. She'd never been to a feast. Her brothers didn't like mixing with the nobility. She stepped toward him. "I'd like to go with you to the feast."

"No," he said, dismounting Adonis. "I will meet you back at the pavilion later." He led Adonis to his tent.

Layne scowled, watching him retreat to the Wolfe tent. She turned and was greeted by the confused and disapproving stares of Colin and Frances.

Frances shook his head in confusion. "What's wrong with you?"

Layne opened her mouth to reply, but Colin cut her off, "Watch yourself, Layne. He might be amazing, but he is well out of your class."

Layne glanced back at the white pavilion, but Griffin was gone.

Layne couldn't help but keep thinking about the feast. Her brothers kept her well sheltered, never allowing her to attend even in the rare few times they had participated in them. But the fact that Griffin had been so abrupt and so commanding in his dismissal of her made her all the more determined that she would attend.

She helped her brothers pack their items as she had done at other tournaments. But as soon as they sent her out of the tent to start packing their horses, she snuck off, heading toward the castle. It was easy enough to sneak away. They wouldn't be expecting her to do it. She knew she shouldn't do it, but she just wanted a glimpse. Just a quick look.

She wasn't foolish. She had taken her dagger, just in case. After the incident with Osmont, she knew she had to be more cautious. She was very careful to remain in the shadows, moving cautiously.

The castle came into view as she cleared the forest, its tall towers stretching high into the sky. The drawbridge was lowered, and the portcullis raised, inviting visitors inside for the feast. She entered without incident and entered the Keep. It wasn't hard to find the Great Hall. Harp music and drums sounded from an open large wooden double door. As she approached, she heard laughter and murmured talking.

The room was packed. Every table was filled. Peasants stood around the walls of the spacious room. She easily joined them, scanning the room for Griffin. Serving girls scurried amidst the tables, placing trays of bread. Often the hand of a seated man would roam over their bottoms, but she could see they were very well versed in ignoring them.

Layne continued to look for Griffin in the

crowded hall. Men shoved food into their mouths, laughing. Someone jostled her from behind and she glanced over her shoulder to see a peasant woman. The woman looked away from her with a mumbled apology. Layne turned back to the scene before her.

Musicians played in the space at the front of the Great Hall near the raised dais. Seated at the center of the dais was the lord of the castle. Lord Frederick, the host of the Norfolk tourney. The seat next to his was empty. That should have been Griffin's spot. As the winner of the tournament, his seat would be in the place of honor next to the host. Where was he? She looked around the room. There was so much activity and so many knights and nobles. She craned her head this way and that, searching the room.

"There he is."

A hand pointed from beside her. She glanced over to see Ethan standing next to her. She followed his direction, her heart beating madly in her chest. Griffin would be in the center of a group of men, speaking about his prowess, relating stories of his skill, basking in the glory of his victory. But what she saw was nothing she was prepared for.

Griffin stood in the center of a group of women. One beautiful blonde gazed at him in adoration and touched his arm in familiarity. At his other side, a brunette laughed and ran her hand along his chest.

Layne's throat closed. It wasn't what she expected. These noble women placing their hands on him, laughing with him. And Griffin in the center of it all, looking warmly at each of them. He belonged there.

And she didn't. She absently touched the material of her breeches, gazing at the velvet of their beautiful dresses. She ran a hand over an errant lock as she looked at their perfectly styled and shining hair.

And he didn't want her here. Because he was embarrassed of her. A lump rose in her throat. Of course he wouldn't want her here.

Ethan chuckled. "He certainly enjoys being the center of all that attention."

She wasn't good enough for him. Her throat closed and her chest felt heavy. She whirled and raced out of the Great Hall, trying to escape. She didn't belong with him, in his life. She didn't fit in. She had never fit in. She was foolish to think there could be anything more. He had warned her not to come. Colin had warned her she was not in his class. What had she expected?

"Layne!"

Layne didn't stop for Ethan's call. She raced out of the Keep, the cool air slapping her face. She battled the disappointment and the failure tightening around her heart, clenching her stomach tight.

Before she reached the drawbridge, Ethan grabbed her arm, halting her. She whirled, yanking it free.

Ethan stared at her, the question in his eyes replaced by understanding and then sympathy.

Layne furiously blinked back the tears burning her eyes. She pushed back the pain in her chest. She lifted her chin and met his gaze.

"You didn't expect to find that."

She shook her head.

"You thought he would be here, waiting for you."

She shook her head more vehemently.

"You thought that because you were under his protection, he cared for you."

It was like a dagger to her chest. She had thought that maybe… maybe he cared for her. Had feelings for her, yes. He had kissed her, after all! Had talked about marriage! She dropped her chin to her chest. How many other women had he kissed?

Ethan took her hands into his. "Griffin has always been the gallant knight who would protect any woman. But that doesn't mean he cares for them. He has too much responsibility to think about. Women have always come second to winning tournaments."

She looked down and ran a sleeve across her nose. "It's not the winning. I think… I came here expecting to see him…" She shrugged. "Glorified. Honored."

"But not by all those women."

She couldn't speak because of the thick lump in her throat. No, not by women. She hadn't even considered…

"You know, when I feel a little down, nothing helps more than swinging a sword."

She shook her head, grateful that her long locks hid her pain. "Griffin said I was not allowed."

Ethan squeezed her hand. "He's not here, is he?"

Slowly, she lifted her gaze to him. No, he wasn't there. He was busy with all those other women. Letting them touch him. The image of the beautiful blonde running her hand over his arm flashed like a burning burst of sunlight in her mind. She couldn't change who she was. "No," she replied softly. "He's not."

Ethan grinned and pulled her out of the castle, leading her over the drawbridge.

CHAPTER EIGHTEEN

Griffin's cheeks hurt from smiling so much. The moon was very high in sky, starting its descent. He had stayed at the feast much too long. There was a lot to do. But those woman wouldn't let him go. Finally, he had to sneak away.

He needed to be on the road by dawn to make it to Woodstock. Woodstock. That was one tournament he was not looking forward to participating in. He wasn't looking forward to seeing Richard. Or Jacquelyn.

Jacquelyn.

He had not thought of her in years. She had been the loveliest women he had ever seen. Glorious blonde hair, always perfect and neatly braided or tucked beneath a veil. Brown eyes that he thought were warm and sincere. He shook his head at that. He had believed her to be everything a proper lady should be. But she had been nothing like she appeared. Not perfect and not warm. She had been kind to him when she believed he was first in line for the castle and lands. But when she discovered Richard was the rightful heir, he discovered her true nature. It had taken her exactly one week to get Richard into bed with her. He remembered she told him she was never in love with him. That he wasn't good enough for her.

So he had set out to prove himself, to prove to her, that he was good enough. And the tournament had become his entire life. He had missed Richard's wedding because of a tournament. He had defied his father's orders to return.

That had been two years ago.

He pushed the thought of his family quickly from his mind and found that it was much easier to do when he thought of Layne. She was nothing like Jacquelyn. Her eyes were so large and so infinitely more pure. He'd never forget how they lit up when he performed a feat of strength, like when he had splintered a piece of the quintain.

He chuckled softly. But it wasn't her eyes that kept him up at night. It was thoughts of her soft lips.

He saw his white tent in the distance and quickened his step. He had an intense desire just to see her. She would probably be sleeping. What would she do if he woke her with a gentle kiss? What would she do if…?

He shook his head. He knew he would do nothing. Carlton was sleeping inside the tent also.

Prickles raced across his neck as he slowed. Her brothers' tent was still up. They should have been long gone on the road to Woodstock.

Griffin's hand instinctively dropped to the handle of his weapon. He approached the tent cautiously, scanning. His nerves were on end. They could all be sleeping. But he knew that was not likely. What could have postponed their departure?

His gaze lingered on the Fletcher tent. Everything seemed in order. All packed and ready for the trip. The horses were tethered to a nearby tree. His gaze swung to his own tent. Adonis whinnied at his approach. Griffin put a hand on the horse's neck to soothe him. Then, he entered the tent. Carlton slept peacefully on his mat.

Dread slithered through Griffin. Layne's mat was empty.

He was about to shake Carlton to rouse him and ask him where Layne was when he heard a soft call in the distance coming from the field of honor. He hesitated and gazed out in the direction of the field as if he could see it from where he stood. Trees and darkness limited his vision. It hadn't been a cry for help. It had been…

He began walking toward the field. Was it Layne? Was she with her brothers? Who could be practicing this late?

Another holler rose. Not a holler for help, but a group cry as if to encourage someone. He made his way through the trees to the field. When he emerged, he saw two people in the field. One he recognized instantly as Layne. Her long hair was pulled back in a braid. She held a sword out before her, toward her opponent.

Two men and a boy lounged against the fence, calling out direction to her. Her brothers.

Griffin stalked across the expanse to the field. As he neared and recognized her combatant, his jaw clenched. Hard.

"Watch his back swing!" Colin advised.

Back swing, Griffin thought. A woman advised to watch out for a back swing!

Layne swung the sword at her opponent who

backed away. She suddenly lunged out with her foot, catching him behind his foot. He went down and she put her sword to his throat.

Her brothers exploded with excitement.

Griffin was not so amused. When he ducked beneath the plank of the fence to enter the field, their excitement died.

When Layne spotted him, she backed a step and immediately dropped the sword.

Ethan climbed to his feet with his usual smirk on his lips. Griffin didn't stop. He delivered a brutal blow to Ethan's jaw that sent him spinning to the ground.

"Griffin!" Layne called and rushed to Ethan's side, kneeling beside him.

At Ethan's side. Griffin's hands curved into balls. His anger was irrational and all consuming. "What do you think you are doing, Farindale?" he demanded.

Ethan sat back on his bottom. He ran a hand across his lip. His fingers came back wet and darkly stained. He shrugged. "Allowing Layne to have a good time. It's more than you do."

Griffin's jaw clamped down tighter and he took a step toward Ethan.

Layne stood in front of him, blocking his path. His gaze swung to his charge. She had disobeyed him. She had been sword fighting with Ethan! And laughing. Laughing with another man, having fun! "You were not to be in the field of honor," he said in a calm voice that completely belied the inner fury churning inside him.

Instead of doing the wise thing and withdrawing to leave the field, Layne stood facing him. There was something in her eyes that he was too angry to recognize or acknowledge. "How was the feast?"

His jaw clenched. "Hear you nothing that I say,

woman? Your place is not to wield swords or cross them with a man."

"What is my place?" she demanded.

"I told you your duties when you first came to my tent. I was very clear on what you were not to do."

Ethan stood. "Griffin –"

Griffin did not take his gaze from Layne. His anger seared through his entire body. "You are not to be here with him."

Ethan's eyebrows rose.

"But you can do whatever you want," Layne countered.

"What is that supposed to mean? Of course I can. I am a man. You are a woman! Act like one."

Layne's mouth dropped slightly. Then closed with a vicious snap. "And how does a woman act? Am I to fawn over you and your great accomplishments like every woman at that feast? Should I touch you and gaze at you with adoration? Should I praise you and run my hands over your strong arms?"

Griffin's scowl was fierce. "You were at the feast? I told you not to go."

"So I couldn't see them! So I couldn't see how you smiled at them and encouraged them and gave them hope."

"It has nothing to do with hope. It is how a knight treats a woman. Kindly. Chivalrously. And if you acted like a woman, you would know that."

Her cheeks flamed red and her lips thinned.

His gaze swept her. "You should wear a dress, not those ridiculous breeches."

"That is quite enough, Wolfe," Colin ordered, stalking across the field. "You can't tell my sister what to wear."

"You should tell her!" Griffin roared. "I shouldn't have to!"

"What happened to being perfect the way I am?" Layne demanded; her fists balled at her side. "You go to one feast and suddenly I'm not good enough."

Ethan stepped up beside Layne, placing a protective hand on her shoulder. "A knight does not insult a woman."

Griffin's anger surged at seeing him touch Layne. What else had they done?

Layne surged forward past Ethan to stand toe to toe with Griffin. "And would it please you if I wore one of those silly snoods on my hair?"

"Yes! And give up doing things a man does! Be the fairer sex for once in your life!"

"Why?" she demanded, her voice thick. "For what end? So I could receive your hope? Your attention?"

A rush of anger and desperation and betrayal crested over Griffin and he grabbed her arms. "How am I to present you to my family when you are dressed like that? When you fight like a man?"

Colin and Ethan were on him immediately, pulling him away from Layne.

Griffin struggled in their hold, trying to wrench his arms free. Frances joined them, pulling him back away from her.

He saw the tears in her large eyes reflected in the moonlight.

He fought to get free. He had hurt her. And he had meant to do it. He was trying to teach her to be a woman and here she stood, fighting Ethan. Ethan, for the love of God! Ethan, the man who could smile and women would drop their clothes. Had Layne been alone with him? His mind raced, clouded by fury. "How am I to explain to my brother, to my father, that you use weapons like a knight? That you wear breeches and tunics like a boy? That you unhorsed me at tournament!" He yanked his arms free. His breathing came heavy. The accusation was out for all to hear. He was not good enough. He was sure that word had reached his brother and his father. They would scorn him, laugh at him. Even if he won every tournament from now until his death, it would never change the fact that he had lost to Layne. Had he been trying to change her so they would never believe it?

For a long moment, Layne just stared at him. "You won't have to. I'm going back with my brothers."

Panic engulfed the anger inside him, drowning it. It clenched his chest tight. Leaving? "No." The word was more a gasp. Then, he straightened and calmed. Rationality took over like a blanket to hide his pain. "Not until they can pay me back." He was in control once again. His anger gone at the thought of losing her.

Layne looked at Colin. Griffin followed her gaze.

Colin shook his head.

"I can loan you the coin," Ethan said.

Layne turned to Ethan.

"Stay out of this," Griffin warned in a low growl. The prospect of having her indebted to Ethan made Griffin furious. And something else. Something he couldn't put his finger on.

"No woman should be treated like this. You speak of chivalry and gallantry toward women and all you've shown Layne is humiliation. I won't stand for it."

Griffin opened his mouth and then closed it. Humiliated? He had never meant... His jaw tightened...

Had she been with Ethan? How could she not? He was handsome and fun. Like Richard. He bowed his head and searched the ground as if for an answer. He had said horrible things to her, things his father had said to him. Things he could not take back. He was not worthy of her. He didn't want her to go. But he could never make her stay. "Make your choice," he said to her and turned away.

CHAPTER NINETEEN

ayne watched him go, miserably alone standing amongst her brothers. She raced after Griffin and demanded, "I would know only one thing before I make my decision."

Griffin stopped but did not turn to her.

"Did you kiss any of those women?"

It seemed like he winced, but she couldn't be certain. Finally, he turned to her. There was such agony in his eyes that she wanted to throw her arms around him and hold him, but she stood stone still.

"Layne," he whispered, sighing her name as if it were a cry of pain. "Those women mean nothing to me. I was expected to be there amongst the nobility. I was expected to be there for the ceremony. I didn't want you to go because I knew... I knew how those noble women acted. I knew they would throw themselves at me. I am a precious commodity, a very eligible knight. They want me to pick a bride. But I want none of them."

Her gaze scanned his face.

He looked at the ground. "No. I did not kiss any

of them."

Relief welled up inside her. She believed him, because she wanted to or because she knew he wouldn't lie, she wasn't sure. She wanted him to tell her he wanted her with him. She wanted him to laugh and smile. But he was so tortured and anguished she knew he would do nothing.

Griffin turned and walked across the field.

She wasn't even sure he knew what he wanted.

"I don't want you with him any longer," Colin ordered from behind her. "I will take Ethan's loan."

Ethan joined them. "I've never seen him act like that before. He's usually so in control."

She said nothing as Griffin vanished back into the dark. She could never be what he needed her to be. She didn't belong with those other ladies. She didn't belong in fine dresses and perfumed hair. She walked toward the tent. He could never present her to his family, because she had unhorsed him. And she couldn't change that.

"Layne!" Colin called from behind her.

But she didn't stop. She needed to think. She needed to clear her head. She needed to decide what to do.

Griffin didn't sleep. He kept waiting for her to walk into the tent. But she never did. He imagined Ethan's hands on her body, his lips kissing her. Like Jacquelyn. Women were not to be trusted. But somehow, this betrayal ran deeper than Jacquelyn's. He had believed Layne was honorable, that she would never do something like that.

When he awoke, the Fletcher tent was gone. He stared at the empty spot for a very long time. An incredible feeling of longing and sadness gripped him.

It was for the best, he told himself. She was becoming a distraction. All that was important was winning the tournament. And he would have enough on his mind with his family at the next tournament at Woodstock.

But somehow, he couldn't quite get his mind over the fact that she was gone.

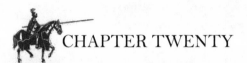

CHAPTER TWENTY

ayne picked up the flasks and extra pieces of bread her brothers had left after breaking their fast, then paused, staring at them. It hadn't been her duty to pick up after them before she was in Griffin's care. With her brothers, everyone cleaned up after themselves. There were no assigned duties; they all helped out with everything. She sat back on her heels. Now, it had just become habit. Yes. Griffin had taught her much. Organization mostly. He was so neat, whereas her brothers were not. But he also taught her heartache. He could do so much better than her. He deserved to marry someone beautiful.

But more than that, she missed him terribly. It was a long moment before she realized she had stopped working and was blankly staring at the bread she held in her hand. She glanced up to find Colin watching her from his seated position across the campfire. She quickly looked away from him.

"You think I was wrong to accept Ethan's loan?" he asked.

Layne shrugged. "It doesn't matter where the loan came from. A debt is a debt." She picked up a bone from the morning meal and placed it into a pot.

"Are you actually cleaning up?"

"We don't want wild animals coming into the camp. I'll just toss these droppings into the forest."

"Did he hurt you?"

Colin's question startled her. "No." She shook her head. "He didn't until… Well, you were there."

"Others have said you were less than lady-like before. It never bothered you."

"That's not what bothered me," she confessed. Her throat closed and she bowed her head to concentrate on her task.

Colin shook his head and leaned forward. "Then what, Layne? The way he spoke to you…"

"He never used that tone before. It was like… like he was embarrassed of me."

"What difference does that make? What should it matter to you what he thinks of you?"

She lifted her gaze to him and he wavered before her eyes. "It does matter."

Alarmed, Colin climbed to his feet. "What is it?"

She looked away again. "I just… admire him. I just think he is a skilled… knight."

Colin was beside her. "Oh, Layne. You didn't… you didn't fall in love with him, did you?"

She let out an exasperated breath and vehemently shook her head. "No," she insisted. "No, not at all." But she knew the words were to convince herself as well as Colin.

"Layne," Colin groaned. He reached down and stroked her hair.

She shrugged him off. "Don't treat me like a little

sister. You know I hate that."

He knelt before her. "But you are my little sister."

She looked up at him and the tears wouldn't be denied. She pressed her face into his shoulder.

His arms went around her.

"He doesn't like me." It was the lamest excuse. And it didn't even touch on the truth, but it was all she could mutter.

Colin stroked her back. "Then he doesn't know what he's missing."

She let him soothe her for a moment, then nodded and wiped at her eyes. She sat back. "We have to concentrate on winning this joust," she said. "We don't have time to think about Griffin."

"You're wrong. He's won the last three tournaments we've been in. He is *all* we should be thinking about."

Layne softly grunted and began to pick up more of the bones on the ground. "If Frances would take his practices more seriously."

Colin narrowed his eyes. "You were around Wolfe for a while. Did you watch any of his practices?"

Layne nodded. "Just one. It wasn't very lady-like to want to watch the practices. Or so he said." She wiped the remainder of her tears away.

"Did you see anything?"

Layne looked up at Colin in confusion.

"Any flaw? Anything we could take advantage of?"

Layne thought back to the practice she watched. She thought of the way Griffin's blonde hair glimmered like gold beneath the moonlight. She thought of the rippling power in his arms, the expert way he handled his horse. "He was amazing," she whispered. "He knows his skill well. And he is strong..." She met Colin's gaze. "He splintered the quintain. It was unbelievable."

Colin nodded. "You told me. But what else? Think Layne. He has to have a weakness. No man is perfect at every aspect of jousting."

Layne shrugged. "If I saw something, so would another opponent. If he has a weakness, he hides it well."

"How did you beat him?"

Layne sighed softly. "At first I thought it was me." She shook her head. "But someone cut his leather stirrup. Someone tried to sabotage him."

Colin put a hand on her shoulder. "You do understand that we have to win this tournament. This is our last chance."

"I know," Layne whispered. "I know."

Tents dotted the Woodstock hillside. The castle rose in the distance, a large wall of stone surrounding it. Griffin had Carlton set up camp as close to the forest as he could. He knew the Fletchers would be there. And he knew Layne was still in danger from the other knights who disapproved of her. Disapproved. He grunted as the word that came to mind. At least they didn't humiliate her. Griffin scanned the hillside but didn't see her tent.

Carlton walked up to him. "The tent is set up. The horses are resting comfortably."

Then it was time to enter the lists. Griffin moved up the hillside, through the competitors' pavilions. There were more colorful tents here than at any other tournament he had attended all year. He skirted knights, nodding his head in greeting, as he made his way toward Woodstock Castle. Laughter and the clang of metal against metal rang out. "Have you seen my brother yet?"

Carlton shook his head. "He's probably in the palace."

Griffin narrowed his eyes and looked toward the field of honor. More likely prancing around on the field, displaying his prowess.

"She is near the forest."

Griffin swung his gaze to Carlton.

"Layne. She and her brothers have set up camp near the forest, around the bend from our tent."

Griffin stared at Carlton for a long moment. How had he known what he was thinking? Carlton had squired for him for years. The boy knew him well. Perhaps too well. Griffin nodded.

Carlton's face softened. Was that sympathy in the boy's eyes?

Griffin faced the wind, feeling the breeze pushing his locks from his face, and pretended that relief didn't surge in his body. She wasn't with Ethan. She was with her family. He took a deep breath and continued toward the castle.

"Your father is at the castle."

Griffin stopped so abruptly that Carlton slammed into his back. He whirled on his squire. "My father is here?"

Carlton nodded. "And your sister."

"God's blood!" Griffin muttered and looked at the looming castle. It was a trap! He had guessed they would be here, but to hear it was actually so... Every instinct inside of him demanded he run. His entire family, here. Looking for him, no doubt. He had made no attempt to avoid them or to hide from them. They knew where he was and what he was doing. But this... This felt different. It felt like they were descending on him like lions on a hunt. He knew it would only be time before they cornered him. But that didn't make facing them any less daunting. He had only this joust to win to prove to his father, nay all of them, that he didn't need them and had no intention of returning.

He faltered for a moment, hesitancy in his step. Perhaps he could wait until later to enter the lists. He groaned inwardly. It would do no good to wait. He would have to face them eventually. He continued toward the castle.

The crowd was daunting. Knights who didn't usually travel the circuit of tourneys were here, either to impress Prince Edward or to win the purse. It made no difference to Griffin. They may be knights, but that didn't mean they knew how to joust.

Griffin made his way into the Great Hall. Tables were set up with banners behind each one. All the knights who had already entered the lists had posted their banners. He scanned the crowd. A group of knights lounged near the hearth, laughing. Other knights sat at dozens of tables, drinking and listening to the troubadour near the dais. More newly arrived knights were still hanging their banners.

It took a moment before Griffin spotted Layne's brothers, Frances and Michael. A moment of anxiety seized him, and he continued to scan the Great Hall, hoping she was not here, hoping her brothers made her stay back at the tent. For her own safety. This was not a place for her. He glanced back at the door. Maybe he should check. Maybe he should make sure she was safe.

What was he thinking? He would enter the lists and practice. She was not his concern. He should be concentrating on who might have sabotaged him and focus on stopping those who might try it again.

After entering the lists, and welcoming all challengers, Griffin left Carlton to attend the remaining formalities and turned to leave the crowded room. He paused when he saw a tall man with blonde hair pushed back from his face enter the room. It was his brother Richard. Richard walked beside a shorter man with dark hair. The way everyone bowed and scrambled around the shorter man, Griffin knew it must be Prince Edward.

Richard greeted the room with a stunning smile, one that had always made friends quickly. He swept in confidently, perhaps a bit arrogantly, but the knights rushed to greet him, surrounding him and the prince in a cocoon of praise.

Griffin grimaced in disapproval and turned away. There was a side entrance he could use to quickly escape before Richard spotted him. As he ducked into the hallway, he almost ran over a woman. With a mumbled apology on his lips, he suddenly recognized her familiar face. The only woman who had ever broken his heart. The woman who had sent him on this journey of escape. Jacquelyn. She was still lovely, after all these years. But he now noticed the coldness in her gaze, the assessing sweep of her eyes, eyes that glimmered like blue ice crystals. Her blonde hair was immaculately styled up, surrounded by a golden veil.

"Griffin!" she greeted and moved forward as if

to embrace him.

He quickly took her hand and pressed his knuckles to it. He had no desire for her to hold him. But he had every desire to remain in control of the situation. "Lady Jacquelyn." He stood tall, releasing her hand. "The years have been kind to you." God's blood! He should have known she would be at Richard's side.

Her lower lip protruded in a practiced pout. One he knew all too well. "We were friends once. Is that how you greet a friend?"

"We were never friends. And after you married my brother –"

"I had hoped you were over me."

He leaned in closer. "Very. Over. You." She had hurt him. Badly. But that seemed like another lifetime. He had no desire for her to turn her venomous attention on him again. He would make it clear he had no interest. "I assume you and Richard are happy."

Jacquelyn cast a glance over his shoulder at the crowd surrounding Richard. She nodded with something close to longing in her eyes. "At times."

Griffin didn't know how to respond to that. He should have known her greed would make her unhappy. One man would never be enough. Now, staring down at her true nature, he was glad she had let him go. "Gwen is here?"

Jacquelyn nodded. "When they heard you were going to be here, they all agreed we had to come. You know, that was why Richard joined Prince Edward in hosting the tourney. He wanted to see you."

Griffin had guessed as much. His gaze scanned the Great Hall as if expecting to find his sister there.

Jacquelyn laid her hand on his arm. "I understand you don't want to come back. Don't fear. I'll keep you informed of their plans. We can be allies." She smiled conspiratorially at him.

Griffin eased his arm from her grip. That was the very last thing he wanted. She was not to be trusted. He didn't think he could believe a word that came from her lips. "I'm perfectly capable of dealing with my family." He turned from her and began to walk down the hallway to the door leading to the inner ward.

"Then why do you keep running away?"

He grit his teeth. Is that what Richard had told her? Or did she draw that conclusion herself? He didn't run. Not any longer.

"Griffin!" He winced at his brother's voice and slowly turned to find Richard moving into the hallway toward him.

Griffin straightened. He couldn't remember the last time he had seen his brother. But the man had not changed. He was exactly the same. Arrogant, confident. He, no doubt, expected to win the joust. Not this time, Griffin thought.

Griffin extended his hand and Richard greeted him with the customary clasping of arms.

"Trying to steal my wife?" Richard asked, holding Griffin's hand tightly.

Old wounds didn't heal. It had been Richard who had slept with Jacquelyn. "She's all yours," Griffin said, dropping his hand.

Richard threw his head back and laughed. "Still the same old Griffin."

Griffin only nodded. When Griffin had last left, they were barely on speaking terms. Richard, embarrassed into silence by his betrayal of his brother with Jacquelyn, Griffin just stewing in wordless anger. Their gazes shifted to Jacquelyn. All because of a woman. Now, she was well in Griffin's past. But the betrayal still hung between them like a curtain of shame. Griffin looked at his brother. "Good to see you, Richard."

Richard grinned his thanks and placed an arm about Griffin's shoulders, guiding him into the Great Hall.

Jacquelyn trailed them.

"No wife yet?" Richard wondered.

"What wife would want to be hauled around from joust to joust?" Griffin wondered. Only one woman came to mind.

Richard laughed, casting a gaze over his shoulder at Jacquelyn. "None that I know of."

"Is that why you haven't participated?"

Richard leaned in close to whisper, "Not that I don't envy you. But, alas, I have a castle and lands to run. There is the constant threat of invasion. And Father... Well, Father is Father. You can never please him."

"You always pleased him."

Richard shrugged slightly. His face darkened. "Not always."

Griffin looked at his brother, wondering what he meant. For as long as he could remember, Richard had been his father's favorite. He always gave Richard whatever he wanted. There were no consequences for Richard. He did what he wanted. And now, with the responsibility of the lands and castle on his shoulders, Griffin was surprised he had straightened up and done what was required of him. He supposed Father was pulling strings in the background. Perhaps that was what his brother was talking about. "Will you joust in the tournament?"

Richard smiled. "An opportunity like this? I wouldn't miss it. Besides, that was part of the reason I wanted to host the tournament." He leaned closer to Griffin, glancing quickly over his shoulder at Jacquelyn. "They can't stop me then."

Griffin looked back at Jacquelyn who wore a scowl of displeasure on her brow. "You've offered a large purse. These men are good. And you are out of practice."

Richard reared back in surprise. "You could never beat me!"

"That was a long time ago."

"So I've heard," Richard agreed. "Champion of every tourney you've entered this year. Impressive."

And it was. Griffin had developed his skill over years of discipline and practice. He studied his opponents, watched and practiced. Practiced until his muscles burned with fatigue. Richard was used to a different life. His muscles were soft from leisure, his skills nowhere near as strong.

"I wonder if you could beat me now."

Griffin's eyes narrowed slightly. "I hope we will have an opportunity to find out."

Richard cocked a grin and slapped him on the back. "Come. Meet my friend, Prince Edward."

"Griffin!"

Griffin turned. A young woman moved across the room toward him, skirting nobles in finery and slipping past other knights in her way. Her brown eyes were bright with eagerness, even as she managed to look down her nose at him. She stopped just before him, a grin tugging the corners of her lips. Her gaze swept him and then she offered her hand to him.

Griffin bowed slightly and took her hand,

pressing a genuine kiss to her knuckles. When he straightened, he smiled. "It's good to see you again, Gwen."

"And you," she agreed. "I suppose you have dragged poor Carlton all through the lands in your attempt at fame."

"Carlton is my squire. Dragging is not really what I have done."

Gwen waved her hand dismissingly, lifting her chin. "Never mind. The least you could have done was send word of your victories. Instead, we had to find out from Sir Ethan."

"Ethan?" Griffin scowled and glanced at Richard.

Richard nodded. "Farindale stopped by the castle months ago. He was on his way to Norfolk."

Gwen nodded. "He told us all about your victories in the tourneys. For shame on not sending word."

Griffin briefly wondered why Ethan had stopped at his home. True, they were good friends once, but had not been close in years. "I would have sent word after I win this tournament."

Richard eyes gleamed with excitement. "A boast!"

"A promise."

"Father is quite irritated with you," Gwen continued. "You know how angry he was when you left."

Griffin nodded. He remembered how red his father's face was, he remembered how he called his name again and again. That was another reason he had not sent word. He didn't want his father to know which tourneys he was entering. The last thing he needed was

Father intercepting him at a tournament, demanding he return home.

"Just as he seemed to be missing you –"

"Missing me?" Griffin echoed, the thought ludicrous.

"Sir Ethan showed up and regaled us with news of your incredible wins. Really, Griffin. Didn't it cross your mind that your family might want to see you compete in the tourneys?"

"Knowing how much you love jousting, dear sister, it never crossed my mind."

Gwen lifted her chin. "I would have set aside my contempt for it to support you."

Griffin's eyebrows lifted in surprise. That was something he thought never to hear from her lips. "That's gracious, sister."

Gwen nodded. "You have no idea."

A noble dressed in a purple velvet jupon with embroidered gold on his sleeves, greeted Richard, pulling him away from the group. Jacquelyn took his place at Griffin's other side.

Griffin looked back at Gwen as she leaned closer to him. "You'd better face Father before he confronts you in front of everyone. He's in the solar and was alone when I left him."

Before Griffin could ask about her statement, she had turned and took Jacquelyn's arm, leading her away. Perhaps that was his clue to escape. "Gwen!" he called.

She paused and looked at Griffin, tilting her head to the side.

"Your dress is lovely," he said sincerely. He knew he would never hear the end of it if he didn't comment on her dress.

She beamed him a radiant smile, curtseyed

slightly so she could spread out the beautiful silken material, and continued into the Great Hall with Jacquelyn.

Griffin hurried out of the room and paused.

Father. He stared at the spiral staircase at the end of the stone corridor. Laughter erupted from behind him. A young man brushed past him into the Great Hall, carrying a pitcher of ale. Trepidation filled him. The last time he had faced his father, he had left immediately afterwards. They had spoken harsh words to each other. While Richard and his betrayal had hurt, it had not been the reason he had left. His father had been the real reason. Not even Jacquelyn marrying Richard could have caused him to flee like he had. He couldn't avoid his father forever. Perhaps he had changed his mind. Perhaps his words would not be so angry.

Griffin straightened his back and headed for the stairs.

Perhaps they would be. But he was a different man now. And he was not running any longer.

CHAPTER TWENTY-ONE

Griffin stood before the wooden door for a long moment. Finally, he lifted his hand and knocked.

It was only a moment before the door opened. A small boy stood there, gazing at him with a thin-lipped glare. "M'lord is resting."

"He'll see me," Griffin told the young lad.

The boy peered up at him through narrowed eyes. "An' ya are…?"

"Griffin."

The boy's mouth fell in a silent gasp and he threw open the door, allowing Griffin entrance.

Griffin entered the dark room. Rich curtains covered the large windows; a low fire in the hearth kept the room warm. Masterfully woven tapestries adorned the walls. A thick rug of fur covered nearly the entire floor. The king, Prince Edward's father, was a friend of his father's. He was sure that was why he had been given use of such an opulent room.

Griffin swung his head toward a cough that came from the bed.

His father was seated in the large, elaborate bed, staring at the closed window. "Open that window, boy. Let some fresh air in! I can barely breathe."

The young boy scampered across the room and pulled at the curtains on the window.

Light splashed across the room, washing across the floor and then the bed and finally his father.

Griffin remained stoic. He tried not to show emotion. His father was not the man he remembered. He looked frail and old, his face gaunt and pale. He locked eyes with Griffin. "Ah. My boy."

"Hello, Father," Griffin greeted.

"Come closer, boy. Sit with me."

Griffin moved up to the bed and sat on the side. The scent of decay and death permeated the air near his father.

A cheer rose from outside and his father swung his gaze to the window. "Prince Edward allowed me to have this room because it is close to the field of honor. I'll be able to watch..." He looked back at Griffin, his gaze sweeping his face. "You've done well for yourself."

Griffin nodded. "Yes, Father."

His father leaned closer. "It doesn't change anything."

His father's words sent a tremor through Griffin. His teeth grit instinctively. "I'm sorry, Father, but it does."

"You are still under my rule, son. You will do as I say."

"I don't want to fight with you. I never did."

"Then do what I say. It's in the best interest –"

Griffin felt the old rage rise in his heart. "For who? You?"

"For everyone! Richard is a dolt! He is going

through the treasury faster than his mother!"

"Don't talk about my mother like that," Griffin said quietly. He wasn't certain his father heard him.

"What will become of Gwen?" His father began coughing and his words trailed off.

Gwen. Griffin would see to it that Gwen was taken care of.

His father grabbed his arm. His grip was weak. "Griffin. Richard does not have the sense you have."

"You made your choice, Father."

"I was wrong. I want you to be my heir. I want the lands to fall to you."

"No!" Griffin stood, breaking free of the tentacle that was his father's hand. "Richard is eldest. It is his birth right. He is heir."

His father inhaled a shaky breath and nodded. "I see how it is. Now that you're independent of us, you think you don't need your family."

Griffin straightened under the accusation. "Gwen will be taken care of. I will see to it. Richard and Jacquelyn will have to live off the wealth of the land."

"Wealth of the land?" His father began coughing again. He doubled over. The young boy rushed to aid his father, but his father pushed the boy away. "That slut makes Richard buy her perfumes from France!" His father sat back in the bed with a sigh. "You are lucky to have escaped her."

"Father, Richard is a capable leader."

"Richard gives her whatever she wants!"

"With all due respect, it is not your say anymore. You handed control of the lands to Richard. I will not argue his legitimacy."

"Traitor!" his father spat. "Coward."

The same words that had drove him away

190

before. He stood. "I came to see you again, Father. I don't want to argue."

"Then do as I say!"

Griffin turned and walked to the door. The door was open a crack and he thought he saw someone shift from the entrance.

A candlestick landed with a thud on the floor beside the door.

Griffin looked back at his father who was reaching for the next object to throw at him from a nearby table, screaming, "Coward!" His hand closed around a book.

Griffin quickly ducked out to see Jacquelyn hurrying down the corridor.

"Do you see them?" Colin asked, his gaze searching the crowded field. Spectators hung over the fence. Villagers brought blankets to sit upon to watch the joust from the surrounding fields.

Layne tried to ignore the stares and pointed fingers. She looked around the crowded field, looking for Frances and Michael. Instead, her eyes caught someone else. Across the field, she spotted Griffin. He was a good head taller than the others around him. She barely noticed them, her gaze settling firmly on him. He was directly across from her, walking along the other side of the fence. His step was confident and sure, his gait full of reined power and fluidity that set a longing to flame inside her chest. When he looked up from the person he had been speaking with in her direction, she tore her gaze from him. "I don't see them."

Colin scowled. "They're here somewhere." He

pushed himself from the fence and moved on. "Come on."

Layne walked beside him, casting a sideways glance toward Griffin. He walked with several other people, a woman on either side of him, a man before him. The four of them were striking in their elegant clothing and highborn walk. They had the air of nobility without making an effort. Her heart sank and she looked at the ground, consciously straightening her shoulders.

Again, she cast a sideways gaze at him, as if craving the sight of him. He was looking in her direction and she quickly looked away. She knew he would never forgive her for leaving him and taking Ethan's loan. How could she ever be good enough for him? Just look at the women he was with!

Again, she slid her gaze toward him. She couldn't help looking at him. He was marvelous to behold. He bent his head slightly to talk to one of the women. His complete concentration was on her. And she was beautiful. Layne's heart fell. Her long blonde hair was expertly folded beneath the golden veil she wore over her head; both her hair and the veil shimmered softly in the sun, as if calling everyone's attention to her. Her nose was delicate and her features fair. Her gown was elaborate and beautiful and worth more than Layne could dream about.

Layne's gaze dropped to the ground. They were from two worlds that didn't belong together. Dust puffed up around her scuffed boots with each step. She couldn't compete with someone like that. Now she understood what he had meant when he said he couldn't present her to his family. Sadness settled around her heart like the dust around her boots.

Griffin spotted Layne immediately. She walked along the opposite side of the field of honor from him and his family. He had come to see the jousts. And apparently, so had Layne and her brother.

"It's a beautiful day, is it not Griffin?"

He looked down at Jacquelyn. She smiled at him, her blue eyes dazzling. But he recalled other eyes that were more dazzling, more sincere and warm. "Yes," he replied. His gaze shifted to Layne again. She was looking down at her feet. Something twisted in his chest. He had humiliated her. He had hurt her. He should apologize to her. But knowing she had made her decision of accepting Farindale's loan only made him realize she didn't want to be with him. She didn't need his apology, nor would she even want it.

He sighed and turned back to see Richard moving toward the berfrois, the sheltered dais that had been built for the tournament. Richard would be seated there, of course. He was host of the tournament. Gwen and Jacquelyn would be seated there, also. Prince Edward and all of his court would be there, also.

Griffin looked over his shoulder at Layne. She and Colin were taking seats on the lawn surrounding the field of honor with her other brothers. That was where he belonged. That was where he wanted to be.

Gwen stopped beside him and followed his stare. "Who is she?" she wondered.

Griffin didn't take his gaze from Layne. For a moment, he hesitated. What could he tell her? That Layne unhorsed him? Never. That she was under his protection for a fleeting moment? No. "Someone I thought I knew," he finally replied and turned away. "But I was wrong."

Richard leapt up the two stairs to the raised dais platform and greeted Prince Edward with a humble bow.

Prince Edward smiled. "Beautiful day for a tournament!"

Richard agreed with a nod. "May I present Sir Griffin Wolfe, my brother."

Griffin bowed. "Your Royal Highness."

"Ah!" Prince Edward called. "Finally. I was fearful I would never get to meet you. Reigning champion and all."

"Thank you, Sire."

"We shall talk later," Edward said. "I have a tournament to open."

Griffin bowed again and moved to stand beside Gwen who had taken one of the seats near Richard.

Edward held up his hands and the crowd quieted. "Lords and Ladies, villagers and merchants, knights and gentry! Welcome all to the Woodstock tourney. Here, feats of strength and bravery will abound. Knights shall joust to prove their skill. And the victor shall receive a purse unmatched in this year's tournaments. Let the jousting commence!"

CHAPTER TWENTY-TWO

Layne's gaze continued to return to Griffin where he stood at the side of the wooden shelter, watching the knights joust. She was getting nothing out of the preliminary jousts. No matter how hard she tried to focus on the competitors, her gaze continually returned to Griffin on the dais. The winds lifted the ends of his hair gently as if desiring a touch. He leaned in to speak to the beautiful blonde as if she were the center of his world. Her stomach rolled. Her heart twisted. She stood, feigning illness, and walked back toward the tent. She hadn't realized how much she liked to be with him, how much she admired him, how much she should have cherished her time with him.

When she emerged from the long stalks of grass into the clearing, she spotted Griffin's white tent near the edge of the forest, just around the bend from their tent. She faltered and then stopped. She glanced over her shoulder. Griffin was at the joust. Maybe Carlton was there.

She headed toward the tent. It had been her

home for a while. And Carlton had been like a brother. She grunted softly. Like she needed another brother!

She walked up to the tent, noticing that Adonis was not there. "Carlton?" she called. She lifted the flap of the tent to check inside, but Carlton wasn't there. She ducked back outside and paused for a moment. She was about to continue to her tent when she spotted Griffin's weapons. His jousting pole and sword were set out at the side of the tent. Wasn't he worried? Wasn't he concerned about the saboteur? The weapons were all out in the open. Almost like...

Tingles shot up her spine and she looked around. There was no one there. No one she could see watching. But that didn't mean someone wasn't there.

She looked back at the weapons, glancing down at his lance. It was if they were set out like a trap.

"What are you doing here?"

She whirled, her hand instinctively reaching for the dagger she now wore tucked into the back of her breeches. It was out in a flash, pointed at –

"Griffin," she sighed. Somehow his appearance, his rugged handsomeness, always caught her off guard and left her breathless. Those sparkling blue eyes left her defenseless. She straightened, lowering the dagger. "What are you doing here?"

"This is my tent," he answered. "I ask you again, what are you doing here?"

The cold hard tone in his voice sent any happiness at seeing him fleeing. She tucked the dagger in her breeches behind her back. "I was looking for Carlton."

"You could have seen Carlton was not near my weapons. What do you want with those?"

She scowled. She didn't like his implication. "If

you must know, I was thinking about your sabotaged lance. I thought it strange that no one was watching your weapons."

"You think the saboteur will try again?"

She looked at him in disbelief. "Of course. Don't you?"

"It doesn't matter what I think." His gaze swept her. "Only what the saboteur thinks."

Layne shook her head, disgusted. "You think I sabotaged you?"

"You want your brother to win."

She nodded. "Yes. Yes, I do. But not like that. Honor is as important as winning."

"I find it amusing you should say so after disguising yourself as a man to joust."

Her disbelief fled in the face of his coldness. She straightened, lifting her chin. "I did not sabotage you. I wouldn't do that to you. I thought you would have learned that by now." She spun around to come face to face with a woman. The woman's blue eyes assessed her with a brief glance from head to toe and then dismissed her.

Layne cast an accusing glare at Griffin before leaving. She had no doubt that the woman was one of the nobles he did not kiss.

Griffin watched her go, regret twisting his heart. He knew she didn't sabotage him. And yet, she had the opportunity at every turn. Had she deceived him so? Even as he thought this, his instinct was to cry out to her not to leave him again. But she wasn't his to stop. He shifted his gaze to lock eyes with Jacquelyn. He quickly tried to hide the hurt and betrayal by turning away from her to look down at his weapons. It didn't appear she had touched any of them. "Why did you follow me, Jacquelyn?"

"I don't have much time to be alone with you." She glanced after Layne and then looked back at Griffin. "I just wanted to... see how you fared. You've been away for a long time."

"You could have asked me these questions in the castle. Why out here? You hate dirt and mud. You wouldn't be caught dead trudging through the combatants' tents." He bent down to inspect his weapons more closely.

"Yes, well, any decent woman would avoid these gong pits." She lifted her foot to inspect the bottom of her slipper.

"Then why come?" He looked at her.

She smiled gently, thrusting out her ample bosom to him, stroking the fabric at her belly. "I'd rather be in the castle. In a warm bed." She looked at him through lidded eyes. "Wouldn't you?"

Griffin stood, appalled. This couldn't be what he thought. Surely, she could not be attempting to seduce him. "Never."

"You like the dirt and mud better? Do you actually sleep here?" She bent over and peered inside the tent, giving him a view of her rounded breasts.

He ground his teeth. This made no sense! Richard was lord of the castle. Why come after him? And then he remembered. He had seen her running from the solar. She must have overheard his conversation with his father. Now, thinking he was the favored son, she was turning her attentions back to him. It was so comically, pathetically obvious.

"I'd like to see where you sleep," she continued.

"You are married to my brother, Jacquelyn. And I would never betray him like that."

She walked up to him, wrapping her arms about his neck. "I can change your mind."

He quickly disengaged her hands and pushed her back a step. "It's time you head back."

She scowled, and in another lifetime ago he would have thought her pout irresistible. But not any longer. "Won't you even escort me?"

"Of course." He bowed stiffly and began to lead the way, careful not to touch her or to let her touch him.

She 'humphed' and hurried past him, walking with her chin held high.

He had a moment of victory. Until he spotted Layne through two trees, near her tent, watching them.

CHAPTER TWENTY-THREE

Griffin stared down the field of honor at his opponent. Daunger sat as still as a stone, staring at him. He had not been in any other tournament, so this was the first time Griffin or any of the other knights were seeing him joust. He was well known for his participation in the melees, known for being rash and reckless and unpredictable. Despite his inexperience in the joust, Griffin suspected he was going to be a dangerous opponent.

Griffin lowered his visor. He had to stay focused, watch for an opening. But as soon as the visor closed and the cheers of the crowd muted, the image of a woman with glorious blue eyes filled his mind. Why had she been near his weapons? Was she really worrying about him?

He grit his teeth. He couldn't think of her now. Firmly, he pushed Layne's image from his mind. But it wasn't as easy as he would have liked it to be. Her vision haunted his days as much as his nights. Everywhere he went, he looked for her, listened for her laughter. He missed her.

Adonis pranced nervously beneath him.

Griffin tugged on the reins, urging Adonis into a circle to calm him.

Carlton lifted his lance to him.

Griffin took it and spurred Adonis. Through the slit in his visor, he saw Daunger charging toward him down the field. He couched the lance, holding it firmly.

Adonis suddenly slowed and threw his head, balking.

Daunger's lance struck Griffin hard in the shoulder. His body half turned in the saddle, and if he was any less experienced Griffin would have been unhorsed. His arm was numb and throbbing as he rode to the other end of the field. He tossed down his lance and turned Adonis toward his side of the field. He passed Daunger who had flipped up his visor and was grinning ear to ear.

Griffin did not look at the grandstand where he knew his family watched. He already felt the incredible weight of their presence.

His arm pulsated from the blow, but he pushed the pain aside. He pushed all other thoughts aside. Dispatch Daunger. That was all that was important. Winning this joust.

Griffin grabbed the lance from Carlton and whirled Adonis, spurring him on. No hesitancy. Just letting the horse and the lance become one with him. The roar of the crowd thrummed in his ears, a distance boom of thunder. His heart hammered in his chest.

Daunger came closer. Closer. His lance aimed at Griffin's chest.

Griffin leaned in slightly. He would not be denied. Not this time. He was rewarded by striking Daunger near his stomach, Daunger's lance struck his arm, succeeding in aiding the thrust forward. Griffin's body twisted slightly, enough force behind the strike to throw Daunger up and out of his saddle.

Griffin's lance pushed him back as Daunger's steed continued on. Daunger fell back into the dirt and dust as Griffin rode past him.

Griffin rounded the opposite end. When he saw Daunger lying on the ground, he straightened. The roar of the crowd was thunderous, drowning out all else. He lifted his visor and waited until Daunger staggered to his feet.

As he rode forward, his body in rhythm with Adonis, he realized something was wrong with his arm. If he lifted it even a little bit, shooting pain erupted through his limb. He held it against his stomach and left the field of honor.

Something was wrong. As Layne watched Griffin ride out of the field of honor, she saw the way he held his arm close to his stomach.

"Damn," Colin muttered, shaking his head.

Layne couldn't tear her gaze from Griffin's disappearing back. The next thing she knew, she was moving through the crowd.

"Layne!" Frances called.

She didn't stop. She squeezed between two farmers, skirted a child racing by. Griffin was hurt. When she cleared the spectators, her walk turned into a run. Tingles of trepidation shivered along her spine. She ran through long stalks of grass. When she finally burst through to the clearing, she saw Adonis outside the white tent. She didn't stop; she brushed the tent flap aside and stepped in.

Griffin whirled. He had already removed his helmet and neck armor and was working on the buckles for his backplate. His blonde hair was damp and hung about his head in wet curls. "What do you want?" His voice was cold.

"You're hurt." She stepped inside the tent and the flap closed behind her.

"It is nothing."

She ignored him. "Sit here." She indicated his mat.

"So it is easier for you to stab me in the back?"

She winced but kept her voice light. "If I wanted to do that, I wouldn't need you to sit." She lifted his arm to unbuckle the straps holding the plates together.

He grimaced and let out a growl of pain. "I don't need your help."

"Of course not. But I would like to help you."

"Carlton will help me when he finishes gathering the lances and returns to the tent."

She ignored his comment and looked into his eyes. "It's your arm."

He clenched his lips and looked away but sat on the mat.

Layne quickly removed his breastplate and backplate, carefully setting them aside. Then, she moved to the hurt arm. He had already removed his gauntlets. She removed the vambrace and then the rerebrace.

She sat back for a moment, staring at him. The way he held his arm, immobile and against his side, was not a good sign. "Where does it hurt?" She leaned in to untie the doublet.

"My entire arm."

She nodded. "You were hit twice in your shoulder." She opened the doublet revealing his firm chest.

He hissed in pain.

She tucked her hand beneath his hairline and ran it gently across his upper back to his shoulder. His body tensed as soon as she touched it. There was a large bump in the back of his shoulder. Even with that little contact, she felt how deformed the joint was and how swollen. She knew what it was. Her father had been prone to these injuries when she was young. She had seen Colin fix it many times. Frances had the same type of injury once. "Can you get your arm out of your doublet?"

"Of course." The answer sounded more like determination than an ability to do the simple task. He took a deep breath and lifted his arm.

Layne pulled the doublet down his arm and off quickly.

He ground his teeth and muffled a heady cry.

She looked at him. "Are you all right?"

This time, he could only nod and didn't look her in the eye.

Layne leaned forward, inspecting his shoulder. She gently ran her fingertips over his arm, up his muscled bicep to his shoulder. The all too familiar lump was there. She felt a twinge of pain and of remorse. She knew what she had to do. "Lie down."

He did as she asked without any protestations. He closed his eyes.

"Can you relax?"

He shook his head.

She stroked his head, brushing his damp hair from his forehead. "Try."

He opened his eyes to look at her. For a moment,

their gazes locked and held. She had missed him and his arrogance. But mostly she had missed his calm reassurance and his insatiable confidence. His heated glances and gentle touches. His…

Layne tore her gaze from his. She needed to fix his shoulder, another thing she was sure he would not approve of, before the idiot physicians rushed in to leech him to death. She sat beside him, facing him. She placed her feet between his arm and his torso. "This is going to hurt."

Griffin's mouth dropped. Then he snapped it closed. "Do you know what you are doing?"

"I find that insulting. Do you really think I would risk your wellbeing?"

"You do want your brother to win."

Layne carefully moved his arm, so it was stretched out away from his body, toward her.

He gritted his teeth as she moved it.

Then she paused, giving him a moment to relax. Her hands wrapped around his wrist.

He opened his eyes to look at her. "That wasn't too bad."

"No," she agreed and suddenly yanked his arm toward her as hard as she could, bracing herself against him with her feet.

He threw his head back and a cry of agony ripped from his lips.

Layne heard the popping noise. She released him just as the tent flap was thrown open and Carlton entered, followed by two physicians.

Layne stood quickly.

The physicians went to Griffin's side immediately, eyeing her with distrust.

Carlton glanced at her unsurely and then at

Griffin.

Layne watched the physicians poke and prod him like a piece of cattle. He fended off their explorations with both hands and Layne grinned. He would be fine. She backed toward the exit.

"Out!" Griffin finally hollered.

Layne made her escape, the physicians quickly following. As she moved away from the tent, she saw a tall blonde man heading toward the tent. She thought he was the lord sponsoring the tournament, but she couldn't be sure. He was accompanied by a stunning woman with golden hair. She noticed the woman was looking at her, watching her. They locked gazes for a moment before the woman followed the lord into Griffin's tent.

Griffin shot to his feet. He jerked forward to go after Layne.

Richard swept the flap aside and entered. "Well done, brother!"

Griffin grimaced, trying to see past him to Layne. Instead, he met his sister's gaze. He was trapped. He moved back into the pavilion, allowing them reluctant entrance.

"Yes, I was amazed at..." Gwen's voice trailed off and a frown of worry marred her brow. "Have you been hurt?"

Griffin realized he was still cradling his arm. His shoulder burned and throbbed. Carefully, he clenched his fist. There was only minimal pain, nothing like the brutal agony he had been feeling moments before.

"Griffin?" Richard asked in the same demanding

tone that his father used.

Griffin ignored him and carefully lifted his arm. There was still some pain, but definitely not like before. He could use his arm again. He glanced at the flap. Whatever Layne had done had worked! He felt a twist of guilt clenching his stomach. At every turn, she was trying to help him. It just didn't make any sense. Why would she help him? Where was her loyalty to Ethan? What about her brothers? If she hoped they would win, then why not leave him wounded and hurt?

"Obviously, the only thing that was hurt was your senses," Richard said. "I joust later this afternoon with –"

Richard went on, but Griffin wasn't listening. He swung his gaze back to look at the tent flap and caught Gwen's stare. There was a strange smile on her lips as she stared at him.

Gwen ducked outside, leaving her brothers to speak of their upcoming jousts. She found Carlton at the side of the tent brushing Adonis. He was a charming young man who would make a fine knight when the time came. She patted his shoulder. "I'm so impressed with Griffin," Gwen said.

Carlton nodded. "Sir Griffin is doing marvelously in the tournaments. He is the most skilled and talented of all the knights. He takes the tourneys very seriously. He practices all the time."

Gwen smiled. "He's always been like that. Maybe too seriously. Every knight needs to have time off."

Carlton shook his head. "With all due respect,

m'lady, Sir Griffin would not win if he didn't practice relentlessly. He will practice for today for his jousts on the morrow."

Gwen nodded as Carlton ran a brush across Adonis's coat. "Yes. There are many here who will be a test to his skill."

"Sir Griffin thinks his biggest challenge will be Sir Osmont."

"Sir Osmont? I believe I've heard the name."

Carlton brushed down Adonis's neck. "They have a past."

"Past?"

"Well..." Carlton stopped combing the horse. He looked over his shoulder at her. "Sir Griffin has often told me that gossip is not a knightly way."

"But Griffin is my brother!" Gwen protested. "I have every right to know."

Carlton looked down with his brow furrowed. "And I would hate to upset you." With a sigh he looked up. "Sir Griffin humiliated Sir Osmont the last time they jousted. He unhorsed him in one pass and made him yield."

Gwen's eyebrows rose in shock. "They crossed swords?"

"Oh, yes," Carlton whispered, barely able to contain his excitement. "Sir Osmont deserved everything he got, if you ask me. He hurt Layne while she was under Sir Griffin's protection and cut off two fingers of her brother's hand."

"Layne? Who is Layne?"

"Only the most brilliant woman I have ever met." His eyes widened in shock and his mouth dropped. He bowed slightly. "Next to you, of course, m'lady."

Gwen's smile was genuine. She did like Carlton. "Who is she?"

"Sir Griffin intervened on her behalf, saving her from the dungeon by loaning her brother's coin to pay off her fine." Adonis threw his head and whinnied. Carlton turned back to the animal to continue brushing him.

That sounded like Griffin. Off to rescue another maiden. "Locked in the dungeon. That is severe. Is she still under Griffin's protection?"

Carlton shrugged, running the brush over Adonis's back. "Nay. She is with her brothers now. Their tent is over there. It's the Fletcher tent."

Gwen gazed in the direction of the Fletcher tent. Layne Fletcher. This was a woman she had to meet. "What did she do to be so punished?"

Carlton faltered in brushing Adonis. "I --" He furrowed his brow in thought. "She dressed up as a knight and jousted."

"Shocking!" Gwen exclaimed, but inside she was intrigued. Griffin had saved this girl even though she defied decorum.

"I only tell you because it is common knowledge. I don't think it is appropriate to gossip."

"We are just talking, Carlton. This is not gossiping. And, as you said, that is common knowledge." But not to her. Nor to Richard. Griffin had been a very busy man since he had been away. "Is she the one that is sabotaging him?"

"What?" Carlton almost dropped the brush. He fumbled with it for a moment, before righting it. "No! Layne would never --"

"So, it is true! Someone is trying to sabotage my brother."

Carlton's shoulders drooped as he opened his mouth and then closed it.

Gwen felt sorry for the boy. Duped by a woman. It was all so easy. She placed a hand on his shoulder. "I didn't hear it from you." But she had heard enough from him; she had heard everything she wanted to know.

# CHAPTER TWENTY-FOUR

After a long day of jousts, many had been defeated. Many were left. Osmont, Richard and both of Layne's brothers had achieved victory in their contests and had made it to the next day's jousts.

When Griffin walked into the Great Hall for the evening meal, he heard Richard's roar of laughter. He spotted his brother and Prince Edward sitting on the dais at the front of the hall, closest to the hearth. Jacquelyn sat beside Richard, with Gwen beside her. His father was nowhere to be seen. Of that, Griffin was grateful. His father had appeared too sickly to come down to the feast.

Griffin clenched and unclenched his hand. It was remarkable how quickly his shoulder had healed after Layne had worked her magic on him. It was tender and sore as if he had received a bad blow, which he had, but he could move it. It should offer no deterrent to winning the joust on the morrow.

Griffin caught himself looking around the room, his gaze swept past the tables of knights and nobles, past all the women. He caught himself with a sigh of disappointment. She won't be here. He was surprised he had been looking for Layne. He inhaled deeply. She was probably in her tent with her brothers. She had helped him. Even though he had insulted and humiliated her. A pain tightened in his chest. He pushed the thought aside and made his way to the head table; many knights called his name to congratulate him on his victory. He nodded in return. There was a different feel to this joust. He was the brother of the sponsor and was expected to act in a certain way. He couldn't help feeling more like a host than a participant. He knew he was expected to sit with his family and part of him was glad he would not have to contend with the women nobles pleading with him to sit beside them.

Gwen spotted him and turned a smile to him as he made his way up the long aisle to the table.

As Griffin neared the dais, he spotted Talvace speaking to Prince Edward. The long, lanky knight leaned over the table to toward the prince. "It truly is amazing that a man who could so easily be unhorsed is expected to win the tournament."

"Perhaps he can now answer for himself," Edward said, indicating Griffin with a wave of his hand.

Talvace whirled to him. His eyes grew wide and then narrowed. "Yes! Tell them of the first time you were unhorsed."

Trepidation slithered through Griffin. "I find it interesting you should be telling the story when you were not there."

"No. No, I wasn't. Perhaps my facts are wrong. Tell us. Was it really a woman that unhorsed you?" Talvace wondered.

All those close enough to hear Talvace's

statement turned to Griffin. He wanted to wring the scrawny man's neck. "There is really nothing to tell. I was unhorsed. Every knight is unhorsed at least once in his lifetime. Some more than others. Isn't that right, Talvace? Perhaps you should be telling the tale of your disqualification."

Talvace ground his teeth, glaring at Griffin.

Griffin made his way around the table to an empty chair beside Gwen.

Richard leaned forward to see Griffin. "Is it true? Was it a woman who unhorsed you?"

Griffin nodded.

Again, Richard roared with laughter. "What happened? Did she cheat? Did she have a longer lance than you?"

"No. She abided by the rules of the joust."

"All except one," Talvace said. "I heard she took her brother's place."

Silence spread across the dais as every eye turned to him.

Griffin tried to remain relaxed as he reached for his ale. Why couldn't they let it go? "She paid her dues," Griffin insisted. "She is of no concern any longer."

"No concern?" Richard boomed. "She is remarkable. The only one who has ever unhorsed my brother!"

"You are being ridiculous, Richard. You have done so many times. As have others. De la Noue recently unhorsed me."

"Who was she?" Richard continued, ignoring his statement. "What kind of woman was she?"

He could be so relentless at times. But this time, Griffin was not going to give him what he wanted. He wouldn't throw Layne to these ravenous lions.

"She is here, Lord Richard, at the tournament," Talvace announced.

Annoyance followed quickly by dread spread through Griffin's entire body. He didn't want his brother to harass Layne. He didn't want Richard anywhere near her.

"Where?" Richard asked, his excited gaze scanning the hall.

"She will not be here," Griffin said trying to remain calm and disinterested. He took a drink of his ale.

"Perhaps," Talvace agreed. "But her brothers will be here. They are competing in the tournament."

Griffin's jaw tightened. Talvace was enjoying this too much. He knew he had to remain calm. Casual. Like this entire affair meant nothing to him. He shook his head. "The younger boy was injured. Most of the Fletchers will stay with him."

"One of them is here tonight," Talvace countered.

Richard's gaze searched the Great Hall. "Where? Where is he?"

Griffin leaned back in the chair. Let him struggle to find Frances. He wanted no part of this.

Jacquelyn wrapped her hands around Richard's arm. "Darling, I want to meet them."

Griffin clenched his teeth. What kind of trouble had he brought the Fletchers?

Richard patted Jacquelyn's hand. "As do I, my dear. You there!" Richard called one of the servants over. "Find Fletcher and bring him to me."

The servant bowed and departed.

Griffin glanced away from his brother…

…right into Gwen's brown eyes. She watched

214

him through narrowed eyes, tapping her lower lip with her finger in a thoughtful manner.

Griffin felt trapped. He had the distinct impression there was no escape for him. What did Richard want with Layne? What kind of entertainment could she provide him? The appetite he had arrived with vanished.

"Why would you keep something like this from me?" Richard wondered.

"I was hardly keeping it from you. It was common knowledge. I knew you would find out eventually. They are a simple family. From the outskirts of Edinfield. Her youngest brother, Michael, was injured protecting her."

"Protecting her?" Gwen asked.

Griffin ignored her thoroughly. He would add no wood to this slow burning fire.

"How old is he?" Richard wondered.

"What happened?" Jacquelyn inquired.

Griffin silently groaned. He glanced at Talvace with a smirk of irritation. "It is a story for another day."

"You know them well?" Prince Edward asked.

"Not well. I traveled with them."

Richard's gaze shifted to the aisle. Griffin followed his stare to see the servant leading Frances up the center aisle. Talvace stepped aside, giving Richard clear view of Frances.

Frances glanced at Griffin before bowing to Richard. "Lord Richard, I want to express my gratitude to you for hosting this tournament."

Richard nodded, but brushed aside his comment with a flick of his hand. "Where is your sister?"

Frances scowled. "At the pavilion with Colin." He looked at Griffin. "Like all good women should be."

Gwen bridled at the comment.

Griffin knew the slight was directed at him and he deserved it. He swirled the ale around in his mug, watching the liquid swirl.

"My brother tells me that your sister unhorsed him," Richard said.

Frances's lips thinned and he cast an accusing glare at Griffin before looking back at Richard. "It's true, Lord Richard. But she has been properly punished. She realizes what she did was wrong and –"

Richard leaned forward. "Tell me what happened."

Frances swallowed. "I believe the story has been exaggerated and retold so many times, it hardly bears repeating."

Richard narrowed his eyes slightly. "Humor me."

"Indeed," Prince Edward agreed. "We would all like to hear the tale."

Griffin looked up in time to lock gazes with Frances. He read the panic in the man's eyes and understood it. It was the same panic that was eating away at the borders of his sanity.

Richard leaned forward, resting his elbows on the table.

Frances shifted slightly and wet his lips. "I was supposed to be the one jousting, but during practice I was hit in the head and rendered unconscious."

"Pity," Richard said without much remorse. He encouraged him to continue with a wave of his hand.

Frances fidgeted more, shuffling his feet, looking down at the rushes.

Griffin knew he was trying to come up with some way to protect Layne. "As I've said, Richard,

216

Layne was punished."

"I care not for punishment. I simply want a retelling of the story."

Griffin locked eyes with Frances and nodded.

Frances took a deep breath. "Layne dressed in my armor and took the field of honor in my place."

Gwen leaned back in her chair. "Hardly befitting of a woman."

"Agreed, lady," Frances said. "But Layne was raised with three brothers. We always included her in our practices, and she was adept at wielding a sword and lance."

"She is not a knight!" Talvace interrupted.

"No," Frances agreed. "When she unhorsed Sir Griffin –"

"You're skipping ahead," Richard interrupted. "Who was her squire?"

"My youngest brother, Michael. Apparently, she had threatened him into it."

"How many passes until she unhorsed my brother?"

"Three."

Richard reared back and slapped the table. He stood. "I must meet her!"

"Richard," Griffin objected.

Gwen stood, also. "I, too, would like a chance to meet her."

"Lord Richard," Frances said, "We've paid the dues agreed upon by Lord Dinkleshire. She will not be a problem again. This I assure you."

Problem? Griffin glared at Frances. Layne was never a problem. She was in danger and that should be her brother's concern. "Richard, Layne's actions have been dealt with. There is no further need for intervention –"

"Have you spoken to her?" Jacquelyn wondered.

Spoken to her? He'd done much more than speak with her! He opened his mouth and closed it. When he looked away, he saw Gwen's shrewd gaze upon him and that infuriating smile of hers. She was finding this much too amusing! "Yes. I have spoken with her."

"Sir Griffin instructed her for weeks after the joust in the art of being a woman," Frances said. "She was under his care."

Griffin whipped his head around to glare at Frances. Those were not the words he would have used. This was rapidly spinning out of control.

"And what does Griffin know of being a woman?" Gwen wondered, staring at him in disbelief.

"Griffin hardly knows how to treat a lady!" Jacquelyn added, laughing.

"How on earth did you do that?" Richard roared.

"I gave her duties. Womanly duties. She was not to touch the weapons or watch practices," Griffin defended, but now his rules seemed trite and useless.

"What did these duties entail?"

Griffin heard the undertone in Richard's voice. "Carlton was there. Nothing untoward happened." He looked at Gwen. "She washed the dishes, cleaned up, mended."

Talvace chuckled lustily. "How well did she learn?"

Griffin rose with such force that he knocked his chair over. "You overstep your bounds, Talvace."

Frances glared at Talvace, his fists tight.

"Yes. Yes," Prince Edward agreed. "We mean no insult."

"She's not under your protection any longer," Talvace replied through clenched teeth.

"Griffin." Richard stood. "Control yourself, brother." He straightened. "Perhaps you are right. We are all tired from a long day of tourney. And we have more skills to test on the morrow." He looked at Griffin and then at Frances. "I will meet your sister on the morrow. She can sit beside us, with your brothers of course, during Griffin's joust."

Frances nodded. "Thank you, Lord Richard. We would be honored."

Griffin watched Talvace retreat to his seat. Richard sat down. Frances walked to his seat. Griffin searched the room for Carlton, but his squire was nowhere to be found.

When Gwen rose and moved toward a side exit, Griffin followed her. Trepidation gripped him in a panicked hold. He seized Gwen's hand. "Please, Gwen," he whispered. "I don't want Richard to meet Layne."

Gwen's eyebrows rose in shock. "Why in heaven's name not?"

He couldn't formulate his thoughts or his feelings. He didn't want Layne humiliated. He didn't want her hurt. He didn't want Richard near her. It was absurd, an irrational fear. Was it because of Jacquelyn? Was he afraid Richard would steal Layne as he had Jacquelyn? No. Was he afraid that Richard would harm her somehow? No. Taint her? Maybe. He grit his teeth. "I can't concentrate on the joust if I must worry about her safety."

"Safety? Richard would never harm a woman!"

"She is not like us. She is noble in name only, not actions."

Gwen grinned. "That much is apparent."

"Gwen!" Griffin called in a painful voice.

"What is it you would have me do?"

Griffin looked at her for a long moment. "Tell one of your ladies' maids to go to her and have her leave the tournament."

Gwen frowned.

"I will put her up at an inn until it is over."

"All in an effort to keep her from Richard?"

"Richard and Father. Yes."

Gwen cocked her head at him. "Are you sure you are not sending her away from you?"

Her observation caught him off guard, and for a moment he was shocked at the truth in her words.

"She is a distraction to your skill, isn't she? And after all, what is more important than winning?"

He shook his head firmly. "I've grown used to protecting her is all. Please, Gwen. Will you do this?"

Gwen smiled sweetly and patted his hand. "Anything for you, my dearest brother." She leaned in and kissed his cheek.

There was something in the way she smiled, a sparkle in her eye, that should have alerted Griffin to the plan she was hatching. But he wanted to believe she would help him and ignored the warning bells going off in his head.

CHAPTER TWENTY-FIVE

"**I** can do it," Michael snapped.

Layne knelt beside his straw-hewn mattress. She wrapped a bandage around his hand, careful to cover the open wounds. They were healing nicely, but it would still be weeks before he was back to normal. "It's my duty, remember?"

"Stop it," Michael said and shoved her, but not hard enough to really push her away.

Layne grinned. "They look good. You've been careful with them, haven't you?"

Michael grunted softly and puffed out his chest. "A man doesn't need to be careful. It's just a little cut. Can't hurt me."

Layne tied the cloth over his palm. "Good." She was glad he was speaking to her again and he was slowly beginning to do everything he used to do, including caring for some of Colin's weapons. "When I see a man, I'll be sure to tell him he doesn't have to be careful."

Michael mocked her with a sarcastic grimace

and stuck his tongue out.

The flap on the tent opened and Frances entered, followed by Colin.

Michael leapt to his feet. "Did you bring us some food?"

"You're back early," Layne commented as she tossed the dirty cloth into a corner pile.

"I was summoned by Lord Richard," Frances said.

Tingles of trepidation danced along Layne's neck. "What did he want?"

"Apparently you have captured his interest. He wants all of us to sit with him during Wolfe's joust tomorrow. Especially you."

Layne scowled. "Why?"

Frances shrugged. "He wants to meet you."

Layne couldn't help the anxiety swirling inside of her. Why? Why would the hosting lord care who she was?

"I don't like this," Colin mumbled.

"He wanted me to tell the tale of how you unhorsed Wolfe." Frances sat on his straw mattress. "I tried to make it sound uninteresting, but he wanted the details. How you did it. Why you jousted."

"Does he want us to pay more coin as restitution?" Colin wondered.

"No," Frances said. "He said it wasn't about the coin or the punishment. He said he simply wanted to meet Layne."

Colin glanced at his sister. "Then it was lucky you weren't there."

"Not so lucky. He insists we sit with him tomorrow."

Layne stared at the dirt floor. What could Lord

Richard want with her? Why during Griffin's joust? She chewed thoughtfully on her lower lip. "I don't think we should go."

"We have little choice. He is the sponsor of this tournament. We don't want to insult him by rejecting his invitation."

"Will Prince Edward be there?" Michael asked with excitement. "I've always wanted to meet the prince."

Frances ruffled his hair. "I'm sure he will be."

"It will be exciting to sit in the berfrois," Michael exclaimed with a glowing face. "It's the best seat to watch the joust!" He glanced at his older brother. "Right Colin?"

When Colin didn't answer, Layne lifted her gaze to see her brother staring at her. "We can't refuse Lord Richard's request. But maybe it's not a good idea for Layne to attend."

Their gazes swung to her.

Layne felt an overwhelming sadness. She would have liked to sit in the berfrois and watch the joust. She would have done almost anything to see Griffin joust again.

"He will ask to meet her again," Frances warned. "He might even command it. Or come to the tent himself."

"We cannot refuse the invitation and Layne cannot stay here alone," Colin said. "Not with Osmont here."

"I can take care of myself," Layne insisted, placing her hand over the dagger she kept tucked in her belt.

Colin inhaled. "I don't want you here alone. It's better if you come with us to the berfrois."

Layne nodded, but she couldn't suppress the excitement she felt at the prospect of seeing Griffin joust, nor the unease at having to meet Lord Richard.

Layne sat on the ground, pulling a needle through Michael's breeches, mending a rip he had received in the seat. He was growing so quickly. He really needed a new pair of breeches. She sighed softly and her shoulders drooped. Why did a pair of blue eyes pop into her mind at the most inconvenient time? Why did the feel of Griffin's kiss keep her awake at night? It was no use dwelling on it. Even now she found it hard to concentrate on the simple task of mending a tear.

A crash outside the tent made her whirl. "Michael?"

The moment of silence stretched, and she warily climbed to her feet.

Michael poked his head into the tent. "You have a visitor."

"Visitor?"

One of the blonde beauties who had been accompanying Griffin swept into the tent. She looked at the breeches in her hand.

Layne's gaze moved from her beautiful almond shaped brown eyes, over her blue velvet dress, to her slippered feet, then back to her eyes.

The woman's dainty eyebrow lifted as she stared at the clothing in Layne's hand. "You'll get better with more practice."

Layne pulled the clothing behind her back. "Who are you? What do you want?"

"I am Lady Gwen Wolfe. I came to meet you."

A tremor of apprehension shot through her. "Griffin's sister?"

"You've heard of me!" She clapped her hands together. "And Griffin said he didn't speak of me."

"He's only said gracious things about you."

"He has?" She narrowed her eyes in disbelief. "Like what?"

Layne hated to lie. The only thing she remembered him saying about his sister was how she manipulated him to get what she wanted. "He said many things, but he never told me how lovely you were."

Gwen smiled. "Griffin might have said many things, but you are correct in saying he would not have told you I was beautiful. I have yet to hear him call any woman beautiful."

Layne stood with her hand behind her back as Gwen looked around the tent. "How do you do it? I find it difficult to live in a large castle with two brothers. And yet, you live in a small pavilion with three."

Layne smiled shyly. "It is a challenge."

Gwen nodded, and looked directly at her.

Layne dropped her gaze to the ground. The difference between them was palpable. She could never be like Gwen. No matter how hard she tried, no matter how much Griffin wanted her to be. No matter how much she wanted to be. "Is there a reason you've come to my tent?"

"Griffin seems fond of you and I was intrigued."

Layne's heart squeezed in her chest. "Griffin wants nothing to do with me. I don't conform to his vision of how women are supposed to act... and look."

"He told you this?"

"He made it clear." He was embarrassed of her.

He could never introduce her to his family.

"Hmmm." Gwen picked up a lock of her hair and gently brushed it over her shoulder. "Sometimes my brother can be a cad." She placed her hand on her shoulder. "You are very beautiful, in a unique way. I think Griffin has seen this. I think he knows. But everything pales in comparison to winning his precious joust. He pushes whatever he views as a distraction aside." Gwen looked into her eyes; a mischievous grin formed on her lips. "Don't you agree?"

"He has to stay focused. He has many strong knights left to defeat."

Gwen's grin shifted to sympathy. "You care for him."

Layne dropped her gaze, not wanting Gwen to see the agony in her eyes. She more than cared for him. She loved him.

"Oh, my dear," Gwen whispered. Then she hooked her arm through Layne's. "Don't you fear. He will notice you again. I will make sure." She smiled at Layne. "We are going to be friends, I can tell. Good friends."

CHAPTER TWENTY-SIX

Griffin had been grateful that Layne had not shown up to his joust. It was for her own protection, he told himself. Without the distraction of her presence, he had easily won the joust. Her brothers had been there, watching with Richard who was furious at the slight. Prince Edward had calmed him.

Griffin had not spoken to Gwen. He hoped she had reached Layne and made her his offer. She must have accepted. That must have been why Layne was not at the joust.

Now, he looked out over the Great Hall at the throng of knights. Most were now out of the competition. Richard was still in, a fact that he found no end to boasting about.

Griffin took a bite of his venison. Tomorrow, Richard jousted against Ethan. He wondered where his old friend had gotten. He hadn't seen him since he crossed him and offered coin to the Fletchers. A thought crossed his mind. Perhaps he had seduced Layne. Perhaps... Griffin grit his teeth and forced the thought away. He ripped into his venison, taking a healthy bite.

And what of the saboteur? Had there really ever been one? Had he made up the cut in his stirrup leather to justify Layne unhorsing him? And the cut in his cinch. Had they really been cut? No. Layne had noticed both, also. He found himself scanning the hall, looking for her.

"Well done, brother."

Griffin looked up to find Gwen taking a seat at his side. "Thank you for speaking to her." Gwen smiled that annoying secretive smile that drove Griffin mad. He leaned close to her. "You did have one of your ladies speak to Layne, didn't you?"

"Well, actually, no."

"No?"

"I spoke to her."

Griffin watched as she took a mug from a servant woman. She was up to something. When the servant passed, he asked, "Did she accept my offer?"

Gwen sighed. "We both found your offer... insulting."

Griffin scowled and growled, "Gwen. What did you do?"

Gwen's gaze swung over the crowd as she sipped the ale.

A prickling of unease and dread danced over his shoulders and up his neck. "Gwen."

"I thought of another proposition for her."

"What did you do, Gwen?" Griffin grumbled.

Gwen smiled as her gaze locked on something in the back of the room.

Trepidation and anger ran through Griffin. He should have known better than to ask Gwen for anything, much less something so important to him. He wanted to grab his sister and shake her until she told him where Layne was. "What did you do?"

Gwen lifted her chin. "I turned her into a woman. Just like you wanted."

Griffin followed her gaze. Standing in the large double doorway, he immediately spotted Ethan. He had stopped to speak with another man. On his arm was a woman. Her dark hair was braided and hung down her back. She wore a simple maroon gown made of velvet that hugged her figure. Even at this distance, Griffin felt something stir inside of him. His breath caught in his throat.

It was only when she laughed at something the man said that he was certain.

Layne.

Gwen grabbed his arm. "Do sit down. You are making a spectacle of yourself."

Griffin was surprised to find himself standing. He quickly sat.

"She is to dine with us. Richard was so upset that he couldn't meet her that I helped make her *presentable*. Just so you wouldn't be embarrassed of her."

Her words were like little daggers slicing at him. But he could not take his gaze from Layne as she turned to Ethan and spoke with him. A dark rage rose inside of Griffin. He swiped at his cup and drained it. "What about Farindale?"

"Ethan is a family friend. He will dine with us, also." Gwen waved her hand dismissingly. "As will her brothers."

For the first time, Griffin noticed her brothers behind her, trailing her in. He slouched in his seat.

Gwen leaned over to him. "Now who is not presentable?"

Griffin clenched his lips and looked away from his deceitful sister.

Ethan led Layne up the center aisle. Griffin's gaze swung to them and locked on the way Ethan's hand held hers, the way every other knight in the room turned to regard her. The way that damned velvet caressed her curves.

"It's remarkable, isn't it?" Gwen asked. "The transformation. Why, I believe even Father would be pleased."

The Layne who moved up the aisle was respectable and conformed to his every idea of a proper woman. This Layne was the one that society dictated she be. But this wasn't his Layne. His Layne was the one that exploded with joy when he splintered the quintain. His Layne was the one who wore breeches and let her hair curl down her back in rebellious, unkempt waves. God's blood. He wanted her. He wanted his Layne. But he feared she would never have him; she would only remember the oaf who had insulted and humiliated her. A lump rose in his throat.

Ethan and Layne stopped before the table.

"Ahhh!" Richard said, rising. "Is this the lady I've heard so much about?"

Colin moved forward. "Lord Richard, may I present my sister?"

Richard pulled the chair beside him away from the table. "Come, my dear. Sit here, beside me."

Griffin stared down at his venison, all appetite gone. He picked at the meat as Layne moved around the table.

"You Fletchers, take a seat at the table. Ethan, you are welcome, also."

Gwen smiled as Layne rounded the table to take

the empty seat between she and Richard.

Gwen elbowed him. She leaned close to him to whisper, "Do greet her. Who is the embarrassment now?"

Griffin grit his teeth and rose. He flung the chair back in his anger at what Gwen had said and it almost struck Layne. She stopped as the chair came to a rest, blocking her path. She turned her gaze to him. He froze, caught in the beacon of her beautiful eyes. All of Griffin's anger dissipated, draining from his body beneath her stare. He floundered. Did he remove the chair from her path? Did he take her hand and kiss it? All he really wanted to do was kiss her lips. His scowl deepened and he bowed his head. "Layne."

Gwen shook her head. "You're a cur," she whispered and pulled the chair aside so Layne could pass.

"Thank you," Layne said to Gwen. She glanced at Griffin. "It's good to see you, Sir Griffin."

He did not miss the formality of her words and the distance that her tone put between them. He watched her move past him and regret suddenly assailed him. She was a remarkable woman. How could he have known she would be so... so... damned beautiful?

She sat and he couldn't take his gaze from her.

Gwen reached out and pulled at his hand.

He realized he was the only one standing. He glanced around and his stare locked on the door in the back of the Great Hall. He should flee. This could not turn out well. He sat heavily.

Colin took the seat beside him.

Griffin greeted him with a nod.

"I'm   delighted   to   finally   make   your

acquaintance!" Richard said to Layne. "My brother has told me many things about you."

"I hope they were not all bad."

That dagger in Griffin's heart twisted.

"Not at all!" Richard exclaimed. "He piqued my interest." Richard leaned closer to Layne. "Is it true you unhorsed him?"

God's blood! Griffin thought, raising the mug of ale to his lips and draining it. Will my humiliation never end?

"I did, but I believe I caught him unawares."

Griffin froze with his head tilted back, the mug to his lips.

"I think my eyes gave me away and Sir Griffin is chivalrous enough to take a fall for a lady."

She was giving him a way out. She was actually making him appear gallant! He shook his head as he lowered the mug.

"That is not what I heard," Richard grumbled.

"But it is the truth!" Layne explained. "No one else was on the field of honor. Only Griffin and I know the truth. I could never have beaten him."

"No," Griffin said softly, the small word tore from his soul. He couldn't let her do it.

Gwen turned to him.

"He has won all the tournaments he has been in. Surely, I could not have unhorsed him. Me, a mere woman."

"No," Griffin said louder. This drew the attention of Layne and Richard. He looked at Layne. "Tell him the truth, Layne. I did not know you were a woman until after you had unhorsed me."

She shook her head slightly, silently begging him not to continue.

"You are no mere woman. You are extremely skilled in the art of jousting and swordplay." He watched her eyes widen in surprise, but he couldn't stop himself. He wanted to say everything he couldn't say before. He wanted to tell her how much she meant to him, how much he missed her. "You can decipher a weakness quicker than I have ever seen. The reason you unhorsed me was nothing short of skill and talent. You know more about weapons than some men know. And you are a brilliant rider."

The table around him was completely silent.

"Your excitement and enthusiasm for the sport is unsurpassed and… I have been a fool for not realizing it earlier." He shook his head. "You belong on the field of honor more than at a celebration for men who are not your equal."

Layne covered her mouth with her fingers.

"But she is not a knight," Osmont shouted and stood from a nearby table. "She should never have been on the field of honor! The day she took up arms against you, she defiled the field."

Griffin rose, his fists clenched. "Just because a man has not been knighted, does not mean he… or she… is any less honorable." He pointed at Layne. "She never hit someone from behind! She has more courage and proper upbringing than you have shown your entire life!"

"Well said!" Ethan agreed, raising his mug from down the table and drinking it deeply.

"You know the rules," Osmont growled. He turned to the assembly who had grown quiet, listening to the exchange. "She was not a knight when she took to the field and jousted against Wolfe. She should never have been there."

Layne stood. "I paid my dues. The matter has been settled. It is not your right or your place to interfere. No matter how much you disagree."

Griffin cast her a fleeting glance. She was beautiful, brave and courageous. He knew she was exactly the woman he wanted to present to his family.

"You dare to speak to me with such disrespect?" Osmont snarled.

"Contempt, disrespect, abhorrence. Call it what you will. What you did to Michael, to me, is unforgivable. Only a coward would hit a woman from behind. Only a coward would take a child's fingers in anger. You are --"

Osmont lunged forward.

Griffin moved instantly to protect her, but the sound of swords being drawn echoed through the room.

Before Osmont was anywhere near Layne, Colin, Frances and the guards nearby had all drawn their weapons.

CHAPTER TWENTY-SEVEN

Osmont came up short, snarling like an animal.

Layne lifted her chin, staring him in the eye.

Beside her, Richard lounged lazily in his chair. "It's disrespectful to insult my guests, Sir Osmont. You will apologize immediately or be removed from the Keep."

Osmont spit on the ground. "I'd rather be trampled by a hundred horses."

Richard leaned forward. "Careful, Osmont. That can be arranged."

Osmont glanced at Layne and then at Griffin. "This isn't over, Wolfe."

Richard rose slowly. "It is over, Osmont. Whatever is left will be settled on the field of honor. You are to never mention this incident again."

Osmont clenched his teeth, bowed slightly and whirled, storming from the room.

Layne knew it was a small victory, but she felt joyful nonetheless. She looked at Michael who stood beside Griffin. She couldn't help but notice the bandage

235

wrapped around his hand that rested over the dagger tucked in his belt. She wiggled her eyebrows but kept herself from grinning.

"You all right, Layne?" Colin asked.

Layne nodded, but turned to watch Osmont walk out of the Great Hall. She might be all right, but it was Colin she was worried about. He jousted Osmont on the morrow.

Layne walked across the grassy field with her brothers and Ethan, back to their tent. She hated the dress. It was cumbersome and she had to pick her legs up high to step through the tall stalks. Her dress got caught on something and she turned.

"I'll help you," Ethan said. As he fought the twigs that grabbed her skirt, she looked back at the castle as if she were called. Standing on the walkway, silhouetted in the moonlight, was Griffin. She was sure it was him. She would recognize him anywhere. Her heart hammered in her chest. He had defended her this night. The things he had said...

Ethan pulled the skirt free.

"Bet you couldn't win a sword fight in that!" Michael said and raced toward their tent.

She would not take that bet. She looked back up at the castle.

Ethan followed her gaze. He laughed low in his throat. "It must have been a shock to see you like this."

"Maybe for him."

"For all of us!" Frances called.

She laughed in mocking reply. But she knew she would do anything to catch his eye again. Even dress in one of these awful dresses.

Colin's horse danced nervously beneath him, but he steadied him with a firm hand. Osmont sat stiffly across the field, his horse unmoving, his gaze locked on Colin.

Colin's gaze shifted to the berfrois. Frances stood with his arms crossed beside Richard who watched with shrewd eyes. Layne was beside him, clasping her hands before her. He could not let his family down. He could not lose.

He pranced Sprite, his steed, back and forth, trying to ease his nerves. When he was ready, he approached Michael who handed him his lance. He spurred his steed forward, down the field, bringing his lance down to point directly at Osmont. He rode his horse, becoming one with the animal, feeling the rhythm, knowing when it was time to strike. Colin leaned forward, preparing for the hit.

He heard Osmont's cry as the lance struck his shoulder, glancing off his armor; but it did not break. It was a brief moment of victory for in the next second, Osmont's lance landed a brutal blow in the side and Colin reeled, teetering. He grimaced as pain speared through his body. His hands tightened around the reins and he clamped his legs around his horse to keep from plummeting to the ground.

His horse circled from the pressure on the reins and reared slightly, but Colin held on and pulled himself upright.

As he centered himself in the saddle, the ringing in his ears cleared enough for him to hear the cry of the spectators around him. He spurred his horse down the length of the field more out of habit than anything else. His head was reeling. He reached Michael and looked down at him. His lips moved, but Colin couldn't hear what he was saying. He shook his head, trying to clear it. The fogginess and disorientation lingered. He had to win. He couldn't let them down. He grit his teeth and reached down for the lance Michael lifted to him.

His breath came to him, muffled inside his helmet. He heard his heart beating in his ears. He lifted his gaze to Osmont. The cocky bastard was prancing at the other end, pounding his chest and lifting his hands to the crowd.

Colin waited a moment for Osmont to reach for his lance before jerking the reins and spurring his horse down the field. He lowered his lance, couching it and clamped his arm down over it tightly.

Sprite charged down the field, and Colin lowered his lance. It struck true, right in Osmont's chest. The lance splintered and Colin wind milled it over his head, riding past Osmont.

Osmont completely missed Colin. The arrogant knight teetered, and the crowd seemed to sway with him.

Colin rode to his side of the field and turned to watch.

Osmont clutched the reins, steering his horse in a circle until he adjusted himself in the saddle. He turned to look at Colin, lifting his visor so Colin could see his snarled grimace.

Colin cocked a grin. Served him right for being overly confident. And for hurting Layne. Colin reached for the next lance. He spurred Sprite, rushing toward Osmont.

Osmont raced toward him, dust kicking up in his horse's wake.

Colin lowered his lance, aiming for Osmont's stomach. He had to win this joust... The thought came unbidden and distracted his focus for the fraction of a second.

He felt the impact against his stomach. His breath was knocked from him as he was lifted up and flew back out of the saddle. He dropped hard to the ground. Pain exploded through his body, and for a moment he saw patches of blinding white in his vision which slowly transformed to a blue sky and thick white clouds.

Damn it. He sat up, pulling his helmet off his head.

Down the field, Osmont threw up his visor and watched him with a wicked grin on his lips. He lifted his hands in the air. The crowd around the field erupted in a thunderous cheer.

Colin began to stand, but a burning pain flared through his right leg and he sat back, clutching his thigh. When he glanced at it, he saw a piece of wood resting on the top of his thigh. It looked like it was just lying there. Strange. He touched the wooden splinter and a searing agony flared from the wood into his leg.

The white piece of lance was not on his leg but lodged in his leg just behind his cuisses. He grimaced.

Michael reached his side. "You all right, Colin?" He followed his brother's gaze down to his leg.

Layne's hands flew to her cheeks. No! Michael knelt at Colin's side. Her younger brother twisted and looked at them, locking eyes with her. She saw the fear and concern on his young face.

She jerked forward, but a hand grabbed her arm. "No, Layne."

She struggled against Griffin's hold, not taking her gaze from Colin. Frances leapt from the berfrois and dashed across the field to Colin's side. "He's my brother!" she whispered harshly.

Griffin tightened his grip. "You can't go out there."

For a moment, concern for her brother overrode the logic in his voice. She tried to pull her arm free of his hold. Colin was still on the ground. Frances made it to his side and spoke to Michael.

Griffin spun her to look at him. "Layne. You can't go out there. When they bring him off the field, we'll go to him."

His words sunk in. She stilled her fight and turned to watch. It was with agonizing slowness that the physicians ran across the field to him. Frances knelt beside Colin and spoke to Colin. Colin shook his head. Fear and concern overwhelmed her. She reached for safety and found Griffin's hand.

Her fingers meshed with Griffin's and he gripped her hand tightly.

Around her, the other nobility were standing, probably to get a better view.

Colin held his leg and leaned his head back, grimacing in pain.

"He's hurt," she whispered. Agony and helplessness filled Layne and she squeezed Griffin's hand. She wanted with every ounce of her being to run

240

to Colin, to see what had happened. She could tell by the agony on his face that it was bad.

"Fear not, my dear," Prince Edward said. "Those are the best physicians in the realm. He will be well cared for."

Frances helped Colin to his feet, bracing an arm around his shoulders. Michael steadied him bearing his weight beneath Colin's other arm. Colin grimaced and held his leg up. They began to make their way from the field amidst applause and cheers. She looked on in horror as it was apparent Colin was not using his leg.

Griffin pulled her off the berfrois, behind Richard, Gwen and Prince Edward, toward the entrance to the field of honor as she craned her head to see her brothers. They skirted merchants selling bread and reached the entrance to the field of honor as her brothers and the physicians emerged.

"What happened?" Layne asked, looking down at Colin's leg. She spied the piece of lance in Colin's leg and her stomach fell. She pushed Michael gently from beneath Colin's arm to take his weight. "Go get Sprite."

Michael nodded and raced back onto the field as they led Colin toward the physician's tent. One of the physicians in a long black robe led the way across the clearing.

Layne held onto Colin's chest and she could feel the stiffness of tension and agony though his body. "It's all right," she whispered to him even though she knew this was bad. Very bad.

He looked at her then, his eyes twin pinpoints of pain. "Not this time, little one," he said softly.

Layne's throat closed and her voice choked off. She helped him to the physician's tent. The physicians took her place at his side and they helped him to a table.

As Frances began to remove his armor, Michael raced up to her. "Carlton is seeing to Sprite."

Layne nodded, but didn't really hear him. Colin's grimaces and valiant attempts at muffling his cries of agony twisted her stomach.

"Will he be all right?" Michael asked quietly, staring at Colin. He was cradling his own wrapped hand.

"You know Colin," Layne said, but couldn't finish the sentence. She had tried for a lighthearted tone, but her voice came out full and thick.

Michael looked up at her.

She couldn't look at him for the tears entering her eyes. How could she comfort her maimed younger brother when her older brother was now in even more turmoil?

She looked down and movement out of the corner of her eye caused her to look over her shoulder.

Griffin stood behind them, a silent sentry. For that, Layne was grateful.

Layne sat on the bank of the stream close to their pavilion, beneath a large oak tree, staring at the rippling water. Colin was in their tent. Frances was with him. He had a joust coming up and Michael had gone to prepare his horse. None of their hearts were in it. Although the fact remained that Frances had to win. He was their last hope. Their only hope. He couldn't lose.

"He'll be all right."

Layne didn't turn. She let Griffin's voice wash over her, but even his calm demeanor couldn't replace the agony in her soul.

She heard him sit beside her.

"It is the danger of the joust," he told her kindly.

She had always known there was danger in jousting, a fall could be severe, but not like this. This was a bad wound. The splinter from the lance had punctured Colin's thigh.

"Colin is strong. He will recover."

But not in time. Not in time to save their father. Not in time to buy them all a comfortable life, a corner of the world where they could be a family. She felt tears rising, but stubbornly blinked them back. Two of her family now needed to be seen to. Counting her father, it was three. Their future rested with Frances.

"Layne…" His whispered word was like a soft stroke against her skin.

She took a ragged breath and tried to get control of herself. She felt a strong tug and found herself in his embrace.

She nestled into the warmth of his arms, melting against him as he stroked her hair.

"He'll be fine," Griffin murmured softly, his arms tightening around her.

She hoped Griffin's words were true. But what of the rest of them? It all rested with Frances now. The entire future of the Fletcher family.

CHAPTER TWENTY-EIGHT

Cheers in the distance rose and fell. Layne sat on her straw mattress; her hands twisted. Frances was jousting. She had stayed with Colin.

Colin lay on his mat, silently staring at the top of the pavilion.

They both knew that if Frances lost, that would be the end of it. They would not be able to pay for the farm. They would have no home. They could make do if it was just her, Frances and Colin. But Michael was a child. He needed food and shelter. And their father... He would not make it. Of that, Layne was certain.

Colin hit the ground with his fist.

"He'll do what he must," Layne said. "I'm sure he will win."

Colin groaned softly. "I should have protected myself. I could have unhorsed Osmont."

"You can't think like that. It's over and you are hurt. You have to recover for next year."

Colin boosted himself onto his elbow to stare at her. "Next year? There will be no next year for us if we lose this. We'll have to sell everything just to survive. Have you thought about where we will go? What we will do?"

Layne didn't like to hear Colin talk like this. He was usually the strong one. He was their rock. "Maybe we could head south. It's slightly warmer and --"

"How will we travel? We have two horses."

"Then someone will walk."

"Walk? It will take us double the time and --"

"Stop it, Colin," she said savagely. "Of course I've thought about it. Every moment of every day. Everything we have, everything, was riding on us winning. We talked about this in the beginning, remember? And we all decided that we would do whatever it took to win. Losing wasn't an option. Remember?"

Colin nodded. "And we did win. We grew overconfident. Then Wolfe entered the jousts."

Yes. Griffin had been traveling a different tournament circuit, like many of the knights. She and her family had gone to smaller tournaments, the faires. And won. They had done well. Until they had no choice but to enter the larger tournaments. At first they had been excited, overconfident from their wins. But that had all changed. "We can ask him for coin."

"And how would we repay him? How are we to repay Farindale's loan? No." He placed an arm over his eyes. "No."

"I can marry."

Colin chuckled humorlessly. "Because those offers are so numerous?"

That stung. She could get at least one offer, she was sure. Maybe. She thought back to when it was simpler, when they were so sure that nothing could go wrong. "Remember when our only concern was if you and Frances had to joust against each other?"

Colin didn't answer.

Layne pulled her knees up to her chest and buried her face in them. She remembered, but it did no good. She had to come up with a plan in case Frances lost. "He can win," she whispered, trying to convince Colin as much as herself.

The tent flap swooshed open. Griffin ducked his head inside.

Dread and trepidation filled Layne.

"He won."

In a rare turn of events, Osmont had lost to Talvace. Griffin had to smile as the overconfident knight rose from the dust, throwing his gauntlets to the ground in a fit of anger. It had been a lucky strike, one that caught Osmont off guard. Griffin wished Layne had been there to see it. But she was with her brothers, practicing. He missed her smile, her laughter.

All the Fletchers seemed to have taken an emotional turn for the worst. Ever since Colin had been hurt, he did not see them smiling or playfully sparring words or fists with each other. They were subdued, as if the joy had drained out of them.

Griffin moved through the corridors of the castle. He wanted to take time before his own joust to clear his mind. He entered the Great Hall and moved through the room. He stopped midway when he saw a hunched form sitting by the hearth, a blanket draped across his shoulders. His father. He glanced at the door, thinking to make a quick escape. But as soon as he did, he heard him call, "Griffin, boy. Come sit here."

Griffin straightened his back, mentally preparing for a fight, and headed over to his father. He grit his teeth as he took the chair beside him.

"I'm old, boy," he said softly with the hint of remorse. "I'm afraid my time will come soon."

Griffin didn't say a word. The old man had used his death as a manipulative tool for a long time. Griffin even had suspicions of how ill his father really was.

"I'm tired of fighting with you," he sighed, and his shoulders drooped further. "I want to go to my death knowing that we are not at odds."

"Father," Griffin said softly, "I cannot be head of your castle."

"It is your legacy, son."

"It is Richard's legacy. I must forge my own path."

His father put a hand on Griffin's leg and for the first time, he noticed how wrinkled and thick with veins it was. It looked fragile, as if a wind would blow it away. "You already have. You've proven yourself a capable warrior, the winner of every joust you've been in. What more could you possibly want?"

What did he want? What was he trying to prove? He had already proven his independence.

His father squeezed his leg. "It's time to come home, son. To take your rightful place."

Griffin shook his head. "Richard is rightful heir. He was raised to be lord of the castle."

"You have more common sense and more leadership abilities than Richard ever did."

Griffin's lips thinned. "I won't do that to Richard." He shook his head firmly. "I won't strip him of his title. I won't betray him like that."

His father withdrew his hand and sniffled, running his sleeve across his nose.

The flames in the hearth snapped and crackled.

"Your loyalty is admirable. Have you considered that Richard does not want to be lord?"

Griffin glanced at him in surprise. "He told you this?"

"Not in so many words." He shook his head. "You have no idea. No idea what has been going on since you left."

Griffin leaned back in the chair, stretching his long legs out before him. Here it was again. He had heard this before. Richard was cleaning out the coiffeurs. Jacquelyn wanted gold and elaborate dresses from France.

"I think you could convince him to step down."

"No," Griffin said. "It is not my place to offer Richard council. He has advisors to do that."

"Advisors that have their hand in his pocket and strings on his wrists. While you have been gone, Richard has become a toy to his advisors. Because he wants to please everyone. He wants everyone to adore him. He only wants to have fun. That's why he's here. He wanted to joust like you. He does not take his role seriously."

Griffin stared into the fire. The last time he had been home, Richard had been a capable leader, charismatic and loved by the people. He had to admit that Richard had come to him seeking his guidance and advice many times. Still, that did not prove Richard was not a capable leader. "Then why haven't you stopped it?"

"Me?" A fit of coughing took over his father's words and he stopped to wipe his mouth. "Richard does not listen to me. I have told him to be rid of that pack of wolves, but he scoffs at me. I'm just an old man." He wiped the spittle from his lips again. "No. It must come from you."

Griffin leaned forward, his arms on his thighs. He wouldn't tell Richard that his own father wanted him to step down. No. He knew how being second best in your father's eyes felt and it was not something he would do to his brother. "I cannot tell him what to do."

His father sighed softly. "It's that girl, isn't it?"

Griffin looked at him. His father watched him with those aged eyes, eyes that seemed to be able to see into his soul. Griffin looked at the fire. His father had not shown him so much interest in all of his life. Why now? Wariness tightened the muscles across his neck. "What girl?"

"Richard's wife."

"Jacquelyn?" Griffin asked in disbelief. "She means nothing to me." And then he straightened, snapping to a sitting position with realization. He was searching for some way to control him, to manipulate him. He rose. "No. There's nothing you can give me that would make me change my mind."

"There is something. And I will find it."

# CHAPTER TWENTY-NINE

Layne sat outside of the tent, looking at the starry night. The stars twinkled like coveted diamonds in the darkness. Colin, Frances and Michael all slept inside the pavilion.

But sleep would not come for her. She didn't want to wander far from the tent. She knew Osmont had packed and left Woodstock after his embarrassing defeat. But there were others that felt the way he did. She still needed to be cautious.

She lifted her gaze to the moon. It was almost full, but there was a little piece missing. Ever since she had jousted, their luck had changed. They had only needed one more tourney to win. One more! And all their problems would have been gone. But she had to go and joust. She had to take Frances's place. That had been when all of their troubles started. That had been the reason Michael had lost his fingers, the reason the other knights had turned against them. It had all been her fault. Somehow, she knew Colin's injury was her fault as well. Osmont had gone at him with a ferocious level of misplaced vengeance.

She bowed her head between her knees. Maybe she should have stayed home with her father and let her brothers handle the jousting. Would it have been so bad to be embroidering all of the time, under her father's watchful eye and guidance so he could seek out the right husband for her? Having her aunt tell her to stand up straight, to agree with what the men said, to be docile and complacent? And never, ever, complain or roughhouse or sword fight or joust. Would it have been so bad?

It would have been horrible. It would have been unbearable. But she would have done it. She would have endured all of it if to give Michael back his fingers, to forgo Colin's injury.

A crunching sound made her lift her head. She scanned the area in front of her but didn't see anything. She was sure she heard something. Like the crunch of leaves or a branch. She slowly turned her head. It was hard to distinguish if someone was there in the dark. She saw Griffin's white tent just downstream of them.

Nothing.

Then she saw a shadow moving toward Griffin's tent. What could someone want at such a late hour?

She straightened. The saboteur! It had to be!

She shot to her feet. She had to stop them. Indecision plagued her. She could rush over and confront whoever it was, but she knew there could be several men involved. She was afraid she might not be able to stop them by herself. She ducked back into her tent. Frances would help her. She moved to his mat and reached out for him but felt only blankets. He wasn't there. He must have been relieving himself or unable to sleep. She glanced back at the tent flap. She didn't have time to find him.

She looked at Colin. He wouldn't be able to help. Not with his leg injured.

She glanced at Michael. She would never risk his life again. Nothing was worth that.

Layne stood, placing a hand over the dagger in her belt. She would have to stop him. She ducked back outside and quickly moved toward Griffin's pavilion, being careful not to make any noise. As she approached, she couldn't see anyone there. Maybe she had made a mistake. Maybe it was just another knight walking back to his tent.

Maybe.

Layne moved closer. She crouched, careful of her steps, placing one foot delicately forward and then the other.

Against the white of the tent, she saw a shadow sit up.

Layne squatted down and froze. She was about halfway between the tents. She watched the shadow. He was doing something near where Griffin's weapons were.

She moved slowly forward, continuing to crouch as she moved. She had to come up behind him. She had to surprise him.

She circled around, keeping the shadow in her line of sight. She had no doubt it was a man. Carefully, she slid the dagger from her belt. She moved on the tips of her toes, silently, careful to move her foot from spot to spot until she was behind him.

Suddenly, he stopped and lifted his head, looking around from side to side like a deer in the line of a hunter's bow.

She crouched down and hid the dagger in the

folds of her tunic so it wouldn't reflect the moonlight. After a long moment, he cautiously returned to his work. She hadn't realized she was holding her breath until she let it out in a slow exhale. She licked her lips and began to move in a bent position. She was almost upon him. What she intended to do when she reached him, she had no idea.

Her heart beat madly, pounding like a drum in her chest. She stood over him, holding the dagger. What could she do? Stab him? Call out?

In the end it was the moonlight that betrayed her. Her shadow washed across the ground and he whirled.

She lifted the blade. The same light that had betrayed her now guided her as it washed over familiar features. She gasped, "Frances!" and immediately lowered the blade.

"Layne," Frances whispered. "Thank the Lord! I thought it was Wolfe. Help me."

Layne stepped up beside her brother, looking over his shoulder. "What are you doing?"

Griffin's weapons lay before him, but they were untouched. Frances held leather reins in one hand. He put a dagger to the reins.

Layne grabbed his elbow and jerked his hand away. "What are you doing?"

"It's the only way," Frances said, shrugging her hand off of him and putting the blade to the leather. He began to saw.

"Stop it!" Layne said. "You can't do this. It's wrong!"

"Wrong? It doesn't matter anymore. All that matters is that I win. I can't lose!"

She held his arm. "This isn't the way. We'll

practice all night, if we must. But you can't sabotage him."

He shoved her away. "I have to," he growled. "You saw him! I can't beat him. I can't defeat him. And I have to! I have to." He turned back to the reins.

"Frances," she said firmly. "This isn't the way. I beat him. You can, too." And then the realization hit her. A chill of doom shrouded her, and she shivered. "You did it. That was why I was able to defeat him. You cut the leather stirrup."

Frances grit his teeth. "Yes. You won because of what I did. And now, I have to win. So I have to do this."

Layne shook her head. She hadn't defeated Griffin fairly. She had known deep in her heart that she couldn't have beaten Griffin, but she had never thought her brother had sabotaged him. "Stop," she said and grabbed the reins. "You can't do this."

"Can't do this? Are you thinking of the family or are you thinking of Wolfe? I saw the way you look at him. Even dressing in a dress to get his attention. Where are your loyalties?"

Surprised and hurt at the truth in his words, she pulled her hand back. "This isn't honorable, Frances. What would Colin say?"

Frances looked at her. His expression was cold and distant. "He told me to do it."

Shocked, Layne stepped back. What was happening? This couldn't be! Not Colin, too!

"He knows where his loyalties lay. The family is all that is important now. We have to win this joust. Any way we can." Frances began to saw his dagger into the reins.

These were the reins that guided the horse, not the cinch or the stirrup leather. If Griffin couldn't control Adonis, he might be seriously hurt or thrown and injured that way. How could she just stand there and let Frances do this? It was as good as cutting the reins herself. She opened her mouth to stop him. But how could she? They had to win. They needed this purse to buy the small farm where they could all live in the winter. They would have food, shelter. Warmth. Michael and her father would be taken care of. They would all survive. Where were her loyalties?

She closed her mouth.

Finally, Frances rose.

Layne stared at the reins on the ground, cut and damaged. Tears rose in her eyes. Every instinct in her being cried out at the injustice of it all. To sacrifice Griffin for her family wasn't right, but what could she do? What could she do?

Her stare shifted to Frances; he was just a dark shadow now. She could just make out the outline of his face, darker shadows against lighter ones. The saboteur. All this time. He had been right beside her. Her mind screamed at the dishonor of it. And yet, he was her brother. It wasn't right!

She should tell Griffin.

Frances walked away, back toward their tent.

She looked at Griffin's tent. Indecision plagued her. She should tell Griffin about the cut reins. But that was how this all started. With her doing something she had no place doing. By taking the field of honor, she had set this all into motion. And now, it was time for her to undo that.

She stood for a moment longer, torn. It wasn't her place. It wasn't a woman's place to warn a man that the saboteur had struck. She turned to walk away. Griffin had tried all this time to teach her a woman's place. A woman's place was not in the affairs of men. Tears stung her eyes, wavering the darkness before her.

He had tried to teach her that women should not know about swordplay or jousting or any of the concerns of men. That women were just docile and amiable and compliant.

She froze. But he had failed. He had failed because she was not like that. And she would not stand by and let this happen.

She turned back to the reins. This was wrong. It was not the right way to win. And everything inside her, everything she was, could not let this happen. Not even if it meant losing the joust. Not even if it meant spending the winter in the open.

Tears streamed down her cheeks, but she lifted her chin in determination. Because she knew what she was going to do. It was the only thing she could do.

Layne glanced over her shoulder looking for Frances, but he was all the way across the clearing, almost to the family tent. She saw his silhouetted form moving toward their tent. She waited a moment more until he ducked beneath the flap and disappeared into the tent.

Then she bent down to the reins. She ran a hand across her cheek, wiping away the tears, and picked up the reins. She ran her finger along the flat side until she found the cut. She looked at it. Yes. It was just like before. Cut enough so that it would fail and rip and be mistaken for a tear. But Griffin knew of the sabotage. He knew. Would he have caught this if she left it? It didn't matter. Because she had no intention of leaving it.

She stood and turned...

...to find Griffin standing there. The moonlight shone on his face dully, making him appear pale.

"Layne?" His gaze dropped to her hands. He took the reins from her limp and trembling fingers. He inspected them, running his hand along them until they snagged on the cut.

Slowly, he lifted his gaze to pin her to the spot. It was like a physical slap. She stepped back.

His brow scowled and he lifted dark eyes to her. "It's you. You are the saboteur."

CHAPTER THIRTY

Griffin stared at her in disbelief, partially because he didn't want to be right and partially because he feared that he was. The reins were cut, the very reins she was holding!

"No," she gasped. "I didn't cut them."

"Then what are you doing here, holding them?"

"I was taking them away. I knew they were cut. And I didn't want you hurt."

"Enough!" he growled. "Enough of your lies."

She reeled as though he had struck her.

He stalked forward and she backed away. He was angry with himself for believing her, angry because he had succumbed to her lies. Angry that he still wanted to believe them, even now when the proof was in his hand! She was the saboteur. He held out the reins. "You cut these, knowing what would happen."

"I didn't cut them. I came here because I saw someone."

"No more, Layne. No more lies. I have the proof I was looking for. I knew you couldn't be trusted. From the first moment you took your brother's place on the field of honor." He whirled away from her.

"You never looked for proof! It's what you've always wanted to see! You've blamed me from the beginning! You refuse to believe that a woman could be better at something than a man. You refuse to believe that I could be."

"You're not!" He turned to her thrusting out the reins. "And this is proof."

"I tried to stop him. I tried to make him stop. But he wouldn't listen, either. He wouldn't listen to me. Just like you. And I don't know what to do. I don't know --" Her voice caught, and she fought to hold down a sob. She blinked back the glimmering tears in her eyes.

Griffin had seen Gwen use tears to soften him, but Layne's tears pulled on his heart. He wanted to give in to her reason; he wanted to believe her. But he stood before her with the cut reins in his hand; the physical proof told him she was lying. His fingers tightened around the reins with conviction. His jaw clenched. Betrayal burned through his body. All this time he had been worried about her and Ethan, but this... This was a worse treachery. She was honorless.

She ran a sleeve across her nose. "They're my family. And I would never betray them." Her body shook with a repressed sob. "But I can't betray you, either." She looked down as if embarrassed. "I love you, Griffin."

Startled, Griffin reared back. She loved him? But how...? Why...? Then the anger crashed down again, threatening to wipe away any softness that might have started to creep into his heart. He had heard those words before. From Jacquelyn when she was manipulating him. She had said those very words to him one night before she took Richard into her bed. But this was Layne. Layne Fletcher. The one woman he so very much wanted to believe. The one woman who had never done or said a deceitful thing in all the time she had been with him. He squeezed his fist. Except this. Had she been untruthful the entire time she was with him? From the very beginning?

"They're desperate to win," she whispered, her shoulders slumped. "*We* are desperate to win. It's our last chance. Frances's last chance. But this isn't the way. This is wrong."

Griffin's gaze swept her. The sorrow in her voice pushed back the anger that had been storming inside him. There was genuine regret in her voice. A true pain in her words.

"I'll go to the dungeon, if you want me to, if you don't believe me."

The dungeon. Griffin had never wanted that for her. Not for a woman. Even one that was dishonest.

She stepped past him.

He looked down at the leather straps in his hand. "If you did not do it, who did? Who cut them?"

She didn't look up at him. An abyss of secrets separated them. "I can't tell you." And she moved off, toward her own tent.

Griffin ran his thumb over the straps, scowling. The evidence was here. It had been in her hands. She must have cut them. She was the only one here. Was it only in his mind that he wanted her to be innocent? The proof was right in front of him.

She must have cut them. She... What had she said? Something about her family? And being desperate. Every knight was desperate to win. She couldn't tell him who had cut them. If she didn't cut them, who would she protect? Who...?

He stiffened with realization. Her brothers. Family. They were the only ones she would do anything to protect. Tingles raced across the nape of his neck. She couldn't betray them. They were desperate to win. They. Her brothers. Griffin's scowl deepened.

Layne dropped to her bottom outside of their pavilion, and wept. She couldn't do it. It went against everything she knew to be right. Everything she thought she was. But now she was unfaithful to her family. Where was the honor in that? Where was her loyalty? The tears continued to fall.

"Layne?"

She recognized Colin's voice, but couldn't even look at him. "You told him to cut them," she whispered in a ragged voice. She adored Colin, revered him as honorable. She felt a deep level of sadness she had never felt in her entire life. She couldn't believe he had told Frances to do something so dishonorable. That was the worst betrayal of all.

The silence stretched.

"What did you do?"

Layne looked up at Frances. She didn't bother to wipe away the raw streaks of tears lining her face. Colin stood beside him. Michael was in back of them, just coming out of the tent. Her family. She stood to her feet. "I told him."

"You told him what I did?"

"Is that what you think I would do?" She wiped at the salty taste that tainted the corners of her lips.

"I don't know. I don't know what you would do

where Wolfe is concerned," Frances said, brushing past Colin to face her in growing anger.

"I told him about the cut reins," Layne said with more conviction. Each word felt like a slice to her heart. Like a betrayal to her family.

"Why did you do that?" Colin asked, mystified.

"Because that's not the way to win. You don't cheat and risk someone else's life. You don't cut the reins!"

"You've ruined our chance," Frances said softly. "It was our only chance." His fists clenched and he stepped toward her. "You've ruined our chance at winning because of your feelings for Wolfe!"

"It has nothing to do with my feelings for Griffin and everything to do with honor! I couldn't live knowing that we won by deceit. I would rather rot in a dungeon cell."

"I hope your high morals will feed us this winter. I hope your chivalry will keep us warm when we are out on the road!" Frances's words were biting sarcasm. "Where is your loyalty to our family! *We* are what is important! And now you've endangered us all!"

Colin stepped between them. "Enough Frances."

"This is all because of you!" Frances continued his tirade. "We are in more debt than we can ever repay! We'll never win this tourney now because you told Wolfe! Our family would be better if you weren't in it!"

Layne's mouth dropped in a gasp. She took a step back as if he had hit her. He was right. He was so right. She whirled and dashed away into the night.

"Layne!" Colin called.

But she didn't stop running. She didn't belong there. She never had.

CHAPTER THIRTY-ONE

"**L**ayne!"

Griffin heard Colin's call and emerged from the tent to see three shadows standing near the Fletcher tent.

One of them separated and ran into the darkness.

Griffin jogged over to the tent.

"Get out of here, Wolfe!" Frances snapped as he neared.

Griffin ignored him to look at Colin. "What's wrong?"

"Family quarrel," Frances growled. "Mind your own business."

Griffin knew for a fact the man he sought now stood before him. Michael couldn't have cut the reins with his injured hand. Colin couldn't have walked far from the tent with his wounded leg. Griffin glared at Frances. The saboteur. He stifled the burning impulse to bury his fist straight into France's face. He clenched his hand, but left his arm hanging down by his side.

"Where's Layne?" he demanded.

"She ran off," Colin told him.

Griffin whirled to look into the night. She had been hurt by his insult. He had seen it in the tears on her face, heard it in her voice.

"I sent Michael after her," Colin said, striking his own wounded leg viciously. "She was really upset."

A sense of dread tightened the muscles in Griffin's entire body.

Lightning split the sky in the distance.

"She'll be fine," Frances insisted.

Griffin spun on him. "A woman alone in the dark? Sometimes you Fletchers forget that Layne is a woman. And there are worse things she might face alone in the dark." He pointed at Colin. "Wake Carlton. Tell him to gather as many men as he can to look for her."

Colin nodded and began to hobble across the clearing.

Griffin started to walk in the direction Layne had gone. Where would she go? There were men out there who were still angry with what she had done on the jousting field. She was in the dark. There were all kinds of danger out there. She was alone. The memory of her bloodied head came to his mind. He began to run.

A rumble of thunder rolled through the night sky.

Layne ran and ran. She didn't know where she was going and with any luck she wouldn't know where she was when she finally stopped. *'Our family would be better if you weren't in it'*. Frances's words replayed again and again in her mind. She thought of Michael's hand. And Colin's leg. No, she told herself firmly. Colin's leg was not her fault.

But Osmont had delivered the blow. Maybe he wouldn't have been so brutal if he wasn't so angry with her. Maybe...

She stopped to catch her breath, leaning against a tree, and looked at the sky through the leaves of the trees. Lightning lit the sky in a blanket of white. Griffin thought she was the one who had sabotaged him. Her! She thought he knew her. She thought of all men, he would have taken her side. But he had accused her instead. He didn't believe her. He never believed her.

She pushed herself from the tree and ran on as thunder boomed around her. She couldn't run fast enough to forget that he wanted nothing to do with her. She wasn't good enough to present to his family. She couldn't run fast enough to erase the memory of his tender kiss on her lips.

Lightning split the sky again, crashing to earth with a large boom.

Layne covered her ears and ran. She turned a corner and stumbled, falling to the dirt. She lifted her face. The first large drops pelted her. At first, she thought a person stood before her and she startled, but then she slowly realized it wasn't a real person. It was the quintain. She turned her head. The empty berfrois was to her right. She followed the darker shadow of the fence around the field. Lightning forked in the sky, splitting the darkness and opening the night. Rain fell in a drenching downpour as she realized she was in the field of honor. She didn't remember passing through the gate that led out into the field, but somehow she must have, because here she stood.

Slowly, she stood to her feet. The sheets of rain blurred her vision of the quintain. The downpour plastered her hair to her forehead. She brushed the soaked strands aside and sloshed through the quickly growing mud to the quintain. She stared up at it for a long moment. Just a dummy. A toy for the knights to practice with. An emotionless block of wood. Griffin had destroyed it. Her brothers had struck it. The other knights had cursed it. And it just came back for more, again and again.

Thunder cracked above her, rocking the ground below her feet.

But this was his field as much as it was the knights' field. This was where the quintain belonged.

Just like her.

She reached out and ran her hand against the wet wood. She may not be a knight, but she belonged here as much as they did. She squared her shoulders.

"Layne?"

She whirled to find Griffin standing behind her. She wiped the rain from her eyes. He looked like a soggy dog. His blonde hair hung at either side of his face; his eyes narrowed against the deluge.

"I didn't cut your reins," she insisted, having to raise her voice against the rain.

"I know."

"You shouldn't treat me like a criminal." She lifted her chin. "I deserve more respect. I've put up with a lot from you. From my brothers." She swept her arm around, encompassing the rest of the field. "From all the knights."

"I know."

She stepped forward to poke him in the chest. "I don't care what Frances says. I do a lot for my family. I take care of them. I protect them and I make sure they are all safe. And sometimes that's not so easy. I am part of the family whether he likes it or not. Because I love every one of them! And I would do anything for them."

"I know."

"And I should be able to sword fight and joust and do anything I want with weapons. Maybe not on the field of honor, but in practice and I should be able to brush Adonis and clean your weapons and --"

Griffin grabbed her and pulled her close to him, covering her mouth with his.

At first she resisted, but then Layne melted against his strength, letting the fight drift away. She wrapped her arms around his body, his strength, and held tight. He brushed his lips against hers, coaxing them open, and thrust his tongue into her mouth, tasting her. His kiss was gentle and tender and demanding. Everything that was Griffin.

He showered kisses on her lips, down her throat. "You're right," he said between each touch of his lips. "You should be allowed to be yourself. You are magnificent."

Shocked, she pulled back to look into his eyes. "You're embarrassed of me."

He took her head between his hands. "I'm a dolt to even think that I was embarrassed of you. You are exceptional. The rarest of beauties in spirit and in mind. If I was embarrassed, it was because I couldn't match up to your enthusiasm. You are a treasure. I've missed you so, Layne."

For a moment, Layne thought she was dreaming. How could he think she was anything but ordinary? She cocked her head at him and looked at him doubtfully. "Have you been drinking?"

He chuckled warmly. "Nay."

The rain suddenly lessened, and the clouds parted to let the moon's light to shine down on them.

Griffin wiped the rain from her cheeks and her forehead and pushed her hair from her face. "I'm sorry for ever doubting you. I know you would never do something dishonorable. I think I've known that from the beginning. Can you ever forgive me?"

Every caress, every touch made her tingle with life and happiness. "Well..."

"I thought of you as a threat to all that I am. To my winning the tournaments, to my family. But in reality, you have only been a blessing to me. At every turn, you have proved yourself. And you have proved me wrong." He kissed her lips tenderly. "You are my strength."

Joy bubbled from Layne's lips.

"I love you, Layne," Griffin whispered showering her with kisses.

Layne pressed her lips to his. She wasn't sure that this wasn't a dream, but she was sure she never wanted to awaken, if it was. Sudden need and desire flamed inside her and she pulled him tight against her. Their clothing was wet, and it was almost like there was nothing between them. He was hot and strong and sheltering. His kiss sent waves of excitement crashing through her. His hands traced her arms, over her hips. Lord, she wanted more.

Griffin stepped back.

A soft groan of protest escaped her lips.

His eyes moved over her face, devouring ever curve. "When I make you mine, it will not be on the field of honor." He grinned at her. "You are soaked through to the bone. We should find you warm clothing before you catch your death of cold."

She blinked, unable to comprehend the sudden turn of events. Griffin put an arm around her shoulders and pulled her close to him as they turned toward the tents.

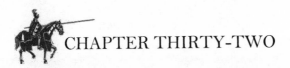# CHAPTER THIRTY-TWO

𝕱rances stared down the field at Talvace. He had defeated the knight before but felt distracted this time. He had trouble getting Sprite to settle down. Maybe the horse was feeling his anxiety. He had to win.

He looked down at Michael who handed his lance up to him.

Sprite still stepped backward, and Frances had to kick him extra hard to get him to start down the lists toward Talvace. Maybe the horse felt as he did? Too much riding on his shoulders.

Frances leaned forward, couching the lance beneath his arm. He stared hard at Talvace, trying desperately to focus. It was no good. He didn't have a good grip or a good angle. At the last moment, he swerved his horse slightly, throwing his lance aside. He passed Talvace, who lifted his lance and rode past him. It wasn't unusual for a knight to give way. And it was customary for the opponent to lift his lance, too. Talvace was a tough opponent, but he did play by the rules. Yes, he did play by the rules. Unlike you, a voice inside him said. He didn't need to cheat to win, did he?

Frances wasn't sure if he could concentrate enough. He came around the field to his side where Michael greeted him with a worried frown. He looked at Talvace across the field. He had won against him before. I can do it again, he told himself. He took the lance from Michael. He could do this. He spurred his horse and lowered the lance. He could unhorse Talvace. He just needed to focus and put the lance tip right beneath his opponent's left shoulder. The force would whirl him from his horse like it had before. Just beneath the left shoulder.

Finally, Sprite moved forward in a steady beat.

Frances pointed the lance and steadied it for a direct hit.

Griffin watched Frances ride from the field. His shoulders were slumped, his head hung. That was not at all the way a victor should be riding. What had gotten into him? He had unhorsed Talvace with a solid strike, yet he was leaving the field as if he had lost.

"Ah, Griffin."

Griffin turned away from the field to see Richard approaching him. Over his shoulder, he saw Jacquelyn speaking to lord Tinley. She had her hand on his arm and was leaning into him with a lowered seductive look Griffin recognized immediately. He frowned. He didn't want a marriage like theirs. Both of them were unhappy in so many different ways.

Richard placed an arm about his shoulders and led him away from the berfrois, away from the crowd. "You are to joust against me and then I will joust against

Fletcher."

Griffin chortled. "You have that wrong. The victor, which will be me, shall joust Fletcher." In reality, Griffin was surprised Richard had made it this far.

"We shall see." He slapped him on the back and stopped to look at him. "Like old times, eh?"

Griffin nodded. He was excited about jousting against his brother; it was something they hadn't done for a long time. He had no doubt he would win, and the thought of knocking Richard on his overconfident arse to claim victory was even more appealing.

"I heard you spoke with Father."

"Spying on me?" Griffin wondered.

Richard cocked a one-sided smile. "I have spies all over. I know everything that goes on in our family. I know much more than you think."

Griffin looked at him. Was he that shrewd or did he really know everything?

"Father is ailing. He is not the man he once was."

"Perhaps not."

"His primary concern is the family and protecting the castle."

Griffin agreed with a nod. "And those are proper concerns, don't you think?"

Richard stared hard at him, that grin of his locked in place. "He told you about the perfume from France."

"Aye," Griffin said.

Richard rolled his eyes. "You know how Jacquelyn is. She wants what she wants. And she's very good at getting it."

"Maybe too good." The rivalry between them raised its ugly head and Griffin felt the stirrings of resentment. "Is it true, Richard? You'd rather be jousting than lord of the castle?"

Richard smiled and purposely ignored the question. "Our bet is still on."

Griffin frowned.

"Surely, you remember, Griffin. The bet we made two years ago before you ran off to play in the jousts?"

"Of course." He remembered the bet. He remembered it very vividly. They had made it right before he left the castle, right after Richard begged and pleaded with him not to go. But at the time, he had to leave. His brother's betrayal had struck him deeply. He had to escape from Father, Jacquelyn and especially from his own brother. He had to get away from all of them. Griffin agreed to the bet so he could be away from Richard. The emotional cut was nothing more than an old wound now; the scar would always be there, but the pain had faded. Regardless of that, the bet had been made and he would honor it.

"I do have to say that when we first made it, I didn't think it would last this long."

"I thought that was why you decided to host this tournament. To see if you couldn't help the others beat me."

Richard shrugged. "Truth be told, it was father's idea to host the tournament. I was more than happy to oblige him."

Tremors of apprehension snaked through Griffin. "Father's idea?"

Richard shrugged. "I wasn't going to argue with him. I was quite surprised, too. But who am I to argue?"

Who indeed? Was Richard better then he was letting on? Was that the reason Father wanted him to host the tournament? Or was it simply a chance to speak with him again?

"Be prepared, brother. I grow weary of being lord. When you lose, you take my place."

"*If* I lose, was the bet we made."

"*If* and *when*," Richard agreed.

Layne ducked into the tent to find Carlton buckling on Griffin's vambrace. Griffin held his arm out for Carlton. He was almost totally covered in plate armor except for his head.

She stopped when she entered and grinned as her gaze swept over him. He was splendid, strong and gloriously to behold. She would never grow tired of looking at him. Her gaze slid to his face. His blonde hair was pulled back and tied with a leather strip. His blue eyes bore into her and a grin twitched the corners of his lips.

When Carlton finished with his arms, Griffin said, "Carlton, go prepare Adonis. Layne will finish with my armor."

Layne's mouth dropped in her joy as she actually inhaled with excitement.

Carlton nodded and left the tent.

Layne moved over to where Carlton had the remaining pieces laid out. He had done a marvelous job of caring for them and keeping them clean.

"When you are ready," Griffin said, laughter and sarcasm in his voice. "An entire field of spectators is waiting."

Layne quickly picked up one of Griffin's gauntlets. She held it out for him so he could slip his hand inside. She pulled it up so it was nice and snug on his hand. When she looked up, he was gazing at her with an intense, heated stare that sent a thrill through her body.

She quickly turned away, feeling a rush of excitement from his look. "You should concentrate on your joust. Actually, that's why I came." She picked up his other gauntlet. He held out his hand and she slipped it over his fingers. "I know you joust against your brother today. And I know how much you would like to win."

"All combatants would like to win. But you are correct. I would like to knock him on his arse."

Layne grinned. "Now is that because he is lord or your brother? Or both?"

"Because he is my brother. I have never beaten him in a joust."

"You lost to him?" Layne was shocked. She had always known him to beat all that stood against him.

"You sound surprised. I could not win every joust. I was young, once. And rash and not as well trained as I am now."

Layne grinned. "Sounds like excuses."

"Perhaps. But I suppose there was a time when you could best Frances."

Layne agreed as she checked his buckles. "There was. Until he grew taller than me. And stronger."

"Sounds like excuses to me."

She smiled. "I guess we grow into our roles." She stepped back. "I may not be able to best Frances, but I can certainly see other things. Ways others can beat you."

"Me?"

She bent and picked up his helmet. "When you first jousted me, I did see something. The way you joust.

You aim for the stomach and then at the last moment, shift to the shoulder. You do it every time."

Griffin scowled as she said the words.

She could almost see him thinking about what he did when he jousted. She handed his helmet to him. "It's something you should be cautious of. Your brother might not be as gentle as I was."

Griffin laughed out loud as she turned toward the tent flap.

She stopped in the doorway. "Be careful."

"Thank you, Layne."

The visor only allowed Griffin to see directly in front of him. The roar of the crowd was distant. He could hear his breathing in the metal helmet. His hair was wet from sweat, but he had learned long ago to place a rag beneath his helmet to help collect the moisture. It didn't stop the beads from running down his forehead.

At the other end of the field, Richard's horse danced beneath him. He knew the animal; it was Richard's favorite. A black warhorse. Adonis's brother. He knew the animal was as powerful as his, but he doubted it had a stronger connection to its rider. Richard let others tend to the animal after tourneys. He had little emotional bond with the horse.

Carlton handed him the lance. He gripped it firmly, then he nudged Adonis. The warhorse started down the list, charging faster with each footfall.

Griffin couched his lance and held it upright until he and Adonis got into their rhythm together, moving as one. When he was close enough, he lowered the lance, aiming toward his brother. The lance moved slightly up and down, but Griffin held it tight, steadying it.

Richard lowered his lance, pointing the blunted tip at Griffin.

Griffin leaned forward to get the first and best blow. His lance struck Richard a glancing blow to his shoulder and teetered off.

A punishing strike hit Griffin's stomach, so hard that he felt himself being pushed back, both from the impetus of his blow to Richard's arm and from the slam to his stomach. He grabbed onto the reins and held firmly, using his knees to hold onto Adonis and keep his seat. He gasped for a moment, trying to catch his breath. His brother was not making this easy.

Adonis instinctively rode to the other side. Griffin circled the horse until he caught his breath. *Looks like Richard really doesn't want to be lord any longer.*

The problem was Griffin didn't want to be lord either. Through the slit in his visor, he looked down the field at his brother. His silver armor glinted in the sunlight. *He knows my moves. He trained with me for a long time. How can I beat him?*

Griffin reached down for his lance. He charged down the field, holding the lance upright before lowering it. *He knows all my moves. He knows how I joust.* He held the lance couched in his arm.

They struck almost simultaneously. Griffin felt the impact push him back against the cantle of the saddle. Griffin's strike again hit Richard's shoulder. Pain flared up from Griffin's side. He grimaced as the numbness spread through his body before fading.

Same thing, he thought. *I hit the same place. And*

then Layne's words came to him. *'You aim for the stomach and then at the last moment, shift to the shoulder.'* Two shoulder hits. And Richard knew it. He knew what to expect. He was shielding his arm, turning it slightly away from Griffin's hits so it slid off.

Griffin grit his teeth. Time to change strategies. Keep it aimed at his stomach. He took the lance from Carlton and spurred Adonis down the lists. He moved the lance down from the ready position and couched it, aiming it dead center at Richard's stomach.

The horses closed.

Griffin leaned in and feigned a slight movement upwards of his lance, hoping to take advantage of Richard's expectations. Richard took the bait, raising his arm to deflect it. Instead, Griffin kept the lance low, delivering a solid, lance-splintering strike to Richard's mid-section. The blow pushed Richard up and back. Because Griffin struck first, Richard's lance missed him altogether.

Griffin reined in Adonis and turned to find Richard in the dirt on his buttocks, mud splattered up over his shiny armor. He cantered Adonis down the side of the field, looking up toward the castle. His father stood in the open window of his room, watching.

Griffin grinned inside his helmet. Whatever his father had planned, it had just failed.

Layne could barely contain herself. She placed her hands together and grinned proudly. She kept her lips pressed together so she would keep her joy silent. Everyone in the berfrois was silent.

Prince Edward stood to his feet. "Well done, Sir

Griffin. Well done!" He clapped. All around him joined in.

Gwen leaned over to Layne. "I don't imagine Richard will be happy about that."

Layne glanced at Jacquelyn who sat in Richard's chair. She leaned back in utter disappointment. "Richard did a marvelous job," Layne said to her to ease her displeasure. "At least he wasn't hurt."

Jacquelyn glanced at her with disgust, shot to her feet and left the stand.

Griffin rode by the berfrois. Layne smiled at him and he bowed his head before cantering Adonis out of the field.

"Well, now we have our two best jousters left," Gwen said. "Who will you be favoring?"

All of her joy evaporated. Her smile slid away. Dread slithered across Layne's shoulders as she looked at Frances standing beside her. They had not said more than a few words to each other after his damning outburst. His gaze was locked on Griffin's retreating back. His jaw was tight, but there was something in his eyes that Layne didn't recognize, something sad.

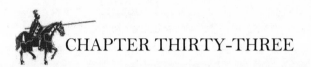 CHAPTER THIRTY-THREE

Layne sat outside the tent, running a cloth along Frances's armor. He hadn't said a word to her all day. She knew he was nervous about the final joust. The joust with Griffin that would decide the tournament champion. And the fate and future of their entire family. As much as she wanted to root for Frances, she wanted Griffin to win, too. She sighed softly. Here she was, silently cheering for her own future and against it all at the same time.

"Good day, Layne."

Layne looked up to see Ethan standing before her. She stood up. It had been a while since she had spoke to him. "Good day, Ethan." She noticed he held the reins of his horse. She also noticed the saddlebags on the rump of the animal.

He nodded when she glanced at him. "It's time for me to head home."

"Home? Don't you want to see who wins the tournament?"

"Either way, there will be heartache that I don't

280

want to share." He smiled. "I'm a bit selfish that way." He shrugged. "I haven't seen my family in a very long time. And, well, spending time with you and your brothers has gotten me missing them."

Layne nodded. She certainly understood that. "If your family is anything like mine, when you get there you might wish you were back here."

Ethan chuckled.

He was very handsome. His eyes sparkled in the sun and dimples appeared in his cheeks. But Layne saw him more as a brother. "I can't thank you enough for everything you've done for me," Layne said.

"You don't have to."

"You know we will pay back the loan as soon as we are able."

Ethan shook his head. "Your debt has been settled."

Layne scowled at him.

"Griffin has paid the debt." He lifted his shoulders. "He said he didn't want you in debt to me. And he can be... convincing."

"He didn't tell me."

"I imagine he didn't want you to know. It's my going away present to him. And to you. Griffin has been my friend for a very long time. And despite all he's done, I still consider him a friend. He's a good man, Layne. He could use a woman like you."

"I know that. But he still wants his proper lady." She knew she could be that and more.

"Convince him otherwise. I think inside, he wants you to." Ethan laughed softly. "He's always leaned more toward the traditional." He tucked a lock of her hair behind her ear. "And you are anything but traditional. I think you will add a spice of flavor to his otherwise boring life."

Layne grinned at him and shuffled her feet. "I'll take that as a compliment."

"You're welcome."

She threw her arms around him, hugging him tight.

Ethan returned her embrace. "If you are ever in Woodland Hills, come and visit me."

Layne nodded and watched him walk away before she bent and continued to shine Frances's armor. She already knew that Ethan was right. Griffin loved her. And that was all she could ask for.

Layne brushed down Frances's horse, preparing it for the joust. She had inspected and cleaned its hooves. She checked for injuries, but the horse was in perfect condition, more than ready for the joust. She just wasn't sure that Frances was. She heard him talking to Colin and he sounded very unlike his normal confident self.

Michael and Colin were inside the tent, trying to reassure him and get his conviction back up.

The final joust. Layne knew that Frances had to win. Her joyful mood had rapidly changed to apprehension. She glanced in the direction of Griffin's tent. She wanted to go to him and congratulate him, but she knew how inappropriate that would be. She belonged here with her family. She should be encouraging Frances, not longing for Griffin.

Frances emerged from the tent. He sat down heavily on the ground near the tent.

Layne continued to comb his steed, but she cast

him furtive glances. "Shouldn't you be preparing or something?"

"Preparing for what?" he asked bitterly. "How to fall?"

Layne dropped her hand. "Don't say that. You can beat him. I know you can."

"Do you really want me to?"

A twist of guilt stabbed her heart. "You have to."

Frances ran his hands through his hair. "I'm sorry, Layne. I am. I just... I can't do it."

Layne sighed and sat beside him.

"And don't go telling me I can. I've had enough from Colin."

"It doesn't matter if you can or not. You have to."

"And how am I supposed to unhorse him? Colin was always the better jouster. He had the best chance. How can I..." He shook his head.

Layne knew deep down that he was right. Colin had always been their best chance at defeating Griffin. Frances was nowhere near as good as he was. But she was not about to speak that truth aloud. Not now. "You've gotten this far."

"But I've never beaten Wolfe!"

"None of us have."

"You did."

More guilt settled about her shoulders. "That was hardly beating. You cut the stirrup leather."

Frances shook his head. "You still had the courage to face him confidently. Not like me."

Layne chuckled. "I don't know if it was confidence or that I was just so excited to be jousting in a real joust." She looked at him closely. The rings were dark under his eyes; strained tightness thinned his lips. The weight of everything was on his shoulders. She wished she could tell him it didn't matter, but it did. "Are you afraid of him?"

"No!" Frances's shoulders slumped. "Not of him. Of the fact that I simply can't lose. This is our last chance. The very last and it's all up to me. Me. What can I do against such a skilled knight?"

"You can beat him." She knew her victory had been tainted, but she had to do something to get Frances's hopes up. "I beat him." The words tasted sour as she spoke them, but Frances needed to hear them.

Frances looked at her with a strange light in his eyes. Realization. Hope. "You did. You beat him. Tell me how to do it. Did you see a flaw in his jousting? There must be something I can use to defeat him."

Layne was torn. She didn't want to betray Griffin, but this was Frances and he was in such agony. Her brother was under so much pressure. Layne considered making something up. Just to give Frances hope. Just to give him a chance. But in the end, it could backfire. She sighed softly and plucked a blade of grass from the ground between her legs. "He corrected the only flaw I saw when he jousted against his brother."

Frances dropped his head into his hands. "Then there's no hope."

"Stop it. You have to look at his style. Watch him. I found a way to unhorse him. You can, too."

Frances looked at her, his gaze sweeping her from head to toe. "You did. You saw what no one else could. You beat him. Laynie, that's it! You do it. You take my place!"

Layne's mouth dropped. She shot to her feet, shaking her head. She spread her hands before her as if they could erase even the suggestion. "No. No. That's how all of this started. I'll not take your place."

Frances grabbed her hand. "It's the only way, Layne! You've got a better eye than anyone else! You can find the flaw! You have to! You have to do it."

"No. No." She tried to pull her arm free, but he held it tightly. Her heart twisted; her stomach clenched. Everything in her cried not to do this.

"Please. Layne. I can't win. I can't. But you can. You're better than me. I knew it the day when Colin told me how good you were. You have to do this."

Layne stopped struggling. Compliments from her brother. He must be telling the truth. Or he was that distressed. "Don't ask me to do this. Don't."

"I can't do it. You can. You can beat Wolfe."

Layne's heart twisted. Maybe she could. But she didn't want to. He began to pull her inside of the tent.

"For the family. You owe it to the family."

"It has been a glorious competition!" Richard's voice rang through the jousting field. He addressed the amassed crowd from the berfrois. He was elegantly dressed in an immaculate blue houppelande.

Lords and ladies, merchants, knights and peasants had come to see the final joust, all congregating on the grassy plains around the field of honor. On the berfrois, Prince Edward sat with the most distinguished of the visiting lords and ladies. Jacquelyn sat straight as a board beside Richard, gazing out over the field. Next to her, Gwen sat, her chin held high.

"The best have made a long track to Woodstock --"

A thunderous cheer went up from the villagers.

"-- to participate in the greatest tourney to ever

grace these great lands. The skill shown by our competing knights has been unequaled. Most have fallen, eliminated one by one, until only two remain. On this most excellent day I give you the final two competitors!"

A roar of approval erupted throughout the field.

Just one more victory, Griffin thought. That's all it would take, and he would be free of his bet with Richard. He would not have to be lord. He could be with Layne and they could make their fortune from jousting. The last thing he wanted to do was be away from her.

He stared down the field at Frances. His horse was still, his helm lowered.

Griffin reined Adonis into a circle. He seemed nervous, maybe detecting his own anxiety. Griffin looked at the berfrois. Richard, Gwen and Jacquelyn sat there. Where was Layne? Why wasn't she there? And her brothers were strangely absent. Why weren't they here to support Frances?

As Griffin rode Adonis alongside of Carlton, the boy handed Griffin the lance. He quickly turned the horse and spurred Adonis.

Frances charged toward him, his horse kicking up mud behind him. He lowered his lance, as did Griffin.

Griffin had him well targeted, directly aimed at his chest, but at the last moment Frances leaned away from Griffin's lance, making him miss entirely.

Frances's lance struck his shoulder firmly. The impact knocked him back, but it did not have enough force to knock him out of the saddle. He grimaced against the sudden pain jarring his shoulder. He tossed his lance aside and rode down the list. He hit him! Frances had actually landed a blow! Anger surged through Griffin, but he forced it down. It would only mar his judgment. He rounded Adonis at the end of the list and rode back to his side of the field.

As he passed Frances, he looked at him. Time slowed. Blue eyes shone at him through the visor. It was all he had time to register before he passed him.

Griffin rounded Adonis. He took a moment to stare at his opponent. Blue eyes. He reached for his lance...

...and froze. It couldn't be. Blue eyes.

"M'lord," Carlton called.

Griffin took the lance. His insides shuddered with uncertainty. He glanced at the berfrois again. The Fletchers were not in attendance. Griffin looked down the lists. Only Michael stood as squire. Griffin's chest tightened in dread.

He looked down the field to see his opponent rushing toward him.

He spurred Adonis instinctively. It couldn't be. She wouldn't! He lowered the lance. He had to see. He had to know. He threw his lance aside and pushed her lance away from him, staring as he rode past.

The crowd around him gasped.

She didn't look at him.

He quickly rode Adonis around her side of the field, glaring at Michael. Michael wouldn't meet his gaze as he passed, and he turned to ride down the list. He slowed Adonis as he neared her. When she met his eyes, he knew. He would recognize those eyes anywhere. Layne! It was Layne! He reined Adonis so he was cantering next to her toward her side of the field. Why? Why was she doing this? Didn't she know what could happen if she was discovered? Of course she knew! She had done this before. During the last joust with him. Didn't the dungeon or a fine hold any threat? Why was she doing this?

Griffin turned Adonis back to his side of the field.

The crowd around the field of honor mumbled with confusion.

He turned Adonis to look down the field to Layne. How could she do this?

How could he? God's blood! How could he joust against her when he might seriously injure her? Didn't she know? Didn't she know that if she jousted him, he could harm her? And if he didn't joust her, he would lose.

And he would spend a lifetime without her.

Griffin paced Adonis back and forth along his side of the field, staring at her. How could he joust her? He would never raise the lance to her. She could be hurt. Her image overlapped Colin's in his mind. She was the one laying on the ground with the splintered lance in her leg. He grimaced. He couldn't do it.

How could he not? If he didn't win, he would have to take over as lord of the castle in Richard's place. He would never see her again. An ache rose in his chest. He would never see her again. Yet, he couldn't risk hurting her, killing her. He wouldn't! It wasn't worth it. He might not be able to see her, to be with her in the tourneys, but she would not be hurt.

She would at least be alive.

With a heavy heart, he took the lance from Carlton. For a long moment, he steadied Adonis with the lance in the upright position. He stared at her. Why would she force him to do this? It didn't matter. He would never hurt her.

He slowly lowered the lance to point it at the

ground in forfeit.

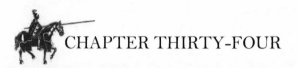 CHAPTER THIRTY-FOUR

Layne quickly rode Angel from the silent, stunned field. She couldn't be caught there. She rode hard back to the pavilion. Griffin had forfeit. And she knew why. Because he knew it was her. There could be no other explanation.

Colin met her outside the tent. "What happened?"

Layne dismounted and entered the tent, removing the helmet. Frances stood from where he was lounging on his mat. Colin entered the tent.

"Griffin forfeit," Layne said with a heaviness she couldn't hide.

There was a long moment of silence.

"You won," Frances gasped.

Yes. She won. But she didn't feel like she won. There was a heaviness in her chest. Griffin had forfeit.

"Hurry," Colin said, lifting Layne's arm. "Get this armor on Frances. They'll be expecting him." He began to unbuckle the armor.

Frances lifted her other arm and began to

remove the armor. "You won," he repeated, shocked.

"No," Layne whispered. "Griffin forfeit."

"We still get the purse."

A lump rose in Layne's throat, cutting off any words she could say. Tears rose in her eyes. Why would he forfeit? Why would he do that? He was jousting in front of his family, to win their respect. And now he had just thrown it all way. Because of her. She knew how much it meant to him to be the best. She locked eyes with Colin for a quick moment before she looked away.

"We won!" Frances hollered.

Then why did Layne feel like she lost?

As soon as the final stage in their deception was complete and they had gotten the armor on Frances, Layne dashed across the clearing to Griffin's tent. She shoved the flap aside.

Griffin stood in the middle of the tent, in full armor, his back to her.

"Griffin," she gasped.

"Why did you do it?" His words were soft, laced with disappointment and resolve.

His broken words were too much for her. Anger surged inside of her. "Why did you give up? Why didn't you fight? Why did you let me win?"

He shook his head. "It wasn't worth hurting you."

Her heart squeezed. She had broken the trust they had built. "Frances asked me. I wanted to tell you. But there was no time."

"Was it worth risking your life?"

She considered his words. If they didn't win,

they would be out in the cold. Not just her, but Michael and her father. All of them! "Yes," she said softly. "I couldn't say no to him, to my family. They needed me."

Griffin turned to her. There was such sadness in his eyes that she felt a keen sense of grief. "And what of me? I needed to trust that you would not joust again, not because it was the knightly code, but because it endangered your life."

"I would do anything for you! But I couldn't turn my back on my family. I couldn't let them be out in the cold. We needed to win that purse!"

"It will always be your family before me."

"I can't let them down. My father... He already thinks I'm a disappointment. Please." She reached for him, but he pulled away. She dropped her hand.

"There really is only one solution."

He was going to send her away. He was going to tell her she was dishonorable, and he never wanted to see her again. "Griffin." It was a ragged plea, ripped from her soul.

"You will have to become my family," he said.

She swallowed hard, not really hearing him. Feeling the pain emanating from him was torture to her soul. She had betrayed him. "I never wanted to hurt you."

"If I am your family, you would obey me in all things."

She blinked. "What?"

Griffin sighed. "My brother and I made a bet a long time ago. If I lost a joust, I must take his place as lord so he could travel the country and participate in jousts."

Layne scowled.

"At first, I had to prove to my family that I was

capable, that I didn't need them." He looked down. "Then, it changed. There was only one reason I didn't want to lose." He looked at her. "Because of you. I wanted to be that strong knight I saw when you looked at me. I wanted to win every joust to impress you."

Layne couldn't speak. She couldn't say a word. Impress her?

"But I couldn't win against you. I didn't even want to." He looked away to the tent flap. "So now, I find myself caught. I must honor my bet to Richard and take his place as lord of the castle. And yet, I don't want to lose you."

"Lose me?" She could only echo his words.

"I can only think of one way to make you stay with me. You will join me."

"As lord of the castle?" Her mind was reeling.

Griffin grinned. "As my wife."

Layne's mouth dropped. Her heart flipped in her chest. Surely he couldn't mean he wanted to marry her? "You want to marry me?"

Griffin took her head into his hands. "I know it is a lot to ask of you. I am not the perfect knight --"

"You are! You are to me." She reached up to touch his shoulders, his arms. Was this a dream? Then she scowled. "Why? Why would you marry me? I'm willful and disobedient. I roughhouse with my brothers..."

"That will stop," he said and pressed a kiss to her lips.

"I am unable to embroider or cook."

"We will have servants to do that." He kissed her again and again. "There is really only one reason I want to marry you. I love you. I have loved you since the first time you unhorsed me."

Layne stared at him in disbelief. It all felt like a dream. A wonderful, magnificent dream. More than she could have possibly ever hoped to dream of. She threw her arms around his shoulders. "Yes! Yes!"

 EPILOGUE

"She's in trouble, there's no doubt," Aunt Emalyn said to Gregory Fletcher. "No knight would ever escort her home otherwise." Her wrinkled eyes turned to Gregory. "I told you to control her."

He was an old man, but he remembered how vibrant Layne was. And how hard to control. Even from an infant, she seemed to let her curiosity get the best of her. When he had received the missive that Lord Griffin Wolfe would be accompanying her and his sons back to Edinfield, doubt and foreboding filled him. While it said nothing about being in chains, he could picture no other reason.

Now that they were nearly home, his excitement and anxiety were getting the best of him. He waited just outside the Manor for his family. How he had missed them! He ached to hear the tales of their tourneys.

"You will be lucky if any member of your family remains out of the dungeon. She was no good from the beginning."

He longed to tell his sister to be silent, but she

had graciously allowed them to stay with her during these hard times. Since his injury, he was unable to joust and provide for his family. The humiliation was almost too much to bear. And he was grateful for all she had done for him.

The gates to the Manor opened for the first person in the long procession of visitors.

Gregory's fingers tightened around the missive crumpled in his fist.

Michael was the first in. He rode a horse that Gregory had never seen before. He came to a stop just before his father, kicking up a cloud of dust. He slid to the ground and hugged his father tightly.

Gregory squeezed Michael. "My son," he whispered, closing his eyes. Michael had grown taller and thinner, if possible. Gregory pulled back to inspect him. He looked healthy and as vibrant as when he had left. He didn't notice his missing fingers as his hands were encased in white gloves.

Other guards rode in and then two men together. Colin and Frances dismounted together and approached their father. They each warmly embraced him. He noticed the way Colin limped and thought to remember to ask later.

Anxiety swirled in the pit of his stomach when he saw Layne was not with them. She rode separately. God's blood! What had happened to her?

"Told you," Emalyn whispered.

Near the rear of the line, Gregory spotted her. She rode at a tall knight's side. And what was that she was wearing? A dress?

The knight dismounted and walked to her horse, helping her dismount.

Gregory stared, stunned. He noticed, too, that

Emalyn had closed her mouth and that gave him some satisfaction. But Layne in a dress? He had never seen such a sight.

Layne looked around, and when she spotted him, she picked up her skirts and raced across the yard to launch herself into his arms.

He was almost knocked over by the exuberance in her greeting. He squeezed her, holding her close. She kissed his cheek and stepped away from him. Her hair was still wild with full curls down her back, but there were small flowers woven into it. Her eyes twinkled as she stepped back.

"Father," she said. She looked back and the tall knight that had helped her dismount walked forward.

Gregory could see by his stature and powerful stride he was of noble birth and impressive lineage.

"I'd like to present to you Lord Griffin Wolfe," Layne finished.

Griffin bowed slightly. "It is an honor to meet you, Sir."

Michael ducked between them. "He wants to marry Layne. Eew."

Layne reached out for him, but he ducked away behind Griffin.

Shocked into silence, Gregory could only stare at Wolfe. And then Layne. Was it the truth or was Michael toying with him? Layne grinned at Lord Griffin and bit her lower lip. For a moment, Gregory saw something he had never seen in Layne's eyes before. Contentment. Together, they turned to look at him.

"It's true, Father," Layne said.

"He must have gotten bashed in the head once too often!" Michael said from behind Griffin.

Frances moved to grab Michael, but he skirted

away from them, dashing across the yard with Frances in pursuit.

"I would have asked you in private for your daughter's hand, but someone beat me to it," Griffin said.

Gregory looked at Layne. He had heard of this Sir Griffin Wolfe. This fearsome, unbeatable knight. The thought of a union between his headstrong daughter and such an upstanding noble knight would never have crossed his mind even in his wildest imaginings. He cleared his throat. "And this is what you want?"

Layne smiled. She looked at Griffin. "Yes."

Michael grabbed his father's hand and pulled him toward the Manor. "Griffin said we could all live with him. In a castle!"

Griffin took Layne's hands into his own. He looked down at her with complete devotion and love and kissed each of her knuckles. "You can be exactly who you are now," he said. "I am completely besotted with you."

Michael circled from a few feet away, still tugging his father's hand and cried, "Eew!"

"I can?" Layne asked. "Good because when I catch Michael, I'm going to give him a sound thrashing." She started after her brother, but Griffin stilled her movement, catching her arm.

"Allow me, m'lady."

The threat was enough. Michael ran into the Manor.

Gregory laughed. Colin and Frances laughed right along with him as they followed Michael into the Manor. Even Emalyn couldn't help but crack a smile as she moved toward her home.

Gregory hugged his daughter. "You have made

me proud, Layne."

Layne's spirit soared. She squeezed her father back, relishing the moment. This was all she ever wanted. She stepped back from him and looked at Griffin. Now, she had more than she could have ever possibly hoped for. Her family would have a home. Her father and her brothers would be taken care of. And she had a perfect knight.

The End

ENJOY THIS BOOK? I COULD USE YOUR HELP

Reviews are the most powerful tools I have to get attention for my books. Just a simple sentence or two of why you enjoyed it would help other medieval romance fans find my books. I would really appreciate a moment of your time and an honest review!
Thank you!

THANK YOU

Thank you for reading Layne and Griffin's story. Jousting in medieval times was an exciting time filled with pageantry and skill. It was also dangerous. Many knights were injured. Even kings were killed while jousting. It's one of my favorite events to write about! I have many more exciting novels for you to read, so please join me on my adventures into the medieval era!

Welcome to my world!

Laurel

ABOUT THE AUTHOR

Critically acclaimed and bestselling author Laurel O'Donnell has won numerous awards for her works, including the Holt Medallion for A Knight of Honor, the Happily Ever After contest for Angel's Assassin, and the Indiana's Golden Opportunity contest for Immortal Death. The Angel and the Prince was nominated by the Romance Writers of America for their prestigious Golden Heart award.

When not writing, you can often find her lounging with her five cats or researching ideas online for the next book. She loves to visit the Renaissance Faire, spend time with family and hear from her readers.

She finds precious time every day to escape into the medieval world and bring her characters to life in her writing.

Subscribe to her newsletter so you don't miss out on upcoming new releases and fun contests. http://bit.ly/laurel-odonnell

Thank you for reading!